A DETECTIVE OUT OF TIME

By Greg Fowlkes

Includes previews from the book

A FICTIONAL DETECTIVE TRIFECTA

~ NOVELLAS FEATURING
THE FICTIONAL DETECTIVE ~

A DETECTIVE OUT OF TIME

© 2018 The Fictional Press
www.TheFictionalPress.com

The Fictional Press is a small, independent press specializing in the publication of fictional works by emerging authors. If you are interested in bringing your fictional works to life in print as well as electronically, contact us! We can help!

www.TheFictionalPress.com

ISBN 13: 978-1-943403-46-2

Printed in the United States of America

BOOKS BY GREG FOWLKES

From the Wizard at Law Series:
The Laws of Magic
Trial by Magic

From the Murder on Mars Series:
Blood Red Sands of Mars
A Death at Station Alpha
A Corpse in Hut Town
Murder at the Mars Club
Blackmail Under a Dark Star

From the Fictional Detective Series:
The Fictional Detective
A Fictional Detective Trifecta
The Fictional Nemesis

Star City Stories: Space Opera Noir Featuring Frank Sladek

The Uncorrupted Corpse

Tequila Visions

Cargo From Paradise

Ice Viking

TABLE OF

CONTENTS

PART ONE (1955)...1

PART TWO (1955)... 29

INTERLUDE ONE (2042)............................... 51

PART THREE (1955)....................................... 77

PART FOUR (1979)... 97

INTERLUDE TWO (2042) 145

PART FIVE (1955).. 165

PART SIX (1925)... 183

INTERLUDE THREE (1955)........................ 205

PART SEVEN (1955) 215

1979..227

AUTHOR'S AFTERWORD.............................235

PART ONE

(1955)

I'm going to tell you a story. It's a strange one, and you probably won't believe it. I'm not sure I do, and I lived it. Some of the names and details have been changed because, well, because they've changed. You might not understand that now, but when I'm finished you will. Assuming you believe me.

The story starts on an afternoon in April. As it turns out, which year matters less than you would think, but it was some time in the 1950's. The place, a medium sized city someplace in the Midwest, where exactly isn't important. It was a nice, bright day, but still too early in the year for the leaves to be out on the trees. It was a Tuesday, and I was sitting at my desk doing nothing in particular when Effie came in and said there was a man to see me.

I should mention that I'm a private investigator. Effie Holmsted is my receptionist. Now in detective stories you may have read, that would conjure up images of a shapely blonde or a slinky redhead. Effie is a widow in her fifties. Her husband died in the war. She looks vaguely Scandinavian or maybe Slavic, but around here that's not worth mentioning. She has the job because she was the first one to answer my ad when I opened up the agency who had the necessary qualifications. Effie can type eighty words a minute and take shorthand. She answers the telephone in a professional manner which clients like and which turns away cranks and salesmen. Sometimes I think Effie is short for Efficiency. The important thing is that she does the job and doesn't ask questions about my personal life. I return the favor.

"There's a man to see you, Mr. Christian. He said his name is Howard Winslow. Here's his card."

Effie handed me a piece of pasteboard with Winslow's name and an address in Boulder, Colorado. There wasn't a phone number. It didn't have a company name or logo on it either. It was a decent printing job, not fancy but not cheap either.

"Show Mr. Winslow in, Effie."

She returned a moment later with Winslow and then left, closing the door between my office and the outer office.

Winslow was a tall man in his late forties. He had dark hair that was graying at the temples. His hair was neatly trimmed, but a shade too long on the sides. He wore horn-rimmed glasses with gold fittings. His left hand held a gray Homburg hat. He had on a conservative gray suit. It was of good material and well tailored, though perhaps not for Winslow. He had a muted tie that was neither narrow nor wide with red, navy and gold stripes. His belt and oxfords were black. He looked eminently respectable or at least like someone trying to look respectable. Winslow gave the impression that he might come from one of those old east coast families, but these days that doesn't mean anything.

I stood up offering him my hand. His grip was firm without him trying to prove anything by it. He looked me straight in the eye. I looked straight back.

"Have a seat, Mr. Winslow." I indicated one of the arm chairs in front of the desk. "What can I do for you?"

"You are Harold Christian?" He said it like he was wanting confirmation rather than questioning the fact. I couldn't exactly place the accent, though I thought it wasn't local. His voice sounded educated and articulate.

"That's me. And you are Howard Winslow?"

He didn't take offense at my question. "That is correct. I want to hire you to find someone, Mr. Christian."

"That's the kind of thing that I do. Who is it that you want to find?"

"I want you to find a man. His name is Harlan Winslow."

"Any relation?"

"Yes." There was a moment's hesitation. "He's my—cousin. It's a matter of an inheritance. I need to find him before Friday."

"Why the time limit, Mr. Winslow? Does your cousin lose out if I don't find him?"

"No, Mr. Christian, I do."

"I see."

"It's complicated, Mr. Christian, and really neither here nor there. I need to find Harlan Winslow before 7:00 PM on Friday. That's all the information that is important to you at the moment."

"Well, there is the matter of my fee—"

Winslow reached inside his jacket and produced an envelope which he slid across the desk in my direction. I opened it and saw five one hundred dollar bills. The notes looked old, not worn, but as if they had lain in storage for a long time. I held one up to the window just to make sure. It looked genuine. Winslow didn't seem to be bothered by my inspection.

"I believe that should cover your retainer and expenses. If you find Harlan Winslow before 7:00 PM on Friday there will be another five hundred dollars waiting for you."

"And if I don't?"

"That will be unfortunate—for me. As for you, you will have made if not earned the five hundred dollars in the envelope. Are the terms satisfactory?"

"Eminently." I left the envelope lying on the desk. "What can you tell me about your cousin? A name isn't much to go on."

"I'm afraid that I can't be of much help, there, Mr. Christian. The only thing I am certain of is that he is, or at least will be in this city by Friday."

"What about particulars? Height? Age? Hair color?"

"Harlan Winslow is forty-seven. Roughly my height and build. I've been told there is something of a family resemblance, though not necessarily a strong one."

"So I'm looking for someone that kind of looks like you."

"More or less." Winslow smiled as if the thought amused him. I didn't get the joke.

"Do you know his occupation? Hobbies? Interests?"

"I understand that he is something of a scientist though he is not currently employed as one. As to the others, I have no information."

"Let me ask you this, Mr. Winslow. Have you looked up your cousin in the city directory or the telephone book?"

"I doubt that my—cousin—would be listed in either. He is, in many ways, a very private person."

"I see. You say that he will be in the city by Friday. Do you know why?"

"No, I'm afraid not."

I thought it over for a minute. On the one hand, it sounded like a wild goose chase. On the other hand, it was five hundred smackers which would help to pay the rent.

"I won't lie to you, Mr. Winslow. I can't guarantee that I will be able to find your cousin. You haven't given me much to go on. Not that I won't do my best, you understand."

"I realize that, Mr. Christian. But trust me; it is very important that I find Harlan Winslow in time."

"In time for what?" I asked.

"That needn't concern you right now, Mr. Christian."

"Alright. If I do find your cousin, how do I get in touch with you?"

"I'll be staying at the University Hotel until Saturday morning. You can leave a message for me there. Otherwise, I'll be in contact on Friday to learn your progress."

"Fair enough. Fortunately, I have no other pressing cases at the moment so I can give the matter my full attention."

"I'd appreciate that, Mr. Christian. If there is nothing else, I'll leave you to your work."

Winslow stood and offered his hand. We shook, and then he left.

The University Hotel is a respectable place. As its name suggests, it was close to the campus and was favored by visiting faculty and lecturers. It was neither cheap nor extravagant, but it was discrete. After Winslow had left I called the front desk and asked if I could speak to Howard Winslow. The clerk put me on hold for a minute or so. When he came back on the line, he informed me that Mr. Winslow wasn't in and asked if I wanted to leave a message. I told him I'd try again later. It appeared that at least that part of Winslow's story was true.

Because it never pays to ignore the obvious, I got out the telephone book and city directory from the lower left drawer of my desk. There were several Winslows in both, but neither of them had a Harlan Winslow listed. For that matter, Howard Winslow wasn't listed, either. So it wasn't going to be that easy.

I told Effie I was going out and then walked over to the public library. Most people don't realize this, but libraries are great places if you're a private investigator. They've got all sorts of useful information and they're free. I looked up both Winslows in Who's Who and several other professional directories. Neither was listed, which really didn't mean much one way or the other. On a hunch, I paged through the collection of year books from the university. A Harlan Winslow had been a student in the physics department, and had gotten his degree in 1942. After that, at least as far as the year books went, he had disappeared. That might just mean that he'd gotten a job or that he'd gone someplace else for graduate work. It was more likely that, like a lot of us, he'd gotten sucked up in the war effort in one way or another. I puttered around the library for another hour, but I couldn't find any mention of Harlan Winslow, either during or after the war. That might not mean anything, or it might mean a lot. Plenty of people with degrees in subjects like physics had vanished behind a veil of secrecy into things like the Manhattan Project.

Out of curiosity, I got a street map of Boulder, Colorado. The street on Winslow's card existed, but according to the map at least, the address was someplace out beyond the city limits. The road hadn't been built out that far. So Winslow had given me a phony address. I wasn't sure what that meant. I wasn't sure I cared. It wouldn't be the first time a client had given me a fake identity. The five hundred dollars were real, though. After Winslow had left I'd checked each one of the bills out.

I splurged on a two dollar hamburger steak dinner at a diner not far from the library. After that I wandered into a bar and ordered a beer. I like beer. Drinking beer gives you plenty of time to think, more than with whiskey, and I needed to do some thinking.

I didn't know what to make of Howard Winslow's story. The way I saw it, it didn't quite add up. Oh, on the face of it, it made sense. Finding potential heirs is actually a fairly common job for a private detective, at least where the estate is big enough to pay for it. Usually, though, it's the lawyer handling the estate that does the hiring, not one of the heirs. They usually don't act so close to a deadline, either. Finding someone that's dropped out of touch can take a long time, a lot more than the three days Winslow had given me.

But that wasn't what was really bugging me. It was that I had this feeling that something was "off" about Winslow. I wasn't quite sure what it was about him, but I had this feeling that something wasn't right. During the war I'd ended up in military intelligence. Nothing glamorous, I hadn't been a spy or anything, more of a glorified policeman, but I'd learned during that time to trust my instincts more than appearances. After the war, I'd done more of the same for a couple of years before deciding I wanted back into civilian life. I won't go into the details here of what I was doing during that time, but it just reinforced the notion of going with my gut rather than my head.

I knew that Winslow hadn't told me the whole story. I was okay with that. Clients seldom do. But I had this feeling that he was concealing something more than the usual dirty little secret, something important. I just didn't have any idea what it could be.

When, after three beers, I still hadn't figured it out, I decided to call it a night. I paid my tab and went home.

In the morning, I set Effie the task of calling all the hotels and motels in town to see if any of them had a Harlan Winslow registered as a guest. Effie is good at things like that. It's surprising how many desk clerks and managers who would hang up in a second on a man asking questions like that will bend over backwards to help someone that sounds like their mother. I told her that if that didn't pan out, she should start on the boarding houses, beginning on the ones near the campus. Now, I had no reason to believe that Harlan Winslow was using his real name, but then I had no reason to think he wasn't. I had no reason, either, to believe that he had any idea someone was looking for him.

For my part, I started calling around to any place that might hire a physicist or engineer. All this was based on the theory that Harlan Winslow had to have someplace to sleep, and, unless he was already rich, he had to have some way to make money. I know this sounds boring as hell, but the reality is, ninety percent of what a private detective does to earn a living would bore you to tears. It's mostly a routine of asking the same questions over and over again of anyone you can think of who might have the answers.

By noon, it was clear that either Harlan Winslow was sleeping in a hollow log out in the woods or he was using a different name. He wasn't gainfully employed, either, at least not as an engineer or scientist. I sent Effie out for sandwiches while I thought about my next move.

It occurred to me that if Harlan really was a scientist or whatever, maybe he had some idea for a new invention that he was working on, on his own. I don't know that much about science or engineering, but I knew enough to think that he'd need some kind of workspace to do it in. I started calling around to real estate agents, the kind that rented out commercial properties. Fortunately, there weren't that many of them. By the time Effie got back with the sandwiches I had a few of leads to check out.

I washed down the sandwich with coffee from the percolator that Effie keeps going on a hot plate in her office. Then I got to work.

By work, I mean I went to each of the locations and asked questions of the neighbors. At the first two places, it didn't take long to figure out that they weren't the ones. One was being used by someone making some sort of spaghetti sauce. At the other, the guy was making some sort of custom hi-fi equipment. I ruled him out because he didn't look anything like Winslow or the description he had given me of his cousin.

The third place was locked up tight and it didn't look like anyone had been there for a month. Taking a peak through the mail slot in the front door, I could see a mound of advertising circulars and other mail that had accumulated on the floor.

It was at the fourth place that things started to look promising. It was an older warehouse that had been subdivided into smaller spaces for starter businesses. I talked to the guy across the hall from the place I was interested in. I used the old dodge of saying that I was working for an insurance company and was checking up to make sure everyone was following the fire code. I've got some phony business cards that I flash around in situations like that. It usually works. I described Harlan Winslow to him and he said he couldn't be sure, but it sure sounded like the guy across the hall. I took that as a yes.

The doors to the place had frosted glass in them. It didn't look like the lights were on. I couldn't hear any noise coming from inside, either. The door didn't have any name painted on it, just a room number. The neighbor across the hall said that the occupant kept irregular hours, but that he was pretty sure that he'd been there that morning. I thanked him and left.

Outside, I'd had the forethought to have parked my car across the street in a position where I could get a good look at anyone using the building's main entrance. I got in the car and hid behind a newspaper that I keep for just that purpose trying to look like someone bored who was waiting for someone else. As long as someone doesn't come by and see you several hours apart, it's a pretty safe dodge.

I'd gone through the paper twice, reading every article and add. It was nearly five and people had been trickling out of the buildings on either side. There was a bus stop down the block at the intersection, and some of them were headed in that direction. The bus came by, stopped, and picked up a handful of passengers. One man got off and started walking in my direction. Despite the fact that he had a hat pulled down low over his face, the light was positioned so I could get a good look at him. Winslow had been right. There was a strong family resemblance between him and his cousin. I didn't have much doubt that I'd found Harlan Winslow.

Harlan had the same lanky build as his cousin. He had on a brown hat that looked as if it had seen better days. From what I could see of his hair, it was brown as well and cut short. He was wearing a dark blue suit, white shirt and a dark narrow tie. His shoes were black with a good shine. He looked to be younger than Howard, maybe in his mid thirties. That would fit in with his having graduated from the university in 1942. He was carrying a big brown paper bag in one hand and a briefcase in the other.

I waited until Harlan entered the building just to make sure, and then decided to call it a day. There was no telling how long Harlan Winslow might be, and I'd done enough work for one day. I drove back to the office. Effie was just leaving. I told her that I'd found the man we'd been looking for and gave her the details. She seemed pleased, but not surprised.

After Effie left, I called the University Hotel. The desk clerk placed a call to Winslow's room, and after a few moments we were connected.

"I take it you have something to report, Mr. Christian?"

"Yeah. I've believe I've found out where your cousin is working."

"Are you sure about this? It's important that you not waste time on a wild goose chase."

"He's rented a work space under another name, I got a good look at him. As you mentioned, there is a marked family resemblance. I don't think I'm mistaken."

"Excellent work, Mr. Christian. I'm very pleased with your efficiency. I'd like to hear all the details. Would it be possible for you to meet me in the bar here at the hotel? Say around eight o'clock this evening?"

"That shouldn't be a problem."

"Good. I'll see you then." With that the line went dead. I was a little surprised. I had thought that I'd give him the address, and that would be the end of things, but Winslow seemed to have something more in mind. As to exactly what, I didn't have a clue, but at least it looked like I'd get a free drink out of it.

As I had a couple of hours to waste, I went and had a steak dinner washed down with a couple of Scotch and soda's. After that, I went to meet Winslow.

It seems as if hotel bars are either busy or empty. They are never somewhere in between. On a Wednesday evening at eight, the bar in the University Hotel fit in the latter category. The bar area wasn't large, more of an alcove off the main lobby than anything else. The only customers were a couple of professorial types sitting at the bar nursing a pair of glasses of neat whisky. I looked around and spotted Winslow sitting at a table off in the corner.

"Right on time I see, Mr. Christian. I took the liberty of ordering for you. Scotch and soda. I hope that will be alright."

"Works for me," I replied. It looked as if he'd ordered the same for himself. Either he'd just arrived, or he'd been waiting for me to drink.

"Good. I have to admit I wasn't expecting results so quickly, Mr. Christian. Please make your report."

I thought that was an odd way to phrase it, like an officer addressing an underling, but then, that was essentially what the relationship between the two of us was. After all, I was just someone Winslow had hired. I went ahead and made my report.

"I started with the usual, calling around to all the hotels and motels in the area. That turned out to be negative. If your cousin is staying in a hotel, he's not registered under his own name. I had my secretary call around to rooming houses, but that's always less of a sure thing. Not every place with a room to let advertises. Based on the fact that your cousin has a degree in physics, I called around to companies that might employ someone in that line. That turned out negative, as well, again assuming your cousin is using his own name."

"So far you've told me what you didn't find," Winslow said impatiently. "While I appreciate your diligence, why don't we move on to the positive results?"

"I was just trying to give you the big picture, Mr. Winslow. It occurred to me that maybe your cousin was working on something on his own. I made inquiries of a number of real estate agents that specialize in renting space for light manufacturing. I came up with a list of half a dozen places that looked promising. I started to check them out yesterday afternoon. I struck pay dirt on the fourth one. When I talked to the man who rents space across the hall he said that his neighbor fit the description that I gave him. I basically described you, Mr. Winslow."

"You led me to believe that you had a more positive identification than that, Mr. Christian."

"Yeah. Well, like I said, it sounded promising, so I parked me car across the street from the front entrance of the building and waited. Along about five o'clock a man got off the bus. I got a good look at him, and like I said, there is a strong family resemblance. I watched him until he went into the building. As I had no idea when he might be planning to leave, I decided to call you and see how you wanted to proceed."

"I presume you have the address of this place?"

"Yeah." I gave him the address including the room number. "Your cousin didn't use his own name with the real estate agent. It's rented to a William Harlan."

"I'm afraid my cousin has a penchant for secrecy, Mr. Christian. It may have something to do with his war time experiences."

"Yeah, I've met people like that," I said. I didn't go into my own background. "That's where things sit for the moment, Mr. Winslow. How do you want to proceed? Or do you want me to drop it? Just so you know, I'm fine either way."

"I appreciate your candor, Mr. Christian. I believe that in our initial meeting I had mentioned that if you found my cousin before Friday evening I would pay you an additional five hundred dollars."

"Yes, you had mentioned that," I acknowledged. I have to admit, at the time I wasn't sure I cared. After all, I'd made five hundred bucks for one day's work. I would have been happy to have left it at that. Maybe I should have.

"I'm willing to complete that end of the bargain, on one condition, Mr. Christian."

"And what is that?"

"That you continue--what is the phrase—the surveillance of my cousin until Friday evening."

"I'm not sure that's necessary, Mr. Winslow. We know where he is working. Given that we know the name he's using, I can probably find out where he's staying. If you want to talk with your cousin, or present him with legal papers or something, you know where you can find him."

"What you say may be true, Mr. Christian, but I would still like you to—keep an eye on my cousin. I presume, given your profession, that you aren't adverse to such an occupation."

"Don't get me wrong, Mr. Winslow. If you want to pay me five hundred dollars more to follow your cousin around until Friday evening, I'm more than willing to do so. It's your money."

"Yes it is, Mr. Christian." Winslow reached into his inside jacket pocket and pulled out another envelope which he laid on the table. He didn't open it, but from the thickness, it looked like it contained a number of bills. "Do we have an agreement?"

"Sure. I'll tail your cousin for the next couple of days. Do you want me to report back to you?"

"Call me here at the hotel Friday afternoon. I may have further instructions."

"And if something happens with your cousin in the meantime?"

"If something happens before Friday, it's probably too late, and I've been operating on faulty information."

It was an odd way of putting it, though, as I found out later, understandable.

"Okay. I'll babysit your cousin until Friday night."

"There's just one more thing, Mr. Christian. Do you have a firearm?"

"Yes. I don't normally carry it, but I own one. I've got a permit and I know how to use it too, but like I said, I don't normally carry it. Too many things can go wrong."

"You might reconsider that position, Mr. Christian. At least until after Friday evening."

I looked Winslow straight in the eye. His expression hadn't changed. We might as well have been discussing the price of butter.

"Just what am I getting myself into, Mr. Winslow? This isn't just about a matter of some inheritance, is it?"

"Oh, but it is, Mr. Christian. The inheritance is mine, and I mean to make sure that I get it. But you needn't be concerned that I am asking you to do anything illegal. In order for me to receive my inheritance, it is absolutely vital that my cousin survives Friday evening."

"What do you mean by that?"

"I'll be frank with you, Mr. Christian. Perhaps I owe you that much. I have reason to believe that an attempt will be made on my cousin's life Friday evening. I want you to prevent that from succeeding. I'm afraid I can't explain any further."

"If that's the case, why don't you just go to the police?"

"What could I tell them?"

"Well, for starters, you could tell them who you think is going to kill him."

"I don't have that information, Mr. Christian. I wish I did. All I know is that someone is going to try and kill my cousin Friday evening."

"Well, tell the police that."

"We're both men of the world, Mr. Christian. We both know that the police react to crime, not prevent it. If I went to the police and told them my cousin was going to be murdered without any supporting details, they'd probably arrest me. Or have me committed. That's why I've approached you. You'll have to trust me."

"It still seems pretty screwy. Why don't you just tell your cousin that his life is in danger?"

"Because he'd be no more likely to believe me than the police would. My cousin doesn't know me from Adam. We've never had the occasion to meet. His probable reaction would be to go into hiding and then I wouldn't be able to protect him at all, Mr. Christian."

For the first time since I'd met him, Winslow was getting himself worked up. He picked up his drink, which till that point he hadn't touched, and knocked off about half of it. I watched him. He wasn't a regular drinker. When he had settled himself down he said:

"Do we still have an agreement, Mr. Christian?"

"I'll watch over your cousin, Mr. Winslow. But if I think for a moment that you've been playing some sort of game with me,

I'm going to go to the police myself. I just want you to understand that."

"I understand, Mr. Christian." He stood up then and added, "Good evening. Oh, don't worry, stay and finish your drink. I've already paid the tab at the bar."

After he left, I sat there wondering just what I'd gotten myself into. Winslow had seemed sincere about protecting his cousin. But how could he know that someone was going to try to murder him? And the information he had seemed to be pretty specific. Sometime Friday evening an attempt was going to be made on Harlan Winslow's life.

Was there something more going on? Why all the secrecy and evasiveness? Did it have something to do with the fact that Harlan Winslow was a physicist? There had certainly been enough in the papers about commie spies and atomic secrets since the end of the war. Was that what this business was about? But I'd had some experience with the cloak and dagger, and somehow this didn't seem to fit the pattern.

I picked up the envelope from the table and opened it. Just as Winslow had promised, there was five hundred dollars, four C notes and two fifties. Like the first payment, the bills looked old but not particularly worn though the series dates were all recent. The two fifties struck me as peculiar. If you were getting a thousand dollars to pay someone, why not just get ten hundred dollar bills? I put the envelope in my jacket pocket and finished my drink.

After I left the hotel I drove back to the building where Harlan Winslow had his workspace. From the street, I could see there was a light on, so the chances were good that Harlan was still there. From the fact that he'd arrived that afternoon by bus it was likely he didn't have a car. It was around nine, and the last bus run was around eleven. If he didn't catch the bus, it meant that he'd probably end up spending the night at his workshop. I decided to wait.

Sure enough, just before eleven the lights went out. A few moments later, a tall figure left the building and started to walk down the street towards the bus stop. I didn't want to spook him, so I didn't start my car until he had made it to the corner. Even then, I didn't turn on the lights. I knew he was going to catch the bus, so there was no point in giving myself away by following too closely.

I had a bus schedule in the glove box along with a route map. Both are things that can come in handy if you're tailing someone who doesn't have a car. If the bus was on time, from the schedule I had about three minutes before Harlan would board it. Right on time, the bus pulled up to the stop on the corner. No one got off, but the tall man got on.

I turned on the lights of the car and headed up towards the corner. Following a bus isn't that easy, not if you don't want to be spotted. The problem isn't that you're going to lose the bus. After all, you know what streets it's going to take and where it's going to turn. But buses stop frequently, and it becomes pretty obvious what you're doing if you stop every time the bus does. Fortunately, at that hour of the night there wasn't much traffic to notice and the rear of a bus is kind of a blind spot for the passengers inside. Unless he was expecting a tail, it was unlikely that he'd spot me.

I had followed the bus for three miles in the direction of the campus when I saw the tall figure get off. As I pulled over to the curb, he didn't even glance in my direction. He went a few doors down the street from the bus stop and entered an apartment building. From the look of it, it was the kind of place that rented studio sized units for short term tenants. It was a pretty good bet that Harlan Winslow was at the place he called home and was going to go to bed for the night. It sounded like a good idea, so I did the same.

I was bone tired, but I couldn't sleep. I kept thinking about what Howard Winslow had said about someone going to murder his cousin Friday night. Despite what you might read in detective novels or see on television, private investigators don't deal with murder as a rule. They leave that to the police. Both sides like it that way. Most of what private investigators do is find people. Sometimes the people want to be found, as in the case of looking for lost heirs. Sometimes they don't, usually because they owe money to someone. Occasionally, a private eye will be hired to keep an eye on someone, though most good ones try to avoid divorce work like the plague, preferring a good clean case of embezzlement any day. But murder, even an anticipated one, was something I wasn't used to dealing with.

I knew a few guys on the force, and I thought about contacting one of them, but Winslow was right. What evidence did I have? All I really had was a comment in a bar from someone that claimed he was the intended victim's cousin. Maybe he was Harlan's cousin, and maybe he was even right about the upcoming murder attempt, but neither of those were things I could go to the cops with.

I finally fell asleep around three and dreamt of flashes of gunfire coming from dark alleys.

It was after nine when I woke up feeling as tired as when I'd gone to bed. I called Effie at the office to see if anything needed my attention. She said no. She was used to my keeping odd hours, and she never let it upset her own routine, which was one of the many things I liked about her. She did say that there had been a call from a woman, but she hadn't left a message.

I thought about staking out Harlan Winslow's workshop, but decided to fry up some bacon and a couple of eggs instead. I knew where Harlan worked and where he lived, and, at least according to his cousin, he wasn't in any danger until the evening of the next day. If his cousin was wrong, that wasn't my problem.

After I'd washed the eggs and bacon down with orange juice and black coffee I was feeling better. I had a hot shower and felt even better. The sun was shining; birds were chirping outside my window, it had all the looks of being a wonderful spring day.

I got to the office about ten thirty. Effie looked up as I entered. She must have liked what she saw.

"That woman called again," she said cheerfully. "At least it sounded like the same woman. She wouldn't leave her name."

"Did she say what she wanted?"

"No. She sounded worried, though. Is there something I should know, Harry?"

"Your guess is as good as mine, Effie. I'm not working on anything but the Winslow case at the moment and I'm not suffering from any romantic entanglements."

Effie never says anything, but I know she has hopes that one of these days I'll settle down with someone.

"Speaking of the Winslow case, Howard Winslow hasn't called, has he?"

"No. Were you expecting him to?"

"Not really," I said with a shrug.

I went into my office, read through the mail, and signed a few checks. I thought about calling Howard Winslow at his hotel, but he'd been pretty clear about me not contacting him until Friday afternoon.

At twelve, I walked to the bank and deposited seven of the C-notes Winslow had paid me. The teller at the bank looked at the bills oddly. He made a big show of holding them up to the light and examining them.

"Nothing wrong with them, is there? I was just paid them by a client."

"No, they seem to be perfectly genuine, Mr. Christian. It's just that judging them by the feel and appearance, I would have thought they were much older than the series dates would indicate."

"Maybe my client has been keeping them in a mattress," I joked.

"That might explain it," the teller smiled. He knew what I did for a living. "The odd thing is, is that the bills all have different dates on them, but they all seem to have suffered the same amount of aging."

"But there isn't a problem with your accepting them, is there?"

"Oh, no, Mr. Christian. I don't doubt that the bills are good." He stuffed them in his till and handed me the receipt for the deposit. I left, before he thought better of it.

I had suspected there was something odd about the bills. If my bank balance had been in better shape, I'd have been tempted to hang onto them until I could have an expert examine them. If it came to that, I still had two of the hundreds and the pair of fifties Winslow had paid me.

After the bank, I had a late lunch and then went back to the office. There was something I wanted to pick up.

I keep a .38 automatic in a safe in my office. Normally, I don't carry it because I don't need it. I have to admit, though, that I was getting spooked. Something odd was going on and I wanted to be prepared.

I got the automatic out of the safe and checked it over making sure it was in working order. I worked the slide a couple of times and then put in a loaded clip. A .38 doesn't necessarily have the stopping power of a bigger gun, but the one I had was smaller and lighter than a Colt .45. That made it easier to carry and hide under a jacket which was a real advantage.

I put on the shoulder holster and checked myself in the mirror. Unless they were looking for it, most people wouldn't spot that I was packing. I reached in a couple of times to make sure that I could grab it if I needed it, and then, feeling a little silly, I left it at that.

In the outer office, I said good-bye to Effie, telling her that I probably wouldn't be back that afternoon. I gave her the addresses of Harlan Winslow's workshop and apartment just in case. She wrote them down without comment like a good secretary.

Outside Harlan's workshop, I parked in the same spot I had used the day before. I'd brought along a cheap paperback to keep me company. Half way through, it occurred to me that I must be doing something wrong. The private eye in the book never seemed to do much real work but he had plenty of good looking dames to keep him busy. Of course he had gotten beaten up twice in the process, so I was ahead on that score.

A little after six Harlan Winslow came out of the building. Instead of heading to the bus stop as I would have expected, he turned the other way. I got out of the car and followed him. He walked two blocks, then turned and walked two more before entering a diner on the corner. That seemed like a good idea, so I followed him. I hadn't eaten since lunch.

I picked one of the stools at the counter. Harlan had grabbed a booth. When the waitress behind the counter, a thin blonde who looked forty but was probably thirty, asked for my order, I had a hamburger with fries and a coffee. From what I overheard, Harlan had the meatloaf special. From the way the waitress talked to him he must have been a regular.

The meatloaf came first, but I ate faster, and was waiting half a block up the street when Harlan emerged from the diner. I followed him back to the workshop and sat in my car for another couple of hours. He locked up in time to catch the ten o'clock bus. I thought about following him, but his cousin assured me that nothing was going to happen until the next evening.

I got up early the next morning and was parked outside Harlan's apartment building before seven. From the schedule I knew that buses came by every hour just before the half hour. Right on cue, Harlan came out of his building to stand at the bus stop at seven twenty. He was dressed pretty much as he always was and he was carrying his briefcase in his left hand. When the bus came by, he got on it.

I didn't bother to follow the bus. Instead, I drove over to his workshop and parked in the street out front where I had parked the day before. I'd beaten the bus by about ten minutes. The bus stopped at the corner and Harlan got off. I watched him walk up the street and enter his building. If he suspected that he was a target for assassination, he wasn't showing it.

There didn't seem to be much point in my hanging around. I went and got breakfast, and then ran a couple of errands before stopping by the office. The person Effie was starting to refer to as "that woman" had called again. Effie had tried in her most motherly way to pump her, but the caller had refused to say who she was or why she was calling. Both Effie and I were starting to think she was a crank.

I was back parked in front of Harlan's workshop at ten thirty. Just before noon, he came out and walked in the direction of the diner. I followed him, but didn't go in. I didn't want to take the chance on him recognizing me. Also, the food hadn't been that great. Instead I found a phone booth and placed a call to Winslow at the University Hotel.

When he answered, I gave him a brief rundown on what his cousin had been up to since we'd met. Winslow didn't seem particularly interested. He asked me to meet him at the hotel in an hour. As I was pretty sure that Harlan would be busy in his workshop through the afternoon I agreed.

Winslow had told me to come up to his room, number 307. When I got to the hotel, I took the elevator up to the third floor. 307 was to the left. I found the room and knocked on the door. A moment later Winslow opened it and let me in.

The room was your basic hotel room. It was nice enough. The hotel had been build just after the war, and the room was a little more spacious than if it had been built earlier. There was a big window on the end, and it had a small private bath next to the door. It was furnished with a bed that looked comfortable, a nightstand, an arm chair with a lamp, and a table and chair positioned in front of the window. The bed had been made. There weren't any personal items in sight, not even a newspaper or book. Looking at it you couldn't tell whether anyone was occupying it or not, despite the fact that Winslow must have been there nearly a week.

"Your cousin went back to his workshop after lunch," I said to start the conversation.

"Good," Winslow replied. Again, he didn't seem particularly interested. He seemed on edge and distracted.

"Look, Mr. Winslow, do you want me to keep following your cousin or not? You've paid me enough that it doesn't matter to me either way."

He looked up at me, his attention suddenly focused. It was kind of chilling.

"I don't care what you do this afternoon, Mr. Christian, but it is absolutely imperative that you follow my cousin when he leaves his workshop at seven o'clock tonight. That is when the attempt will be made on his life."

"If you don't mind my saying, that seems pretty specific. How do you know that? As far as I know, you didn't even know that your cousin had a workshop until I told you."

"I didn't."

"But you know someone is going to try and kill him at seven tonight?"

"Yes."

"Then you must have some idea of who this killer is."

"I can't tell you that, Mr. Christian."

"Why not?"

"Because I don't know. That's why."

I was getting a little tired of Winslow's evasiveness. I'll put up with a lot for a grand, but I don't like having games played with me.

"Look, this whole business is starting to sound kind of screwy to me. If you don't know who is trying to kill him how can you be sure that something is going to happen. Did you see it in a crystal ball or something?"

"Something like that," Winslow replied. He almost sounded amused by his answer.

"Something like that?"

"Let's just say I've seen the future, Mr. Christian."

I didn't like the smile on his face.

"Let's just say I've seen the future, too, and it doesn't involve me." I slammed my hat on my head and headed for the door.

"Mr. Christian! I've paid you a thousand dollars. You owe me something for that. I've told you that a man's life is in danger. Can you really ignore that? What if you should wake up tomorrow morning and read in the paper that Harlan Winslow had been shot and killed just after seven this evening? How will you feel knowing that you might have prevented it?"

I turned to face him. The smile was gone from his face.

"All that I am asking is that you be there tonight at seven o'clock. I think I've paid you enough for a few more hours of your time. If my cousin makes it safely to his apartment tonight, then you can consider that our business is concluded. You've will have made a thousand dollars for not an inordinate effort on your part. And you will have saved a life."

"And if no one tries to rub out your cousin?"

"Then I will have been proved a fool," Winslow answered. He didn't seem bothered by the possibility. "But you will still be one thousand dollars richer."

I couldn't argue with his logic. Or the grand that he'd paid me. "OK, I'll be there at seven tonight. Are you sure that that is when it will happen?"

"Yes. At a little after before tonight my cousin will be passing the mouth of an alley on Third Street. A shot will be fired from the alley. It is up to you to make sure that it doesn't kill my cousin."

"Third Street is where your cousin has his workshop," I said.

"Yes, so you've told me."

"Any other hints that might be useful?"

"No, Mr. Christian, I'm afraid that's all I can tell you, because that's all I know."

"I guess that this seeing the future stuff has its limitations?"

"That's one way of putting it."

"Do you mind my asking why you just don't go introduce yourself to your cousin and tell him he's going to be bumped off? Or better yet, why don't you take him out to dinner someplace so he's miles away from Third Street at seven?"

"That wouldn't be a good idea, Mr. Christian. I can't explain it to you, but that's the way it is."

"I see." I didn't, really, but it didn't look like I was going to get any more answers out of Winslow. "I guess this is good-bye, then, Mr. Winslow."

"You'll do it, then? You'll save Harlan?"

"I'll do my damnedest."

I figured that I had nothing to lose. If Harlan came out of his workshop at seven, I'd tail him and keep him from passing any alleys. If he didn't come out at seven—well then it really didn't matter. As Winslow had said, I was getting paid in either case.

I had an early dinner and drove back to the workshop on Third Street. I hadn't looked closely at the block before, but a couple of buildings up from the one Harlan was in, there was an alleyway on that side of the street. It wasn't much, maybe eight feet wide. Once the sun set, it would be plenty dark enough to hide a gunman.

I parked in my usual space and waited. Five o'clock came and then six. It got dark and most of the people in the buildings on either side of the street had gone home or gone out for dinner or whatever they had planned for Friday night. The light stayed on in Harlan's workshop. Just before seven, the light went out and a few moments later Harlan came out the front door.

I got out of the car and started to follow. Maybe I rushed it a little, because Harlan Winslow looked back over his shoulder and then sped up. I didn't want to spook him into running, or worse, ducking into the alley, but I had to catch up to him. I quickened my pace to match his.

I was maybe thirty feet behind him when he reached the alley. There wasn't anything else I could do, so I called out, "Excuse me, Mr. Winslow." I tried to sound as friendly as I could

He was maybe a step into the opening of the alley when I called out. He turned, uncertain as to what to do and then took a step back towards me. Just as he did, a shot came out of the alley.

I pulled out my automatic and ran past Harlan and into the alley. I could hear footsteps running away, but it was too dark to see anything. I didn't bother to follow.

Harlan Winslow was standing there wide-eyed staring at the pistol in my hand.

"Are you alright, Mr. Winslow?"

"Yes. How do you know my name? Who are you?"

His eyes kept focusing on the gun in my hand. I put it away and said:

"My name is Harry Christian. I'm a private investigator. I can show you my license if you like, but maybe right here isn't the best place."

"I don't understand." Harlan seemed confused by what had just happened.

"I just saved your life, Mr. Winslow."

"That shot—it was meant for me?"

"I think so. That's why I'm here."

"I still don't understand. Why were you following me?"

"Your cousin hired me to protect you."

"Cousin? I don't have any cousins. Not that I know of, at least." The shock seemed to be wearing off and was being replaced with suspicion.

"Look, you'll be late for your bus if you don't hurry. Why don't you let me walk you down to the bus stop and we can leave it at that."

Harlan looked nervously at his watch and then glanced up at the corner. The two of us walked up to the stop.

"What's this all about, Mr. Christian?" Harlan asked when we had reached the bus stop.

"I'm not sure I can explain, Mr. Winslow. But here's your bus. You'd better get on."

"Aren't you coming with me?"

"No. I've got a car parked down the block. But don't worry, Mr. Winslow. Everything will be alright now."

He boarded the bus and it drove off. I walked back to my car and drove to the nearest phone booth. I called the University Hotel, but the desk clerk informed me that Howard Winslow had checked out that evening. He hadn't left a forwarding address. After that, I went looking for a bar.

PART TWO

(1955)

I was in a good mood as I headed to the office the next Monday. And why shouldn't I be, I thought to myself. The fine spring weather was holding, I'd just earned a quick and easy grand, and I'd managed to save a man's life in the process. I wasn't really sure about my part in the last item, but at least Harlan Winslow wasn't dead.

Even Effie couldn't dispel the good mood, though from the expression on her face I could tell there was something she wasn't happy about.

"That woman is in your office. I didn't know where else to put her."

"What woman?" I asked.

"The one that kept calling last week refusing to leave her name or business." Effie likes to run the office on what she considers a businesslike basis and either one of those errors was apt to upset her. On the other hand, Effie has great instincts about people, so maybe there was cause for concern.

"Did she give her name this time?"

"She said she was Miss Helen Hollander," Effie replied skeptically.

I knew what she meant. While it was quite possible that her parents had saddled her with that name, it had the unfortunate distinction of sounding made up like something out of a mystery novel.

"Anything else?"

"Just that it was important and that she'd wait."

"I guess I might as well see her, then. If I buzz you, you know what to do?"

Effie just looked at me. We had worked out an arrangement for dealing with cranks. If I buzzed her on the intercom she'd come in and say I had an appointment or an important phone call or something to serve as an excuse for getting rid of the crank.

I entered the inner office, hung my hat on the rack and got a good look at Miss Helen Hollander. She was worth the examination. She wasn't necessarily pretty, but she certainly was good looking. Miss Hollander was a tall brunette of an athletic build, the kind that comes from swimming or playing lots of tennis. Her hair was cut shorter than is fashionable in a style that was unusual but not unattractive. She had on very little makeup. I thought she looked to be in her early thirties. She was wearing a suit of good quality, though the fit could have been better. The skirt of the suit was a little too short, not that that was a bad thing. She had nice legs. Her feet were shod in sensible shoes.

I noticed the way she sat in the chair in front of my desk, not straight up at the front as many women do, but leaning comfortably against the back. She seemed comfortable in her body. If I had to take a guess, she had been something of a tomboy as a young girl.

As I entered, she stood to face me.

"I'm Harry Christian. Effie says you're Helen Hollander."

She held out her hand to shake. Her grip was firm but it wasn't as if she was trying to prove something by it.

"I want to hire you to find someone, or rather two people. That is, if it's not too late." There was an edge to her voice as if she was afraid that it was too late. She continued, "I tried all last week to contact you, Mr. Christian, but your secretary kept saying that you were out."

She spoke with an accent I couldn't quite place. Actually, she didn't have an accent. She sounded like a good Midwesterner, but the effect was of someone trying to sound that way, like an English actor trying to sound like an American. It was close, but there was an over emphasis on certain vowels and an over careful enunciation of some of the words.

"I'm afraid that I was busy on another case, Miss Hollander. But that's all wrapped up now and I'm at your complete disposal. Just who do you want me to find?"

I tried to figure that out before she answered. Usually, when a woman of that age is trying to find someone, it's a husband who's gone missing, but Miss Hollander wasn't wearing gloves and there was no sign that she'd ever worn a wedding ring. She didn't strike me as the type that would chase after a man, either.

"As I said, it's actually two people. The one I'm most interested in is named Howard Winslow. The other is a relative of his, Harlan Winslow, though I suspect he may be using a different name."

That should have set off the alarm bells in my head. In my line of work, I've come not to believe in coincidences. Nine times out of ten, what seems a coincidence just means someone knows something more than you do. This seemed all wrong, Miss Hollander coming in and asking me to find last week's client. The smart thing to have done would have been to buzz Effie and then escort Miss Hollander out the door, locking it behind her. I didn't do any of those things. I'm not sure why.

Instead I asked, "And why do you want to find these men?"

"I'm afraid that I can't divulge that information, Mr. Christian."

Now most women, most clients for that matter, would have come prepared with some lie to tell me. A few would have said, "I can't tell you that," before breaking down in hysterics. Miss Hollander had done neither of those. She'd used the phrase "I can't divulge." I'd heard that exact phrase repeatedly when I'd been in intelligence during the war.

"Just who are you, Miss Hollander?"

"Does it matter?"

"It matters to me. I like to know what I'm getting myself into."

"I'm willing to pay your going rate. And I'm not asking you to do anything illegal. I just need to find these two men. It's important."

"You still haven't answered my question. Who are you?"

"I told you, my name is Helen Hollander."

"You'll have to give me a little more than that, Miss Hollander. After all, anyone could come in here and give me that name."

"I'm afraid I can't tell you any more than that. You'll have to trust me, Mr. Christian."

"You'll have to do better than that. You come in here asking me to find two men. One of them was my client. The other, well, oddly enough he was the man my client asked me to find, a man who someone tried to kill."

"And did you? Find him, I mean." From her body language, the answer to that question seemed unusually important to her.

"That's neither here nor there at the moment, Miss Hollander. I just find it very strange that you come in here asking for those two. It's too much of a coincidence, and I don't believe in coincidences. Now either you explain yourself, or I'm going to have to ask you to leave."

I stood up so as to make my point. She rose as well, turned toward the door and then turned back.

"All right, Mr. Christian. I'll tell you what I can."

"That's better. Now, why don't we sit down again?"

We both made a big show of sitting.

"OK. Now why don't you tell me your story?"

"I work for the government, Mr. Christian." The way she said made it believable.

"What branch?"

"It's a department you may not have heard of—"

"You'd be surprised, Miss Hollander. I used to work for the government myself—"

"I know." That stopped me for a moment. Clearly, I hadn't just been some name that she'd picked out of the phone book. But then, I'd known that already.

"OK. You say you work for the government. Can you prove that?"

"I can show you my ID card," she said reluctantly

"That would be a start," I replied skeptically.

She reached into her purse and pulled out a slim wallet. I thought I caught sight of the butt of an automatic, but I might have been mistaken. She flipped the wallet open and handed it over to me.

I have to say that the ID card was pretty impressive. I'd never seen anything like it. It certainly wasn't a simple piece of pasteboard. I took the card out of the window in the wallet. It looked to be made of some kind of plastic. There was a photo of Miss Hollander. There was no mistaking that fact. It was in full color and had the appearance of depth to it. There were a bunch of numbers which might or might not mean anything and an official looking seal, too. It also said that Miss Hollander was a doctor, but I was guessing it wasn't of medicine. I put the card back in the pocket in the wallet and handed it back to her.

"This says you work for the National Time Laboratory. I've don't think I've ever heard of that. Is that part of the Bureau of Standards?"

"Department of Energy, actually," Dr. Hollander replied.

"You don't say. Says you're a doctor, too."

"Ph. D. Mathematics." The straightforward way she stated that made me suspect that it was true. I'd met a few female Ph. D.s during the war and Dr. Hollander fit the profile.

"Mathematician, eh. Interesting. It still doesn't explain why you want to find Howard Winslow."

"Doctor Winslow works for the NTL as well. He took a piece of equipment without authorization. I'm trying to get it back."

"What kind of equipment? Some kind of clock?"

"Something like that. I'm afraid I can't tell you anything more, Mr. Christian. It's classified. But then you'd know about things like that, wouldn't you?"

"Would I?" Dr. Hollander seemed to know a lot about me, certainly more than she could have learned from my ad in the phone book.

"You worked for the government, yourself, I believe. In New Mexico? During the war."

"I'm not supposed to talk about that, Miss, sorry Dr. Hollander. But let's just say that I know about things being classified."

"I understand. And you'll understand why there are some things I won't talk about."

"Fair enough. So this Howard Wilson stole a clock from the government and you want to get it back?"

"That about sums it up."

"Which is why they sent a mathematician."

"Excuse me?"

"To sum it up. It was a joke, Dr. Hollander."

"Yes. I see."

I had to say that she was playing the part of a dead pan government agent very well.

"That doesn't explain why you're interested in Winslow's cousin."

"Cousin? Oh, you mean Harlan Winslow."

"Yes. So they aren't cousins?"

"No. Not that it matters."

"But they are related?"

"Oh, yes. They are related. In a manner of speaking."

"I'm not sure I understand."

"It's classified."

"Alright. You still haven't explained why you're interested in him."

"It has to do with the clock."

"The clock. The one Howard Winslow took?"

"Yes."

Ordinarily, I would have found her evasiveness tiring, but instead it was becoming more of a game. "I know that Harlan Winslow is some kind of engineer. This must be a very special kind of clock, Dr. Hollander?"

"It is."

I took a good look at the woman sitting across from me. Despite all the glib banter, there was a tension to her. I'd seen that kind of tension before, during the war. Right before they set off the first A-bomb. It wasn't fear as much as anticipation. Like knowing something big was going to happen any moment.

"Look, Miss Hollander, or Dr. Hollander, or whatever your name is, we can play games like this all morning, and it's not going to get us anywhere. Now why don't you tell me who you are and what you really want? If you don't, you might as well stop wasting my time and get out of my office."

"I told you Mr. Christian, I work for the government. You've seen my credentials."

"That was your first mistake, Miss Hollander. As I said, I used to work for the government. One of the things I did was look for phony credentials. I've seen a lot of them in my time. Yours stick out like a sore thumb."

"I assure you they are genuine."

"Come off it. If you are going to fake documents, you have to at least try to make them look like the real ones. Your ID is too good. Real ones aren't plastic and they don't have color photos in them, color photos that look like they have three dimensions to them. Not to mention that I've never heard of the National Time Laboratory, haven't heard of it because it doesn't exist."

"It does exist, Mr. Christian. Just not—now—"

"What is that supposed to mean?"

She paused, as if deciding what, and how much to say. It obviously wasn't an easy decision for her to make.

"I'm going to trust you, Mr. Christian. Partly because of what I know about you, and partly because I don't think I have any choice. You haven't heard about the National Time Laboratory because it doesn't exist—yet. The reality, Mr. Christian, is that I am from the future. A future where the NTL does exist. A future from which Howard Winslow came, just as I came. That clock he stole wasn't an ordinary clock. It was time machine."

My jaw dropped. Not because I believed her, but because, as a lie, it was so outrageous.

"Really? A time machine? Like H. G. Wells? Is this some kind of gag, Miss Hollander? Or is this just some kind of con. If it is, I have to admit it's a doozie."

"It's not a gag and it's not a con. It's the truth."

At the time I thought that either she was a really good actress or she actually believed the yarn that she was telling me.

"And I suppose you've got a time machine, too? Maybe if you showed it to me, I'd believe you."

"Alright. If that's what it takes."

She opened up her purse and pulled out a small metal object, maybe five inches long, two and a half inches wide and a half inch thick. The flat face of it looked almost like a television screen except that it was in color. There were a lot of numbers on it that kept changing at a dizzying pace.

"Technically, this is a Time Stream Controller or TSC, not a time machine, but the purpose is the same. It controls the rate at which the person holding it passes through time. It can speed that rate up or down, or even make the rate negative, that is move wielder into the past. This is what Howard Winslow stole, or at least one much like it."

"Let me get this straight. That little gizmo lets you travel in time?"

"We usually just refer to it as the dingus, not gizmo. But yes."

"OK. Prove it. Take me to the future. Or the past. Then maybe I'll believe you."

"That would be very unwise, Mr. Christian."

"Why?"

"Time travel is inherently dangerous. It would be too easy for you to do something that would affect the time stream."

"I don't get you."

"Think about it, Mr. Christian. Suppose you were to go into the past and kill your own father before you were conceived. What would happen to you then? Would you even exist?"

"I never knew my father. He skipped town before I was born, so killing him probably wouldn't be such a big deal. But I get your point. I kill my father, then I don't exist. But what happens then? If I don't exist, I can't go back in time to kill my father so I would exist—"

"To go back in time and kill your father. That's what is known as a paradox, Mr. Christian. Time travel is rife with the possibilities for them. That's why it's so important for me to find Winslow and get the controller that he stole back."

"If they are so dangerous, why did you build the damn things in the first place?"

"Because we could." It wasn't an apology or an explanation. It was a statement of fact. I had the feeling that we'd reached the point where Miss Hollander should be trying to hold back a grin, except she wasn't smiling. I wasn't, either. I couldn't decide if she really believed in this crazy notion about being a time traveler or whether she was trying to con me. I decided to play along for the moment and see if she hung herself.

"OK. Let's say, just for the sake of argument mind you, that I actually, for one moment, believe this whole story. What is supposed to happen next? And why me?"

"The why you is easy enough. After it was discovered that one of the dinguses was gone and Howard had gone missing, a thorough search was made of his apartment and office. Your name was found in one of his notebooks along with an advertisement for your agency taken from a phone book from this year. That's one of the reasons I've been trying to get in touch with you, because there is a good possibility that he will try to contact you."

I noticed that she had referred to Winslow by his first name. Had there been something between the two of them? Was that what was behind this time travel delusion, that she had developed a romantic obsession over him that had not been returned? It wasn't out of the realm of possibilities. Winslow wasn't that much older than she was, and women often developed an interest in older men.

"I take it you know Winslow fairly well?"

"As I told you, Howard is—was—will be—" She hesitated in frustration before going on, "The English language doesn't yet have the right tenses for time travel. Howard was the chief scientist on the time travel project. As a mathematician involved in developing some of the formalism of the theory behind the project I worked quite closely with him."

"I see—" I commented.

"What's that supposed to mean?" she asked angrily.

"Nothing, I guess. Go on."

"As I said, it is more than likely that Howard Winslow will contact you. If he does, I'd like your help in getting the controller from him and getting him back to the future where he belongs."

"And if he doesn't contact me?"

"Well, you are a detective, aren't you? I'd like to hire you to find him. As I said earlier, I'm ready to pay you for your services."

She reached into her purse and pulled out an envelope and laid it on the desk. I picked it up and looked inside. There were five one hundred dollar bills. I had to smile. It was almost as if what she and Winslow knew about private investigators had come out of pulp novels. The reality was that my clients rarely paid in cash and Effie was quite capable of generating an invoice—and making sure it was paid. I put the envelope back on the desk. The odd thing, though, was that the bills had the same aged appearance of the ones that Winslow had given me.

"OK. Say I agree, which is more important to you, getting back this dingus Winslow has or getting Winslow, himself?"

She didn't hesitate. "The dingus, of course. It has the potential to be much more damaging to the time stream in the wrong hands. Howard, by himself, is less of a risk. The fact is, your time just doesn't have the technology available to allow him to create another time controller."

"Should I resent that comment?"

"It's a question of progress, Mr. Christian. Could the Wright brothers have built a jet engine? Even if they had had a set of blueprints? They didn't have access to the materials, or jet fuel, or the precision machining necessary. I assure you that it's the same with time travel. You can't imagine all that goes into this tiny device here," she said as she picked up the dingus and laid it back on the desk.

"Out of curiosity, Miss—sorry, Dr. Hollander, what year have you come from?"

"2042. June 10, 2042 to be precise."

"And what's this future like? Flying cars and robots and rocket ships to Mars, I suppose?"

It was her turn to smile.

"The future is less different then you imagine, Mr. Christian. We haven't gotten to Mars yet, though men have landed on the moon a few times. No flying cars, either, I'm afraid, and you wouldn't really recognize the robots as such."

"That's disappointing."

"Oh, there has been progress in other areas, I can assure you. Polio has been eradicated. Small pox, too. People live longer and better—when they're allowed to."

"Do I detect some disenchantment?"

"I'm afraid that the future still has politics—and war."

I couldn't resist the note of sadness in her voice. At that moment, she didn't sound like a crazy woman.

"Aren't you afraid to be telling me this? Afraid that I might change the future?"

"I haven't really told you very much, have I? Besides, what could you do with it? Write a story for one of the science fiction magazines?"

"I see your point. Well, as much as I'd like to oblige you, Dr, Hollander, you can keep your money. I'm afraid I can't help you."

"Can't or won't?"

"I can't help you because Howard Winslow already contacted me last week. That was the case I told you about. As far as I know, he's already long gone. I don't know whether he's gone back to the future or just to Peoria, but he checked out of his hotel Friday night and didn't leave a forwarding address. I asked."

She looked shocked as if her world was crumbling around her.

"If only I had been able to see you last week," she said, shaking her head.

"You didn't leave a number with Effie where I could get in touch with you," I pointed out, gently.

"No, I didn't. I thought I had time," she said with regret. "Ironic, isn't it?"

I really felt sorry for her. That didn't stop me from asking, "Can't you just take that dingus and go back a week and start over?"

"It's not that simple, Mr. Christian. I can't explain the math to you, but doing that would cause—knots in the time stream."

"I take it that's a bad thing?"

"Very bad. You have no idea how bad it can get." She seemed to have regained her composure. Or maybe, to maintain her delusion, she had just rationalized a way out of having to do what I had suggested.

"I'm really sorry that I can't help you, Dr. Hollander. I want you to believe that." I thought that she needed help, but not the kind that I could give.

"I am, too, Mr. Christian. Would you mind telling me what Howard came to you for?"

I paused a moment over that. Could it really hurt?

"Normally, I don't discuss my client's affairs with other people, Dr. Hollander. Professional ethics, you understand. But, in this case, maybe I can make an exception. The simple answer is that Winslow asked me to find someone. He said he was a cousin of his and that it had to do with an inheritance."

"And the man's name?" I got the feeling that she already knew the answer.

"Harlan Winslow."

I noticed that her grip had tightened on her purse.

"And did you find him, Mr. Christian? Did you find Harlan Winslow?"

"As a matter of fact I did."

"And what happened then?" She hadn't raised her voice, but she was emphasizing the question.

"I don't understand. I found Harlan Winslow and I told his cousin or whatever where."

"But what happened then? What happened to Harlan Winslow?"

Though I couldn't see why, I could see that she was really upset.

"Why—nothing happened to Harlan Winslow."

"Oh, no. I've failed," she said before slumping back in the chair.

Part of me wanted to get up and comfort her. Part of me wanted to call a mental hospital. Instead I just said, "I don't understand."

"Don't you see, Mr. Christian? Harlan Winslow was supposed to die on Friday night. A pistol shot from out of a dark alley. That's the way history records it."

I asked myself, how could she know about the shot? The police hadn't been involved and I hadn't told anyone, not even Effie. I was pretty sure Harlan Winslow hadn't been going to tell anyone. The only way that she could have known is if she had been there—if she had fired that shot. And I had seen what looked like the butt of an automatic in her purse.

"That's not what happened, Dr. Hollander, and we both know it. I was there. I stopped Harlan Winslow from crossing the mouth of the alley just as the shot was fired. I probably saved his life. But you knew that, didn't you? Because you were there. In the alley."

She looked confused. She raised her head and glared at me. "What are you talking about? Do you think that I shot Harlan Winslow?"

"Thankfully, no one shot Harlan Winslow. Only one shot was fired and it missed. After that, I walked him down to the bus stop and put him on the bus to his apartment."

"No, that's not the way it happened. It can't be." She wasn't hysterical yet, but she was getting close to the edge.

"That's the way it happened. And you know it. Let me ask you this, how many bullets are in that automatic of yours?"

That stopped her. She looked surprised, but calmer, somehow, as if the rational part of her mind was regaining control.

"How did you know about that?"

"I'm a detective, remember. Why don't you let me have a look at your gun? That will prove whether you fired that shot or not."

At that point, I didn't really care whether she had fired the shot or not, I just wanted to get my hands on her pistol before she shot me—or herself.

I was surprised when she reached into her purse and pulled the gun out, holding it carefully by her thumb and forefinger. She placed it on the desk and slid it across to me.

I picked it up. I didn't recognize the make or model. It was lighter than I would have thought, as if parts of it were made of plastic rather than metal. It was of medium caliber. The gunshot that had come out of the alley had sounded like a .38 which was close enough. I ejected the magazine. As far as I could tell it was full. There wasn't a round in the chamber. From my time in Germany after the war, I recognized the cartridges as being nine millimeter parabellums or something similar, the same as used in a Luger. I looked down the barrel. The pistol hadn't been fired recently. Either that or it had been given a thorough cleaning.

"Are you satisfied?" Dr. Hollander asked. She seemed in control again.

"Maybe," I answered noncommittally. "If you weren't there Friday night, how did you know about the shooting? And why did you think Harlan Winslow had been killed?"

"Because he was. Or at least, that's the way it was supposed to happen. Did happen. Should have happened. This damned language can't express it. What I mean to say, Mr. Christian, is that in the past of my future, Harlan Winslow died last Friday night from a gunshot fired from an alley. And I can prove it."

She rummaged around in her purse and brought out another envelope. "Take a look at that!" she said as she slid it towards me.

I opened the envelope. There was a clipping from a newspaper inside. The paper was yellowed with age and brittle where it had been creased. The headline ran "No Suspects Yet in Friday Shooting." The article went on to say that the victim, identified as one Harlan Winslow, had been shot and killed by an unknown gunman around seven o'clock Friday night. The victim had been walking on Third Street from a workshop that he rented to the bus stop on the corner. From the evidence, the police thought that the shot had come from an alley that opened onto Third Street. The police experts said the bullet jacket from a nine millimeter pistol had been found at the crime scene. The fact that it had been ejected indicated that the weapon was an automatic. Though the victim had been living under an assumed name, he apparently had no criminal record. From the header the article had been taken from the Sunday paper. I'd read the Sunday paper. There'd been no mention of Harlan Winslow or a shooting. The city isn't big enough to support multiple editions of the paper.

"Where'd you get this?"

"It was found in Dr. Winslow's apartment when it was searched after he stole the time controller."

I turned the clipping over. I remembered reading the story on the other side. The hairs started to rise on the back of my neck. Could it be possible that Dr. Hollander's story was true? That she really was from the future. I knew that there were ways to artificially age paper, but would there have been enough time to produce a fake that good in twenty-four hours? The clipping genuinely looked like it could be ninety years old. But what did that mean? Had I accidentally altered the future? I refolded the clipping and pushed it back towards her.

"Now do you believe me?"

"I don't know what to believe, Dr. Hollander," I said truthfully.

She sat there in silence, waiting to see how I would react. I ran through all the facts that I had. They didn't add up—unless. I was no longer so sure that she was delusional, which I found pretty scary. Finally I said:

"If Howard Winslow came back to kill his grandfather, he didn't succeed."

"That's just it, Mr. Christian. He didn't come back to kill his grandfather, he came to save him."

"How can you be so sure?" I asked.

"Because he was obsessed on the subject. Remember, that I worked closely with Dr. Winslow. He is a brilliant man, but he was born with a chip on his shoulder. He had this idea that fate had been stacked against him, not only in his life, but in previous generations. His father had been grown up poor; he'd never gotten an education, largely because father had been killed when he was just a baby.

"The people on the project used to talk about what we would do if we could go back in time. That was before we could actually do it, of course. Most people, if you ask them if what they would do if they could go back in time will say something like, "I'd warn the Titanic," "I'd stop John Wilkes Booth from killing Lincoln," or "I'd kill Hitler before he came to power." That's not what Howard said. He wanted to go back and prevent his grandfather's death."

"What about those paradoxes you mentioned?"

"We talked a lot about those, too. You can't help talking about them when you're working on time travel. We talked about them, we read all the time travel stories that feature them, we argued about them long into the night. Most of us were damned scared of what we were trying to do. But Howard didn't believe in the paradoxes—or he just didn't care."

"OK. I understand your concern. But, from what you've said, he came back and saved his grandfather's life, or rather arranged that I saved his grandfather's life, which I wouldn't have done otherwise. So Harlan Winslow is still alive. What's so bad about that? Usually saving a man's life is considered a good thing."

"Morally, perhaps. But in this case—is saving one man's life worth the risk of changing everything?"

"OK, I get that. But you haven't answered my question. What will happen now?"

She paused before answering, almost as if she was running calculations in her head to determine the answer.

"The short answer to your question is I don't know. I can't know. In the future I came from, which is actually my past, Harlan Winslow died last Friday at seven o'clock. If he didn't die then, the future is different, which means my past is different. I have no idea what I will be going back to when I return to the future."

"You sound frightened. Can one man really make that much of a difference?"

"In this case, yes. You have to understand that the very origins of the time travel project are rooted in the work of Harlan Winslow. What he was working on in that workshop on Third Street were the first preliminary experiments in controlling the time stream. Nothing dramatic, mind you, just altering the flow by a few microseconds a second. But his death interrupted that work. All his notes and schematics were bundled into a trunk and laid dormant for over fifty years. As I said, his son never got a proper education and wasn't capable of doing anything with them. It was only when his grandson, Howard Winslow found the trunk that time control research resumed. Howard was still an undergraduate then. It took him nearly thirty years of hard work before he created the prototype dingus.

"Now imagine what might happen with Harlan still alive. He continues his work. Maybe it takes him thirty years to achieve real results. Maybe even longer given the primitive technology he has to work with. Even so, what if he succeeds forty or fifty years early? Imagine for a moment what World War I would have been like if they had had atomic weapons?"

I had a better idea than most what she was getting at. I'd been at the Trinity site when they'd set off the first A-bomb. It wasn't the kind of thing you'd I'd forget.

"I get your point, Dr. Hollander. But do you really think it's that bad?"

She shook her head. The spring sunshine was streaming in through the office window and caught her hair as it moved. For a moment she looked like a Madonna or an angel. Then she just looked like a very frightened woman.

"I really don't know. No one does. There are all sorts of theories about time, none of which have any sort of experimental verification. Some of the people on the project talk about time having some sort of inertia, so that no matter what one does to change things, in the long run it won't matter much. Of course, they also talk about the butterfly effect."

"Butterfly effect? I'm not following you on that one."

"That's the theory that if you were to go back in time to the Jurassic and step on a butterfly, the whole course of the world changes maybe to the extent that mammals never achieve dominance of the earth and humans never evolve. There've been stories written about it. Now that you know time travel is possible, Mr. Christian, you should read one of them—if you don't want to sleep at night."

"That's a cheery thought," I replied.

It dawned on me that somewhere during our conversation I'd actually come to believe in Dr. Hollander. "What are you going to do?"

"I really don't know, Mr. Christian. It seems I've failed in my mission to find Howard Winslow and the TSC. There's no telling where—or when—he is now. Worse, I wasn't able to keep him from altering the time stream. No matter what I were to do now, the damage has already been done."

"Has it? It's only been a few days. Maybe I can still find Harlan Winslow for you."

"And then what? Will you kill him? I have a feeling that it's too late for that, even if either one of us had the stomach for the job. The only thing for me to do is return to the future and hope it's still there."

"You don't sound very comfortable with the possibilities," I said.

"I'm not," she said with resignation. "I want to thank you, Mr. Christian. You've been very patient with someone you must think is crazy." She gave me a smile, then, the kind of smile the Leonardo painted on the Mona Lisa. I smiled back. I realized that one way or another she was going out of my life.

"Don't forget your money, Dr. Hollander," I said, glancing at the envelope with the five C-notes.

"Keep it, Mr. Christian. I think you've earned it. Besides, chances are it won't do me any good in the future."

"You're sure there isn't anything I can do?"

"No. But thanks for the offer."

She picked up the dingus from the desk and did something with her finger on the front of it. Then she was gone.

There wasn't any flash of light, no whoosh of in-rushing air. Just one moment I was looking at her and the next I was staring at the wall behind her. It had all been real then, I thought. She really had been a time traveler, or at least something not ordinary. And I was the guy that had changed the world for ever.

I got up and walked over to the door to the outer office. When I opened it, Effie was sitting at her desk doing some typing. She looked up at the sound, looked into the empty office. For a moment it looked as if she was going to say something, but she didn't. The inner office only has the one door. I knew she must be wondering what had happened to "that woman" but Effie isn't one to ask questions she might not like the answers to.

I shut the door and sat back down at my desk. I keep a quart of rye in the bottom drawer for emergencies. I was pretty sure that this qualified. As I poured a couple of fingers of the amber liquid into a water glass I noticed that my hand was shaking.

They steadied with the bite of the first sip. Had any of it really happened? Was it all a dream that I was going to wake out of? I looked down at the desk. The two envelopes were still there. I opened them to check the contents. One contained five hundred dollars in old/new bills. The other contained the newspaper clipping of a murder that had never happened.

I took the two envelopes, put them in a larger manila one, and put them in the same safe where I keep my gun. As I locked the safe afterwards I wondered if they'd still be there the next time I opened the safe.

What was I going to do? What could I do?

I could play detective, was what I decided. I placed a couple of phone calls. The first was to Harlan Winslow's apartment building. The manager told me that Harlan had moved out sometime on Saturday. He'd packed up all his stuff and taken it with him. His rent was paid until the end of the month, so the manager didn't seem particularly upset with the situation.

The second call was to the guy who had the space across from Harlan's workshop. He remembered me, so he was willing to talk. When he'd come in this morning Harlan was gone. It was the same story. Everything had been packed up and moved out sometime over the weekend. I thanked him and hung up.

So that was that. Both Winslows had taken a powder, whether in time or space was anyone's guess. Dr. Hollander was gone as well, vanished in the blink of an eye. And I was left with fifteen hundred dollars and a half-empty glass of rye.

INTERLUDE ONE

ONE

(2042)

I wasn't there for the next part of the story, so I'll have to tell it as Dr. Hollander told it to me. That was later, of course, though it was some eighty-five years before the events happened. Helen was right when she said the tenses in language just weren't meant to work with time travel. Whatever the case, this is what she said happened when she returned to the future.

The first thing Helen noticed was that the room was different. It was the same shape and size as the room from which she had left for the past, but there were subtle differences. And some that weren't so subtle. Like the four uniformed guards holding what appeared to be some sort of automatic weapons. When she had left the NTL facility to go to 1955, there had been a couple of security men, but they had been nothing more than glorified watchmen meant to go around at night and make sure all the doors were locked and the windows secured. They had been nice, friendly middle-aged men who'd always checked up on her when she worked late and asked if she wanted a cup of coffee. These guards were young, fit, and didn't look at all friendly. She couldn't see them bring her a cup of coffee, either. They were wearing military style uniforms. The uniforms had shoulder patches that, from where she stood, looked like hour glasses. A similar looking logo inside a shield had been painted on the wall behind them. When she had left the wall had been painted a rather institutional beige. There had been no logo.

The TSC had a "snap-back" feature that was supposed to being you back to the same time and place that you had left. Actually, it brought you back to a time five seconds later so as to avoid embarrassing paradoxes. Sort of now you're there and then you're there, but in the meantime you had been off in some other time for however long it had taken. In the tests, the effect had been like a simple blink out, a little disconcerting, maybe, but not something you worried about.

Obviously, Helen thought, that hadn't happened here. Either something had gone wrong with the dingus—or something had gone horribly wrong with time. She was afraid it was the latter. She didn't get the chance to explain herself.

"Freeze!" It was one of the guards. She noticed that all four of them were pointing their weapons at her. Instinctively she raised her hands. That didn't seem to appease them, but at least they didn't shoot.

"OK, lady. Just who are you? And what are you doing in a secure facility?"

She took a moment to decide how to frame her reply. She didn't see any better alternative than to tell the truth. Either they would believe her—or they wouldn't.

"My name is Dr. Helen Hollander. I work for the National Time Laboratory. I'm a time traveler."

She wasn't expecting the reply she got. "You're not one of ours." Obviously, then, the guards knew about time travel. They were familiar enough with the process, too, not to question what she was.

The guard that had spoken to her said something into a communications device clipped to his shirt. She couldn't hear the reply, but he was obviously notifying someone up the chain of command.

She found herself escorted by two of the guards to a small room down a long corridor that she couldn't remember being there. The only furnishings in the room were a metal table and two metal chairs that appeared to be bolted to the floor. The table had a stout bar on it convenient for attaching handcuffs. The guard pointed at the chair farthest from the door, the implication being that she should sit. She sat.

The NTL facility she had left hadn't had any interrogation rooms. There had never been a need for any. There'd been a debriefing room, but that had had a conference table, comfortable chairs, and a coffee maker. It was as if they were expecting to detain people who dropped in on them unexpectedly. Helen didn't find that reassuring.

The head guard took her purse and the TSC and left. The other guard remained, standing between her and the door. At least that hadn't thought it necessary to chain her to the table.

She waited. She wasn't sure how long. They'd taken her watch along with her other things, not that it had been anything more than a watch, even if it had been an antique. The room didn't have any windows, so there was nothing to mark the passing of time. She started to get hungry. She needed to use the bathroom, too, but she wasn't going to raise that point with the guard until she was desperate.

After an eternity the door opened. It was a different man. This one wore a dark suit, though, from the way he wore it, it might as well have been a uniform. His hair was cut short on the sides in a style that was vaguely military.

He'd brought in a cardboard box and a coffee cup. The box had her purse and the TSC. He set them the box on the table and then sat in the chair she wasn't sitting in, the one closest to the door. It was clear he hadn't brought the coffee for her.

One by one, he took the items out of the box and laid them on the table. When he was done, he set the box on the floor next to him. Then he emptied her purse and spread the contents out in front of him. He made a show of examining each of them, though Helen was pretty sure that he had already done that before he had come in. He seemed particularly interest in the pistol. Finally, he picked up the wallet with her ID card. He opened it up and took out the card for an inspection.

"This says that you are Dr. Helen Hollander, and that you work for the National Time Laboratory. Is that correct?"

"Yes."

"Very impressive credentials, I must say. They almost look like the real thing."

"That's because they are," Helen commented.

"Is that your real name, Dr. Hollander?" he asked with exaggerated skepticism. He seemed intent on annoying her.

"Yes," she answered, trying not to rise to the bait.

"I see," he said slowly, stretching out the word "see." "The problem is, Dr. Hollander, that we have no record of anyone of that name, nor is there any such thing as a 'National Time Laboratory.' Would you care to expound on these facts."

"I assure you I am Dr. Hollander, and I do work for the National Time Laboratory. I'm a time traveler, but then you already know that, don't you?"

"Yes, Dr. Hollander, I know that."

He set the ID card down on the desk and picked up the TSC.

"And this device? I assume that it is your time machine?"

"Yes, that what we call a Time Stream Controller, though usually we just refer to it as the dingus. I assume you are familiar with such things?"

"Yes, Dr. Hollander, though ours are a bit more sophisticated."

"That model is a prototype," Helen replied defensively.

"I see. Just what year do you come from, Dr. Hollander? You clothing would appear to be appropriate for the mid twentieth century, but I assume that it is a costume to blend in with—shall we say the natives."

Helen found that she had taken an intense dislike to her interrogator. Maybe it was a pose, but he seemed to have taken all his cues from watching old movies of Gestapo agents. Still, she didn't see any point in denying what they both knew was true.

"I come from the year 2042. The tenth of June."

"Interesting. Today is June 10, 2042. I had thought that it might be possible that you were a time traveler from an earlier time which would explain the crude nature of your controller, but that would appear not to be the case. If what you are telling me is true, that is."

"Oh, it's true enough, Mr. whatever your name is. I left this very facility on this date to travel back to 1955. I returned to the exact moment I departed, but obviously something has changed. This is no longer the National Time Laboratory, is it?"

"No, Dr. Hollander, this is the National Bureau of Time. It would seem that in your time travels, you have managed to alter history."

"It wasn't me. It was someone else."

"Of course. By the way, you can call me Colonel Smith, if you find that more convenient."

Helen didn't comment.

Col. Smith put down the TSC and picked up the automatic pistol. He seemed to be fascinated with the weapon, but then Helen thought he was the type that would be.

"Tell me, Dr. Hollander, do all the agents of your NTL carry weapons when they travel?"

"We don't have agents, Col. Smith. The NTL is a scientific agency. But in this particular case, it was thought—prudent."

"And why was that. Dr. Hollander?"

"Because I had been sent after someone who had stolen a TSC. I was supposed to recover it, one way or another."

"And did you?"

"No. As you can see, I only had the one dingus on me."

"So you failed?" Smith seemed intent on getting her to admit it.

"Yes. I failed," Helen admitted. "Does that make you happy?"

"Let's not get emotional, Dr. Hollander. Now you say that you went back into the past to retrieve a controller that had been stolen. I assume that it was stolen by one of your colleagues at the NTL. Would you care to give me his name?"

She thought for a moment about refusing, but she didn't see any point in doing so. She was stuck in a present that wasn't of her own making, and it appeared that she would have to live with that.

"His name was Howard Winslow. He was/is chief scientist at the NTL."

That didn't get the reaction she had expected. Smith looked up from the pistol straight into her eyes, then he put the pistol back in the box and began to gather up all her other belongings.

"I'm afraid, Dr. Hollander, that this interview is over for the moment," Smith said as he stood.

"Wait a minute. Just like that? What's going to happen to me?"

"I find I must confer with my superiors, Dr. Hollander."

"Look, I've been stuck in this room for hours. I haven't had anything to eat, and I need to use the bathroom. Badly."

Col. Smith smiled. "I'll see what can be arranged." Then he turned and left.

A few minutes later a guard came in and she was escorted a short distance down the hall to a bathroom. Despite the fact that it was marked "Women" the guards followed her in. There didn't seem to be much point as the bathroom had no windows and only the single door, but she supposed they were following orders. She went into a stall and relieved herself, taking a long time at it. There was no telling when she might next get a chance. She was escorted back to the interview room where she found a sandwich, a bowl of soup, and a cup of coffee waiting for her.

It wasn't great soup, but she hadn't realized how hungry she was. She finished all the soup and the sandwich, too, which wasn't bad, ham and Swiss on rye. She lingered over the coffee until it had grown too cool to be drinkable. Then she waited. It might have been an hour, it might have been two.

Finally the door opened again, and a tall man entered. He looked to be in his late fifties. He was wearing an open collared short sleeved shirt and slacks and his hair looked like it could do with a trim. Helen thought he looked surprisingly like one of her co-workers at the NTL, Dr. Feuerstein.

He turned to the guard and said, "You can wait outside." The guard looked uncertain, but then the newcomer said, "Please." The guard left.

The newcomer took a seat. "I apologize for your circumstances, Dr. Hollander, but you've presented us with quite a problem. My name is Nathan Feuerstein, by the way. I'm the head of Temporal Research at the NBT."

"I know a Nathan Feuerstein," Helen said. "He is one of my colleagues at the NTL."

"I see," Feuerstein replied. "That's very interesting. To think that my—counterpart followed a more or less parallel path despite the changes to the time stream—"

"Then you understand what happened?"

"I won't say that I understand, Dr. Hollander, but I know that something has happened and that the world you left no longer exists, at least not in the same form. As you must know, temporal theory is complex and even after twenty years we are still trying to get a handle on all the nuances."

"You've had time travel for twenty years?" Helen asked, amazed.

"Yes. I take it that in your time line time control is a more recent development?"

"As far as I know, I was only the second time traveler," Helen answered. She found herself opening up to this man who was very like the Feuerstein she had known. "There had been experiments with inanimate objects and animals for a few years, but only over short intervals."

"Interesting. Your ID gives your name as Dr. Hollander. I take it you are a scientist, then?"

"A mathematician, actually. I specialized in knot theory. I was brought into the NTL to help work out what happens when the time stream loops back on itself."

The scientist in Feuerstein took over. "I say. That's something we should have thought of. I can see the applicability. I'd be interested in knowing how far you have gotten in your researches, Dr. Hollander."

"Not very far, I'm afraid. As you said, temporal theory is complex, and we've been reluctant to carry out experiments that intentionally cause paradoxes."

"Understandable, and yet—"

"That wasn't my doing. One of my colleagues stole a TSC and went back in time with the intention of altering time. I was sent back to stop him, but as you see, I failed."

"But why would a scientist, someone who must have realized the consequences, want to change time? Surely he must have known that it would have an impact."

"I'm afraid that he is mentally unbalanced. Brilliant, but obsessed with the past. You see, his grandfather was murdered. The result was that his father grew up in poverty. He felt that this was a wrong that he could right. He used to talk about the possibility endlessly, but none of us thought that he would actually do anything about it. But then he did—"

"And thus brought about your present predicament. I take it he managed to prevent his grandfather's murder?"

"Indirectly, yes. He hired a private investigator to follow his grandfather. The detective interrupted events and saved the man. I was too late to stop him. So now I've come back and found my own time gone."

"Most unfortunate for you, Dr. Hollander. But perhaps not so unfortunate for the man who was saved. Who of us can say which is the better outcome? Might I ask the name of your colleague?"

"I don't see how it can mess things up any more than they are. His name is Howard Winslow. That seemed to mean something to the man who was interrogating me earlier."

"Yes, it did. You see, Dr. Hollander, Dr. Howard Winslow is the director of the NBT as was his father before him, Dr. Henry Winslow. In fact, all of our time travel research has been based on the work of the current director's grandfather, Harlan Winslow."

"So Howard Winslow is your boss?"

"That's putting it mildly, Dr. Hollander. Howard Winslow is a very important man in the government. I'm not sure if you can imagine the uses that time technology can be put to."

"Oh, I think I have some idea," Helen said disapprovingly.

"You must understand, then, what an awkward position this puts you in. The director is going to be very interested in you, I'm afraid."

"And why would that be?"

"Because, if what you have told us is true, then you are an example of the very reason the bureau was created."

"And why was that?" Helen asked.

"After the current director's father, Henry Winslow, created the first working temporal controller, he immediately realized the implications of what he had done, the fact that someone equipped with such a device could go back in time and intentionally alter history for their own ideological purposes. He informed contacts that he had in the government of his fears. Fortunately, they took him seriously. The result was that the

National Bureau of Time was created to prevent such acts of temporal sabotage. Henry Winslow was made its director, a post that his son now holds."

"That was convenient," Helen remarked.

"You must understand, Dr. Hollander, that time travel is a closely held secret. The public has never been informed of the possibility, and only a select group of individuals know of the existence or purpose of the bureau."

"I see," Helen said. The NBT was starting to sound more like a secret police force than a government agency.

"You can see the position you are in, Dr. Hollander. By your own admission, you went back in time to alter history."

"Hey," Helen objected indignantly. "You can't blame that on me. It was all the work of the counterpart of your director. I was trying to stop him."

"Can you be sure of that? That it wasn't your actions that changed history. You have said that the purpose of you mission was to make sure that Harlan Winslow was murdered. Isn't that correct?"

"Well, yes. But that's because that's the way things happened in my past. Harlan Winslow was murdered. It was only because of the interference of Howard Winslow that he didn't die."

"There are twelve billion people alive today who would beg to differ with you, Dr. Hollander. If you had succeeded in you mission, their lives today would be different. Oh, for some, the changes would be small, perhaps not even noticeable. But for others, the changes would be major, perhaps even catastrophic. Surely you can see that, can't you?"

"And what about the twelve billion people in my present?" Helen asked.

"I'm afraid that your present and the people in it no longer exist. If they did, you wouldn't be here, would you?"

Helen paused. She found she didn't have an argument with which to refute Feuerstein's statement.

"I didn't mean to impugn your motives, Dr. Hollander. I'm sure that you were operating with the best of intentions and with the full support of your superiors. However, you must agree, that from our point of view your actions risked our very existence."

"But I didn't do anything! My mission was a failure. I wasn't able to prevent Howard Winslow from changing the past. Can't you understand that?"

"Oh, I understand that perfectly, Dr. Hollander. Your mission failed because it was doomed to fail. Whether you were the causal agent or not, you had to fail. If you had succeeded, we wouldn't be here in this room, would we?"

Dr. Feuerstein sat back rather smugly. Helen couldn't remember her Feuerstein ever looking smug. He just hadn't been that kind of person.

"OK, I get it. There's no point in arguing the matter, is there?"

"No, I'm afraid not, Dr. Hollander."

"So what is going to happen to me?"

"That is a matter under discussion. As I said earlier, you present us with a problem, Dr. Hollander, a paradox, if you like. Since your arrival, we've been checking the government databases looking for the existence of your counterpart. The fact is, Dr. Hollander, you don't seem to exist. The only Helen Hollander on record was a graduate student of philosophy, but she was born in 1951. Obviously, that is too old to be you. Isn't it?"

"No, that would have been my grandmother," Helen said.

"I don't see how that is possible. Helen Hollander, that Helen Hollander, died childless in 1979."

"That can't be right," Helen argued.

"Our records are quite thorough, Dr. Hollander. Oh, I have no doubt that in your timeline she had a child, your mother, but in this timeline, neither you nor your mother have ever existed. I'm sorry if that distresses you, but that is the way things are."

Helen was stunned. She loved her mother. She was a caring, intelligent woman of great character. As for her grandmother— she had been truly remarkable, an academic, an author, a political activist who had been active well into her eighties. How could that past have ceased to exist? Had she somehow been responsible?

"I can see this is something of a shock to you. I understand completely. But to answer your question, at least in the short term, nothing will happen to you. You will be our—guest—while your—fate is decided on. We are, after all, a government agency, Dr. Hollander, not barbarians."

"That's reassuring," Helen remarked.

Feuerstein looked at her, a half-smile on his face.

"There is one thing I'd like to ask you out of curiosity, Dr. Hollander."

"What is that?" Helen was getting tired of the interrogation, but she realized she didn't have much choice in the matter.

"You said that you are a mathematician. A specialist in knot theory, I believe."

"That is correct."

"Excuse me, but you would seem to be an odd choice for a field agent."

"We don't have field agents, Dr. Feuerstein." Helen had long since given up on worrying about tenses. "You have to understand that the NTL is not an enforcement agency, and we don't have nearly the resources that the NBT evidently has. When it was discovered that Dr. Winslow had taken one of the two prototype controllers we thought we had to act quickly."

"Despite the fact that you had all the time in the world?"

"Did we? You have to understand that we are much newer at this game than you appear to be."

"But why you specifically, Dr. Hollander?"

"I was available. It was felt that I was the best equipped to avoid potential paradoxes that might crop up because of my theoretical work, though that doesn't seem to have been the case. Another factor, though less important, was that my mother was a historian."

"I'm afraid I don't understand," Feuerstein commented.

"Her field of study was the cultural history of the twentieth century. Growing up, I'd been exposed to everything from the

Jazz Age to grunge rock. It was thought that this knowledge would give me the best chance of blending in."

"Yes, that would make sense. It always amazes me how little we know about the relatively recent past. I'd like to thank you for satisfying my curiosity, Dr. Hollander."

"Think nothing of it," Helen replied.

"On the contrary, I value this little talk we've had. Be assured that I will put in a good word for you with the director." He looked at his watch. "I must be going now. I have a meeting in a few minutes. I believe that someone will be along shortly to show you to more comfortable quarters."

Feuerstein stood up and extended his hand. Despite herself, Helen accepted it. He wasn't her Feuerstein, but he did seem to share some of the character of the man she knew.

Some fifteen minutes after he had left a guard entered the room. Helen couldn't be sure if he was the same one as had watched her earlier or not. They all seemed to look alike.

"Follow me." It was half an order, half a request. Helen didn't see any reason to resist, so she followed.

They walked down enough corridors that Helen was completely lost. The NBT facility was much larger than the NTL had been. She found herself wondering just how many people the NBT employed.

Eventually, she was shown into a room. It wasn't big, but there was a bed, a table and several chairs, a dresser, a small refrigerator and a microwave. There was even a television screen on the wall. Off of the main room there was a small bathroom with a shower. Next to the bathroom was a closet. When she opened it, she saw that there were several outfits in what looked to be her size. She opened the drawers of the dresser and found some sweaters and underwear, again in her size. The NBT seemed to be nothing if not efficient.

It reminded her of nothing as much as a college dormitory room. Except for the fact that it didn't have a window. When she tried the door it was locked. She knew that there was no point in pounding on the substantial door and asking to be let out.

Instead, she undressed and took a shower. She felt that she had earned that much.

After her shower, she dressed in a pair of slacks and a comfortable looking sweater. The refrigerator was stocked with juice, water, and soft drinks, all of brands she recognized. There was nothing alcoholic which was a shame. She could have used something to drink. There were some packs of popcorn on top of the microwave. She took one and popped it into the microwave and then grabbed a soda from the refrigerator.

While the popcorn was popping, she turned on the TV. No effort seemed to have been made to censor the content. She flipped through the channels, finally settling on the news. As she ate her popcorn and drank her soda she thought how normal it all seemed.

When she finally dozed off her sleep was disturbed by dreams of her mother and grandmother. They were of the time the three of them had all shared a house when she had been nine years old. In the dreams Howard Winslow came knocking on the door of their house, but when her grandmother went to the door to answer, she slowly turned transparent and faded away to nothing. The dream repeated, except this time it was her mother who went to the door. Helen tried to dissuade her mother from opening the door, but she did anyway, meeting the same fate as Helen's grandmother. The dream replayed a third time, only this time Helen was the only one in the house when the knocking came. She woke in a cold sweat, her heart thumping loudly.

After that she fell back into a restless sleep until she woke to a knocking on the door. For a moment she had an irrational fear of what would happen if she opened it, but finally she said, "Who is it?"

"It's breakfast, Dr. Hollander."

"Come in."

The door opened. Instead of Howard Winslow, it was a man dressed like a hospital orderly carrying a tray. Through the door she caught a glimpse of a uniformed guard with an automatic rifle.

"I'll just set this tray on the table, ma'am if that's alright." His voice was tired but kindly.

"That will be fine. Thank you."

He placed the tray on the table and left. After the door shut, she heard it being relocked.

Breakfast consisted of an omelet, toast, and orange juice. There was a small carafe of coffee, as well. Helen hadn't realized it, but she was ravenously hungry. It didn't matter that the omelet had all the lack of character of institutional food, she cleaned her plate. The coffee wasn't particularly good, either, but it seemed to steady her nerves.

In the bathroom she found a toothbrush in a plastic wrapper. She brushed her teeth and tried to make her hair behave. She thought about taking another shower, but decided against it. She had no idea if or when they might come for her.

With nothing else to do, she turned the television back on and switched to a morning news program. At first, there was nothing to indicate that things had changed, but then she began to notice subtle differences. There were still stories about Washington politics and international tensions. She recognized some of the names, but others were new to her. She had been so tied up in her work that she hadn't been paying much attention to current affairs, but had there been a border dispute between Poland and Belarus? She couldn't be sure. After an hour, the one impression she had was that this new world she was in was even more messed up than her old one had been.

When she found the news program growing repetitive, she flipped channels to one of entertainment news. She didn't follow the film industry much, so she wasn't sure how much was different. Again, she knew some of the names, mostly of older actors and actresses, but wasn't familiar with others. That didn't really mean much, though. She found herself tuning out what the hosts of the show were saying and watching the background of the video clips they played.

She noticed that the cars seemed more angular and larger than they had been in what she was beginning to just call "before." The emphasis seemed to be on looking impressive and powerful rather than luxurious. There were other differences, too, like a subtle shift in vocabulary. Every once in awhile there would be a word that she just didn't recognize. The technology was slightly different, too. Some devices seemed to be improvements, but some looked as if they were less capable. There didn't seem to be any consistency as to which was which.

She started looking at the hemlines of the women's dresses and the collars of the men's shirts. Helen knew that you could tell a lot about a culture by its fashion. Her mother had spent a whole year working on a paper about hemlines in the movies and the political climate from 1920 to 2020. She'd read the paper, of course. She'd spent her childhood proofing her mother's and sometimes her grandmother's publications. She felt a sudden pang at the memory. From what she could remember of the paper, this society seemed more conservative and repressive than the one she had left.

She started flipping through channels at random looking for clues as to the state of society. She didn't like what she saw. There was more discrimination against minority groups and more social stratification. Her own world certainly hadn't been free of prejudice, but here it seemed to be more widely held and even approved of.

She hadn't realized how much time had passed until there was another knock at the door. She looked at the clock on the wall and saw that it was noon.

"Lunch, Dr. Hollander."

"Come in."

It was the same orderly who came in through the door bearing the lunch tray. He set it on the table and picked up the one holding the breakfast dishes.

Helen automatically said, "Thank you."

The man smiled and replied, "You're welcome, Dr. Hollander. The choices for dinner are chicken or beef. Which would you like me to bring you?"

As he didn't mention the preparation of either, the choice probably didn't matter. At least they were feeding her. She picked one more or less at random.

"I guess I'll take the beef. Say, would it be possible for me to get something to read? I'm going crazy watching TV."

"I'll see what I can do, Dr. Hollander," the orderly replied, and then left. Again she heard the door being locked.

Lunch consisted of a salad that looked as if it had been put together by a nutritionist. That didn't stop her from eating it.

Half an hour later, the orderly returned.

"They said that you could have a reader, ma'am. It has access to all the books in the library here. I hope that is alright."

"I'm sure that will be just fine. Thank you."

He set a reader on the table and left.

She flipped the television back to a news channel and muted the sound. It proved fairly easy to operate the reader. The principles were the same as the ones she was used to. The available library looked to be extensive.

She started to do a quick check of the contents. As much as she could remember books that had been published prior to 1955 were the same. Titles from the years immediately after were more or less the same, though she noticed that a few that she would have expected to exist were not listed. The closer that she got to the present, the more gaps there seemed to be. That was to be expected, Helen, thought, as the changes accumulated.

She selected a book on recent history and browsed it for a short time, but she found it unhelpful. She couldn't decide what things were really different and what were just gaps in her own knowledge of current events.

After the history, she selected a book on knot theory, something that she did know about. Going through the list of citations, she recognized most of the papers, but again there were papers missing and ones present that she didn't recognize. None of the works of her thesis adviser were listed, and they should have been.

Helen realized that the only thing any of this proved was that the world she was in wasn't the world she was from, but then she had known that all along.

In disgust, she grabbed a soft drink from the refrigerator, selected a mystery from the 1930's, which she started to read sitting on the bed with her back propped up against the headboard.

Dinner was delivered just after five-thirty, slices of roast beef in some sort of brown gravy with mashed potatoes and green beans. There was another carafe of coffee, though she would have preferred a glass of wine. The gravy was oniony, but not bad. The beef was overdone.

After the orderly cleared the dishes, she tried to watch some television, but, somehow, she just couldn't maintain interest in it. She knew it wasn't her world that she was watching. She turned off the television and read until she dropped off to sleep.

The next day was more or less a repeat of the previous one, except for the fact that she chose the chicken for dinner. It was becoming obvious that they were trying to soften her up with isolation. The only question was, for what?

On the third day a guard came for her just before ten o'clock. He was polite but uncommunicative. He escorted her to a conference room where he indicated she should sit at the end of a long table. He left her alone, but Helen had no doubt that he, or another guard, would be waiting in the hallway outside the door.

The room didn't have a clock. She wondered if that was intentional or not. After what she estimated had been fifteen minutes, she started to fidget. She felt like a schoolgirl waiting for the principal.

Finally the door opened. It was Col. Smith accompanied by several other people in uniform. They took up seats on one side of the table. They didn't make small talk amongst themselves. Five minutes later Dr. Feuerstein joined the conference, taking a seat opposite Smith.

"Dr. Cooper and his assistant will be here shortly," Feuerstein commented to no one in particular. Col. Smith glanced at his watch. Helen noted with curiosity that they still wore watches. Most people didn't in her timeline.

A few minutes later two men in white coats came in. Presumably one of them was Dr. Cooper. They took seats at the table on the same side as Dr. Feuerstein. Clearly, there was a division between the military and the scientists. There was no conversation between the two sides. No one had taken the seat at the head of the table.

After ten minutes of sitting in silence, the door opened again. Everybody on both sides of the table stood. Helen decided that it would be politic if she joined them. They all remained standing until the most recent arrival took his place at the head of the table. That was when Helen got a good look at the newcomer. It was Howard Winslow.

Except, of course, it wasn't the Howard Winslow that Helen knew. The age was the same, and so was the general height and build, though this Winslow seemed heavier and less fit. There was a gray pallor to his complexion, as if he worked long hours and didn't get outside much. There was a hardness to his eyes, too, that had been missing in the Howard Winslow that she knew.

"So this is our time traveler?" Winslow said without preamble.

Col. Smith answered, "Yes, director."

"And there's no doubt about that?"

"She appeared out of nowhere in the landing stage room. There were four guards present at the time," Col. Smith stated.

"We've examined the device that she had with her," Dr. Feuerstein interjected. "There are differences in the implementation, but there doesn't seem to be any question but that it is a time stream modulator."

"Could it have been stolen? Or built from leaked information?" Winslow asked.

"It's not likely. There are certain parts that don't look like anything that is available here."

"Here?" Winslow asked.

"On this timeline, Director," Feuerstein said.

"It couldn't be the Chinese? Or the Europeans?"

"We don't think so, Director." This came from the man she assumed was Cooper.

Helen found the exchange interesting. This Winslow appeared to be more of a bureaucrat and less involved with the technology. Her Winslow had been the chief scientist of the NTL.

"Very well. We'll accept for the moment that she is really a time traveler." Winslow turned his gaze on her, examining her for the first time. "Dr. Hollander. That is your name and not an alias?"

"Yes," she answered.

"And your degree is in?"

"Mathematics. Knot theory, to be exact."

"Interesting. I assume that has some relevance, Dr. Feuerstein?"

"It seems plausible. It might be useful to untangle paradoxes. Or avoid them."

"I'll take your word for that, Dr. Feuerstein. I find it odd, Dr. Hollander, that this NTL you claim you work for would choose to send a mathematician on a mission."

"The NTL doesn't have the resources that your organization appears to have, Dr. Winslow."

"Director Winslow," Col. Smith corrected.

"Director Winslow," Helen repeated, emphasizing the first word.

"Dr. Hollander, you say that you went back to April of 1955. Is that correct?"

"Yes."

"Curiously enough, that is the time that my grandfather avoided an assassination attempt. A coincidence—"

"It wasn't a coincidence," Helen agreed. "I was sent back to 1955 to retrieve a prototype time stream controller that had been stolen by the chief scientist of the project. His name was Dr. Howard Winslow. You can probably guess why he chose 1955."

"So you are saying that my—double—went back to 1955 to prevent the murder of my grandfather."

"That is correct."

"I take it that he was successful—despite your efforts."

"Yes," Helen replied thinking that if she had succeeded in stopping Winslow, she wouldn't be sitting here.

"How many agents does this NTL have trying to alter the time stream?"

"The NTL doesn't have agents," Helen said. "We are a research organization." Helen wondered how much of the details of the NTL she could risk revealing.

"And this other Howard Winslow? What happened to him? Were you supposed to rendezvous here?"

"We weren't working together. But to answer your question, I don't know what happened to Dr. Winslow. After the incident with your grandfather he disappeared."

"But he was in possession of a working time stream modulator?"

"If you mean, did he have a TSC, then the answer is yes."

The director turned and asked, "Col. Smith, has there been any sign that this Dr. Winslow is in the present?"

"There hasn't been any sign of such a person surfacing, Director. But, rest assured, we will be keeping our eyes open for him. I've also instituted a historical search to see if he may have gone to some other time."

"Good. Though I admit I'm not sure what to do if we should find this other me," Winslow said with a chuckle. "Should we arrest him or pin a medal on him for saving my—our—grandfather?"

"I think we should be careful about what we do with regards to this counterpart to you, Director," Dr. Feuerstein said. "We're not sure exactly what paradoxes might arise if there were two of you at the same time and place. The results might not be predictable--or pleasant."

"Yes. I see your point," the director said, then after a moment continued, "Perhaps Dr. Hollander might have some insight on that subject."

Everyone at the table looked in her direction. Helen felt like saying, "don't look at me," but she remained silent.

The director stood. "Well, gentlemen. And Dr. Hollander. I'm afraid I have a meeting with the president, so I must leave you. Col. Smith, Dr. Feuerstein, I will be expecting a full report and your recommendations on this situation. Good day."

Everyone stood until the director had left the room.

After he was gone, Col. Smith addressed Dr. Feuerstein, "Well, you've heard the director, Feuerstein. We need to get to the bottom of this mess. Perhaps you can get this woman to cooperate. If not—remember, time is limited."

With that, he got up and left the room followed by the rest of his staff leaving only Feuerstein, Cooper and the other scientist.

"I see that you and Col. Smith don't exactly get along," Helen commented.

"Col. Smith can be an ass, Dr. Hollander. A prime example of the military mind. But don't sell him short. He's no fool—and he can be ruthless when he thinks it necessary."

"I'll keep that in mind, Dr. Feuerstein," Helen replied.

"I'm not sure you realize just how precarious your position is, Dr. Hollander."

"I have some idea."

"The world you came from no longer exists. The events of 1955 ensured that. The present that you are in is the only one you have."

"Are you sure of that? It seems to me the timeline has changed once. What's to keep it from changing again?"

"Col. Smith, for one. Let me make this clear, Dr. Hollander. You will not be allowed to leave this facility, either through the door or by use of a TSM. You are stuck here. But that doesn't have to be unpleasant. Cooperate and you will be given considerations."

"And if I don't?"

"I'm afraid that in that case things could get very bad. The NBT has the authority to terminate anyone that it deems a threat to the time stream. That is its primary mission, to insure the integrity of the time stream. You may not realize it, but people are very nervous about your appearance. And the thought that there is at least one more rogue time traveler on the loose isn't helping any."

"Look, I appreciate your being frank with me, Dr. Feuerstein, and I understand my position. I'm willing to cooperate as much as I can, but I still have some questions."

"Such as?"

"Some of the people in this world had counterparts in mine. You for instance, or the director. Why not me? In our earlier conversation you said that the woman who was my grandmother died in 1979. I'd like to know more about what happened to her. What kind of woman she was. How she died."

"May I ask why, Dr. Hollander? After all, she wasn't your grandmother. As I explained, she died without having any children."

"Still, up until her death she was very much like my grandmother. As such, it appears that she's the closest thing to family I have."

"I thought it might come to this," Feuerstein said with a sigh. "I suppose it's natural for you to want to know that kind of thing. I had a dossier prepared on Helen Hollander. I hope that it will answer some of your questions."

He opened his briefcase and pulled out a file folder. It was surprisingly thick. He slid it across the table top towards her.

Helen opened the folder. The first thing that confronted her was a picture, evidently taken from a university ID while she was in graduate school. Helen had seen photos of her grandmother during those years. There was no question but that it was the same woman. There was a copy of a birth certificate. All the details matched what she remembered. There was a death certificate, as well. The date was November 1, 1979. The cause of death was listed as multiple gunshot wounds to head and torso. As she read the police report, tears welled up in her eyes.

"I'm sorry. You'll have to excuse me. I was very—close to my grandmother."

"I understand, Dr. Hollander. I'm sorry this causes you distress, but I thought you would want to know." For a moment he sounded like her Nathan Feuerstein, a kind and thoughtful man. Were they really so different? "Perhaps you'd like to be alone for a moment."

"Please, I'd like that," Helen said.

The three scientists left the room, while Helen continued to read the file. The police had never solved the case. Ballistics had been unable to match the bullets that were recovered to any known weapon. Also, they had been of an unusual type and caliber. There were reports of two men seen in the vicinity of where the body was found, but nothing to tie them to the murder. They had not been found in the investigation that followed the discovery of the body.

The rest of the file consisted of a paper trail of her grandmother's life, her grades in school, her vaccination records, a few newspaper clippings of events in her life. There was even a copy of an unfinished draft of her doctoral thesis. There was no question that the woman described in the folder was her grandmother, except that her grandmother had died only a few years earlier after a lifetime of achievements and this woman had died when she had been only twenty-eight.

Someone had killed her. Who? Had it just been a random act of violence? Or, Helen thought, had it been agents from the NBT seeking to preserve "the integrity of the time stream?"

Helen wiped the tears from her eyes. That's when she saw it. Dr. Feuerstein had left his briefcase open on the table. Inside was the dingus, her TMC. She reached out and picked it up. She pressed the on switch. It was still charged, still functioning.

The display gave a snap back date of April 1955. There was nothing here for her, Helen decided. She pressed the button.

PART THREE

(1955)

I took a swig of the rye and set the glass back on the desk. When I looked up she was sitting there, right where she had been when she had disappeared into thin air. Except it wasn't exactly the same woman. For one thing, she was dressed differently. She had been wearing a skirt, blouse and jacket. Now she had on a clingy sort of sweater in a heathery color and a narrow pair of black slacks. She looked tired, too, as if the weight of the world were on her shoulders. She had been crying. It couldn't have been more than ten minutes since she'd done her vanishing act, but I wondered how much time had passed for her.

Clearly, it had been more than ten minutes. It was odd that I found myself thinking in those terms, that time could pass at different rates for different people. Despite the improbability of it all, I had bought into her story. Was it because I had seen her wink out with my own eyes, or was it something more? I didn't have an answer.

"You look like you could use a snort," I said, pointing at the bottle of rye with my eyes. Maybe it wasn't the most original line, but she did look like a stiff belt would do her some good.

"Thanks, I'd appreciate it," she replied. There was just a trace of a smile, as if she were out of practice.

I fished a second glass out of the desk drawer. "All I've got is rye. I don't have any ice, either, but I can send Effie out to get some if you'd like."

"Rye will do fine, Mr. Christian, and I can handle my whiskey straight."

I admire that in a woman. I poured two fingers of the amber liquid into her glass, looked at her, and then poured another finger's worth. I topped off my glass, as well. I had a feeling we were going to be having a long talk. I slid the glass across the desk towards her. She picked it up in her long, thin fingers and raised it to her mouth. I noticed that she wasn't wearing any polish on her nails. They had been bright crimson earlier.

"I need your help, Mr. Christian," she said after she had taken a sip of the rye. She had been right, she could handle her whiskey straight.

We were interrupted by a rap of knuckles on the glass of the door to the outer office. The door opened and Effie walked in. She got a glimpse at Dr. Hollander and her eyes went wide as she tried to figure how Dr. Hollander had managed the disappearing act.

"I thought I heard voices," Effie explained uncertainly. I'd never seen Effie looking flustered before, but she must have noticed the change of clothes, as well. Effie is no prude, but my office doesn't have a closet, so there was no place Dr. Hollander could have changed.

"Dr. Hollander and I have some business to discuss, Effie. I'd appreciate it if we weren't disturbed."

"Of course, Mr. Christian." Effie only uses my last name in the presence of clients—or when she disapproves of something I've done. She turned on her heels and closed the door behind her firmly enough that the glass rattled.

I looked at Dr. Hollander. There was a smile on her face, this time a real one.

"I'm not sure your secretary approves of me."

"You'll have to make allowances for Effie. She's probably wondering what kind of hanky-panky we've been up to in here. And how we managed it. But I see it's made you smile. It looks good on you. You should try it more often."

She looked at me in that appraising way women have with men that they don't quite know. I'm not sure what she saw.

To avoid awkwardness I said, "You mentioned you needed my help."

"Yes. I think my grandmother is going to be murdered. I want you to help me prevent that."

I could see that she was serious. I did a little mental math and the numbers didn't add up.

"Your grandmother would be—"

"Right now she'd be three, I think."

"I take it that her demise isn't exactly imminent. Or is it?"

"No. Her murder, if it happens, will take place in 1979," Dr. Hollander said.

"You say if it happens—"

"In the time that I come from, she lived to be eighty seven. She died peacefully in her bed in 2039."

"You'll have to excuse me, Dr. Hollander, but I'm not used to all this time travel business. I guess I don't understand how your grandmother can have been murdered in 1979 yet die in her bed in 2039. Is this one of those paradoxes we were talking about earlier?"

"Yes, in a way. Maybe it would be best if I explain where I've been and what's happened since I left your office earlier."

"Yes. It probably would be," I agreed.

She took a sip of rye and then began. "You should know that the TSC, the dingus has a function that can take you back to the exact time and place you left from. We call it a 'snap-back' and it's a way of getting home. That's what I used when I left. Except that when I arrived in 2042 it wasn't the 2042 that I'd left. Oh, it was the same place, the same date and time, but everything else was different."

"In what way?" I prompted.

"Well, the first thing is it wasn't the NTL anymore. The facility was part of something called the National Bureau of Time. But it was more than just a change of name. The whole purpose was different. Instead of conducting scientific research the bureau seemed to have become some sort of policing agency."

"Policing what?"

"Time itself."

"Time? I'm afraid I still don't understand."

"How can I make this clear to you, Mr. Christian? When you interfered with time and prevented Harlan Winslow from being killed in that alley, you changed the course of history. Instead of growing up in poverty, his son grew up to be a scientist, and building on some of his father's ideas he was the one who invented time travel rather than his son. Except, he made a working time controller some thirty years before one was developed in my time line. Realizing the implications, he went to people he knew in the government. That's how the NBT was created. He was made its first director. His son, Howard Winslow is the current director. The purpose of the bureau is to make sure that the future, their future, isn't changed by other time travelers. From what I learned, their methods can be quite ruthless."

"You said that Howard Winslow is the current director of this bureau? The same Howard Winslow that hired me?"

"No, that's just it. That Howard Winslow came from my timeline, the timeline where there is no bureau and the TSC isn't invented until 2042. That Howard went back in time to your present and hired you to find his grandfather who had been murdered when his father was just an infant. It was the act of you saving his grandfather that changed history so that when I returned to the future it was a future in which the NBT existed and I didn't!"

"Excuse me. Did you say you didn't exist?"

"Or I won't exist. Whichever way you want to put it. When I arrived back in 2042 Howard Winslow exists, except he is the director of the NBT and not just a scientist. The counterparts of some of the other people that I knew also still exist and are involved with the NBT. But there isn't a counterpart of me. Not just working for the NBT, but anywhere. I will never exist in that future. Neither, for that matter, will my mother."

Dr. Hollander seemed to have run out of steam for the moment. I took a gulp of rye and tried to wrap my mind around what she had been telling me.

"OK. I kind of get the idea that my saving Harlan Winslow changed things. I'm still not convinced that was a bad thing, but I understand the principle. What I don't understand is what that has to do with your grandmother."

"I have reason to believe that it is the NBT that will be responsible for my grandmother's death in 1979. And I think the reason that she is going to be killed is to prevent me from being born."

"Why would they want to do that?"

"Because they think that I might change history, might alter time so that the NBT doesn't come into existence."

"And why would they think that, Dr. Hollander?"

"Because I will if I can! Remember, I originally came back to this time to stop Howard Winslow from preventing his grandfather's death."

"OK. If that's true, how does that make you any different than this NBT? You are trying to prevent them from changing your future; they're trying to stop you from doing the same to theirs. What's the difference?"

"Because I don't go around killing people to do it!" Her voice had risen enough that I was afraid that Effie might come in, but she didn't.

"I'm sorry for the outburst, Mr. Christian. It's just that you don't know what a wonderful woman my mother is, or what a truly remarkable woman my grandmother was. I can't bear the thought of history without either of them."

"Fair enough. You want my help in saving your grandmother. Why don't you tell me about her?"

"As I said earlier, she was a remarkable woman. She was a professor of philosophy. Her work involved an examination of the ethics and the impact of science and technology on modern life. She was well known in her field and active up until her death. She served on a number of government panels and—oh, I'm not telling this very well."

"Why don't you start with her name? In my line, I find it's best to start with the basics," I said trying to encourage her. For no good reason other than habit, I had gotten a pad of paper out and was jotting things down as she said them.

"Her name was Helen Hollander. Dr. Helen Hollander. I was named after her."

I looked up at her. I guess the obvious question must have been on my face.

"I can see what you are thinking, Mr. Christian. No, my grandmother never married. Neither did my mother for that matter. That sort of thing will become a lot more common in the future than it is now."

"I see," I replied. I'm not sure I did, but an unconventional upbringing hadn't seemed to have harmed the woman sitting across from me, so maybe it didn't really matter.

"My grandmother never let the conventions worry her. She played the piano and loved the theater. She liked fine wines and drank her whiskey neat. She was good at poker and better at blackjack when she felt like it. She was kind and caring for the poor and downtrodden, and had little use for fools and the mean spirited."

"It sounds like I would have liked her," I said. It was the truth.

"My mother says that I'm a lot like her. I've never seen the resemblance, myself."

"Maybe you're too close to see it," I interjected. "She doesn't sound like the kind of person that deserved killing. What about your grandfather."

"My grandmother would never talk about him. Not even his name. I got the impression that it was a brief affair, though. Not a one night stand, but it didn't last long. Just a few days. He must have made quite an impression, though, because she never married after that."

"So your mother never had a father around when she was growing up—"

"No. I didn't either, though after I went away to college she did move in with a man. But I never thought of him as a father."

"Don't tell Effie about any of this. She has some rather old fashioned ideas at times."

"I saw that," Dr. Hollander said with that hint of a smile again. "It's strange, though. My grandmother never talked about my grandfather, but I think she wrote about him."

"Oh?"

"Yes. In addition to being a professor, my grandmother was an author. She wrote a series of thrillers that featured a hard-boiled hero who made a habit of rescuing damsels in distress. They were quite popular back in the eighties and nineties. They even made movies out of a couple of them. Because of that, we never had to worry about money. The hero was named John

Overholt. I think he was modeled after my grandfather," she said wistfully.

"I never seem to have time to read that kind of stuff," I said. "What about your mother? Are you sure that it's not you but her that the NBT wants to eliminate?"

"I don't think so. Though I suppose it is possible. My mother is a professor of history. Twentieth century popular culture to be exact. I guess academics run in the family. I grew up surrounded by the sights and sounds and fashions of the whole century. Despite that, my mother is a warm and very grounded person. Much less flamboyant than my grandmother was. I can't see any reason for anyone to want to prevent her from existing."

"OK. I get your point. Both your grandmother and your mother are wonderful people. So are you, from what I've seen of you. None of you deserve to be snuffed out of existence. But I don't see how I can help you."

Dr. Hollander finished what whiskey was left in her glass.

"What I want, Mr. Christian, is for you to go to 1979 with me and save my grandmother."

That caught me by surprise. I was just getting used to the notion of Dr. Hollander being a time traveler. The notion of me becoming one had never crossed my mind.

"Why me?"

"Mostly because you are the only person I can trust. You're the only person in the past who knows that time travel is possible. I'd rather not have to tell anyone else."

"But why me? Why take anyone at all? Why not just go to 1979 and recruit help locally?"

"I realize how ill-prepared I am for this job. I'm not a secret agent or a detective. I'm a mathematician. Look at how I bungled tracking down Howard Winslow. I don't know who or what I'll be up against. I need someone who can handle themselves and who knows what the stakes are. Frankly, if I had a choice, I'd take John Overholt, but he's not real. You are."

"Yeah, maybe that's true, Dr. Hollander, but that doesn't mean that I'd be any good flitting around in the future. I'm no Buck Rogers."

"I think you'll find that 1979 is a lot less different from 1955 than you think. It's only twenty-four years, after all, and human nature doesn't change that quickly."

"Maybe not, but still—the future—"

"Look, what I need help with is exactly the kind of skills that you, as a detective, possess. The ability to find someone, to keep that person under surveillance, and to protect that person. That's the kind of thing you do, isn't it?"

"OK. When you put it that way, I can see why you might think I could help you. But you still haven't told me why I should."

She looked at me across the desk, resolve in her eyes. I hadn't really noticed that her eyes were blue before. A deep, piercing blue.

"I thought I made myself clear, Mr. Christian. My grandmother is going to be killed and it will be your fault. You owe it to her to try and prevent that from happening."

"Look, I'm sorry about your grandmother. I really am, Dr. Hollander. And maybe what you say is true, that by keeping Harlan Winslow from being killed I'm in some way responsible. But that doesn't mean I should go running off to the future trying to make up for it. From what you've said, everything I do has an effect on the future. If I have fried eggs instead of scrambled for breakfast some people a hundred years from now will live while others will die. And maybe that's true, but I can't go around living my life worrying about it. It's not my job. I'm just a two-bit shamus trying to eke out a living."

"Alright, Mr. Christian. What if I hire you to help me? Howard Winslow hired you to protect his grandfather. Why can't I hire you to save my grandmother? There's five hundred dollars of my money in that envelope that I left here. That ought to pay for your services, shouldn't it?"

Put that way I could see that she had a point.

"I usually get paid extra if travel is involved, Dr. Hollander."

There was that hint of a smile again. She knew she had me hooked. All she had to do was reel me in.

"Then you'll help me?" she asked expectantly.

"Let's say that I'm considering it, Dr. Hollander. There's one thing I don't understand, though."

"What's that?"

"Let's say, for the sake of argument, that I agree to help you. If the reason that your grandmother is going to get rubbed out by these time police in 1979 is that Harlan Winslow survived being killed last Friday, why don't you just go back those three days and make sure he doesn't. It seems to me you wouldn't even have to do anything violent. All you would have to do is make sure I wasn't on that street to interrupt him just as he was crossing the mouth of that alley. You could steal the distributor cap from my car or let the air out of a couple of the tires. There are any number of ways you could keep me from being there. Wouldn't that have the same effect?"

"It's not that simple, Mr. Christian. I wish it were. I can't explain it to you without a lot of math that you wouldn't understand, but the fact is that if an object makes multiple appearances at the same time and place the time lines get confused."

"Get confused?" I said, reflecting my own condition.

"Yes. Confused, tangled, intertwined. It's hard to explain. We think that it's some sort of quantum entanglement effect that even I don't really understand, despite the fact that I was the one who worked out some of the equations describing it. Maybe the best way to describe it is that a knot forms in the time stream. It's one of the areas of time travel that we don't really understand very well."

"A knot in time? What does that mean?"

"Imagine a rope suspended in space," Dr. Hollander said, sounding like she was lecturing to a group of particularly dense freshmen. "That's the time stream. Now if you put some slack in the rope you can get a situation where three different parts of the rope can be at the same level. You can visualize that, can't you?"

"Sure."

"Now if you pull the rope taught again, you end up with a length of rope just like you started with."

"OK. That makes sense." I responded, though I still couldn't get what the doctor was getting at.

"Now imagine making a loop out of the rope and threading an end through the loop. What do you have?"

"A knot."

"Exactly. And what happens when you pull the rope tight again?"

"You still have the knot. But it's tighter."

"Yes. And if you pull the rope too much the knot gets so tight you may not be able to untie it."

"OK. I get that. But what does all this have to do with time?" I was getting a little annoyed with Dr. Hollander at this point.

"I said the rope represented the time stream. Maybe a better way to put it would have been to say it was a hose rather than a rope, and time is the water running through the hose from one end to the other. So what happens if you put a knot in a hose? It depends on how tight the knot is. If it's loose, the water keeps flowing, but if you pull the ends of the hose, at some point the knot will become so tight that the water will stop. That's what we think happens with the time stream when it gets tangled."

"So what does that mean?"

"I don't know, Mr. Christian. Let's just say the possibilities scare the shit of me."

I didn't know whether to be more shocked at Dr. Hollander's language or what she was implying about time.

"We tried it once with a couple of rabbits," Dr. Hollander answered. With a shudder she continued, "We didn't try it again."

"What happened" I pressed her.

"Both of the rabbits disappeared. Vanished. There was a lot of smoke and light, too. It was pretty scary."

"So what you're saying is that if you or I go back to last Friday or any other time where we had existed, we'd vanish in a puff of smoke? Like a magic trick?"

"It's a little more complicated than that, but yes. There are limitations to the effect, we think. If one appearance of the time traveler were in China and the other here in North America we think they'd be safe. Or if someone ten years older were to go back and visit his younger self, there would be enough differences between the two that it wouldn't cause a problem. The truth is, we don't really know what the range limits are. We, the people at the NTL, are still new to the business of time travel, and, needless to say, we've been a little reluctant to experiment when the consequences could be so dire. I tried to do some calculations. The best estimate I was able to come up with is that the range of the effect is proportional to the mass of the object. For the average human it would be about ten meters, say thirty feet. But that could be off by a couple of orders of magnitude."

"What does that mean?"

"It might be ten centimeters or a kilometer, say four inches or five eighths of a mile. Give or take."

"That's not very precise," I commented.

"That's why we've been reluctant to experiment. There's another possibility. We think that the rabbits vanished because the time stream was trying to heal itself, and don't ask me what that means, because I don't know. Let's just call it some kind of conservation effect, like the conservation of momentum or energy. But what happens if instead of a simple knot you get a really complicated one, one with multiple loops all entangled. One of my colleagues at the NTL, a brilliant physicist, thought that if that happened and such a knot was drawn tight, time might cease to flow."

"That doesn't sound good," I put in.

Dr. Hollander just shook her head. "No. It wouldn't be. It would mean the end of the universe. Or at least this one."

I let the last statement slide. I was beyond my depth as it was.

"That brings up another question—"

I was interrupted by a knock on the door. It was Effie.

"It's five o'clock, Mr. Christian. Do you need me for anything or is it alright if I go home now?" She eyed Dr. Hollander suspiciously. Effie takes my virtue seriously.

"No, you can go home now," I answered. "Oh, before you go, could you call down to the diner and have them send up some sandwiches and coffee. Dr. Hollander and I have some things to discuss and we're probably going to be at it for a while."

"Of course, Mr. Christian."

After Effie left, Dr. Hollander said, "You said you another question."

"Yes. It's something that's been bothering me. You said that when you went back to 2042, things had changed. People had changed. What became of those people, the ones you left behind when you came here the first time?"

"The short answer, Mr. Christian, is that I don't know. I wish I did. That question has been bothering me, too. Those people, as you called them, were my friends. At least most of them."

"Did they cease to exist? Like the rabbits?" I persisted.

"I can't give you an answer to that. The best I can do is give you is another analogy. Instead of a rope, think of time as an infinitely long multi-dimensional wire extending from some time in the primeval past to some time in the infinitely far future. Now think of time as a current that is flowing on that wire from the past to the future. Imagine that at some point along the wire another wire is spliced in, a wire that extends into some other far future. What happens when you cut the original wire just above the splice? I can't give you an answer as to what happens then, Mr. Christian. Does time still flow in the segment of wire that has been cut off? Kind of like what happens with a magnet if you cut it in half. Does time instead cease to exist in the cut off segment? Or does it become frozen in place because the current of time has been cut off like a wire disconnected from a battery? I don't know enough about the nature of time to give you an answer. I don't think anyone does."

"OK. Fair enough. So how do you know that preventing your grandmother from being murdered in 1979 will bring things back the way they were?"

"I don't, Mr. Christian. All I know is that my grandmother will continue to be alive. That is enough for me."

It might have been enough for her, but I wasn't sure that it was enough for me. This business of trying to change time seemed like a dangerous thing.

"OK. Say I agree to go with you to 1979 or whenever. What's your plan?"

"My plan?"

"Yes. What exactly are you trying to do and how are you going to go about it?"

"I'm going to prevent my grandmother from being murdered. I thought you understood that."

"I understood, alright, but how are you going to do it? Do you know where your grandmother will be? Do you know who it is that kills her? How they go about it? Do you know where exactly she will murdered?"

"All I know is what I read in the police report they let me read."

"They?"

"Dr. Feuerstein. He let me see the dossier that the NBT had compiled on my grandmother. It included a death certificate and a police report. I read both, but I admit at that point I wasn't paying attention to the details."

"But that's just the sort of thing you'll—we'll need. What can you remember?"

"She was shot. I know that. The police suspected that it was two men who were seen in the vicinity, but they were never caught nor were they able to identify them."

"And the location? The time?"

"It was November 1, 1979. 4:30 in the afternoon, I think. The police report said that she was on her way home from the university."

"That's something. And these two men? Any description?"

"Medium height, average build. Dark clothing. It all came from one witness who saw them walking away after they had heard the shots. They may not have even been connected to the murder."

"Not a lot to go on. You say shots. There were more than one?"

"Yes. She was shot in the head and torso. The police report said the bullets recovered from the body were of an 'unusual type and caliber.' Is that important?"

"I don't know about 1979, but 99 percent of the guns out on the street are of only a few calibers. .22, .38, .45, maybe 9 millimeter if it's foreign. Ballistics is usually pretty good at narrowing it down. The fact that they thought the slugs were 'unusual' points to the murderers being from somewhere else, or, in this case maybe I should say some when else. So maybe you are right about them being enforcers from this NBT, though even the FBI doesn't go around shooting people just because they feel like it."

"The NBT isn't the FBI, and I think that the 2042 I just came from is a lot different than the one I left originally."

"Granted. So maybe we are looking for two NBT agents, or maybe it was just a kid planning a stickup with some antique gun he stumbled across and your grandmother was just in the wrong place at the wrong time."

"Does this mean you'll help me?"

"I'm not promising anything yet, but I won't try to stop you either. And, either way, I wouldn't want you to get yourself killed because you were unprepared. I kind of like you, Dr. Hollander. You've got real moxie."

"Thanks. I think."

"What about Howard Winslow? Is he still running around with one of these time travel dinguses? Is there any possibility he might have been involved?"

Dr. Hollander shook her head. "I don't know what happened to him. He didn't show up back in 2042 as far as I know. The Howard Winslow that I met when I went back wasn't the same man that I knew. He was—different."

"Sounds confusing," I commented.

"It is. It's one of those areas of time travel that we don't really understand very well. It's as if at the instant you prevented his grandfather from being killed, another, a different Howard Winslow was created and the original, the one I knew, was cut off from the time stream in the same way that I've been cut off."

"So the Winslow that hired me is just wandering around loose somewhere in time?"

"That would be my best guess. There was no indication that he had taken up residence in 2042. Not that they were telling me everything. But I didn't get the impression that they were hiding the fact from me. As far as I know, Howard still exists and he still has the prototype TSC. He could be anywhere in time, even here in 1955."

"That's a cheery thought. Would Winslow, the original I mean, have any reason to want your grandmother dead?"

"Not that I know of. Unless he somehow saw me as a threat."

"Well, you did try to stop him from preventing his grandfather's death—"

"Does he even know that? We never came in contact."

"Good point. We'll put him on a back burner for the moment and concentrate on the two men that the witness spotted."

We were interrupted by a knock on the hallway door. I went out to check and it was a boy from the diner with the sandwiches and coffee. I paid him off with a decent tip and went back into the office.

"Dinner," I said as I put the bag on the desk.

"Thanks, I haven't eaten since breakfast in 2042."

While we were eating, I thought about what it would take to keep Dr. Hollander's grandmother from getting killed. After we were done, I outlined my plan.

We spent the next few hours hashing out the details, but the essence of the plan was pretty simple. From the newspaper clipping we knew that the attempt on Dr. Hollander's grandmother would be made on the afternoon of November 1st, 1979. We'd use the time controller to arrive in 1979 a few days earlier. That would give us time to reconnoiter and arrange for any necessary logistics like getting a car. We'd find the doctor's grandmother and then keep her under observation trying to spot the two suspicious men that had been in the police report and the newspaper clipping. If and when they made their move I would stop them.

I admit, that was the weak spot in the plan, but I couldn't think of any better way to handle the situation. We didn't have much information on the assassins other than the fact that they had been spotted in the vicinity of the crime scene. Despite the best efforts of the police at the time they had never been able to find them after the fact and hadn't been able to trace their movements beforehand. Probably because they hadn't been looking in the right place, like 2042. Of course, we couldn't even be sure that the two of them had been involved at all. For all we knew, they could just have been Jehovah's Witnesses or Fuller Brush salesmen

We discussed alternate plans like kidnapping Dr. Hollander's grandmother and holding her someplace safe until the magic moment had passed, or preemptively killing the presumed assassins before they struck, but they all seemed pretty dicey to me. There was too much chance of our being detected or worse, arrested. We'd have a lot of explaining to do to the cops. When they couldn't find any trace of our existence they'd probably lock us as Soviet agents, presuming that in 1979 there still was a Soviet Union. Discarding other possibilities, we settled on the plan as I had originally outlined it.

That left some practical matters to deal with. If we were planning on arriving a few days ahead of November 1st, we'd have some expenses to handle, like someplace to stay, eating, getting a car. Fortunately I always kept some ready cash in the office safe. I had about seven hundred and fifty bucks on hand. In 1955 that could carry one for quite a while; in 1979 I wasn't so sure. It would have to do, though, unless we planned on waiting until I could get to a bank. Of course with a time control dingus that didn't really matter, but I could sense that Dr. Hollander wanted to get moving.

At least we didn't have the problem that Dr. Hollander and Winslow had had of finding pre-1955 bills in 2042. The money in the safe would all still be legal tender in 1979.

There was one other thing in the safe that I took out, a short barreled, nickel plated .32 revolver that I had taken off a punk that had tried to rob me once. I'd kept it in case I ever needed a gun that couldn't be traced back to me. I didn't have any extra bullets for it, but the cylinder was full.

I handed it to Dr. Hollander asking, "Can you use this?"

I knew from the way she checked it out when she took it that she could. She just nodded a bit grimly. They had taken away her purse in 2042, but she found some way to hide it. I had my own automatic as well and a shoulder holster with a few extra rounds. It would have to be enough, but then I was hoping to avoid an extended firefight.

We didn't have to worry about taking a change of clothes or anything with us as it turns out the time dingus couldn't really handle much in the way of excess baggage. At least we wouldn't be arriving in 1979 in our birthday suits as some time-travel stories make out. Showing up buck naked at the end of October would be uncomfortable at best. That's when it occurred to me that we'd be arriving just in time for Halloween.

"Is there anything that we've forgotten?" I asked.

"Not that I can think of. When do you want to go?" Dr. Hollander asked.

"I guess there's no time like the present," I told her, not recognizing the irony of what I'd just said.

She pushed the button on the time dingus.

PART FOUR

(1979)

One moment we were in my office. The next we were in a clearing in some forest. If I was to believe the woman I was holding, we were in the future as well, though as it was almost pitch black, it was hard to tell. I guess that at that point I really was starting to believe her. After all, if the dingus in her hand could whisk us from my office to the woods in the blink of an eye, why couldn't it move us through time?

I realized I still had her wrapped in a bear hug of an embrace. We disentangled awkwardly.

"Where are we?" I asked.

"We're in a park on the edge of town. The Arboretum. It's the one place I know of that has remained clear from the thirties into my time. I thought it would be a good place to arrive because there wouldn't be anyone around to see us."

"Makes sense," I said. Dr. Hollander had obviously given the practicalities of time travel more thought then I had. "Let's get out of here. I don't know about you, but I'm freezing." It was the end of October and neither one of us was dressed for the weather.

"I'm pretty sure that the entrance to the park is this way." She pointed to a path that led through the trees. If the time of day matched that of when we'd left, there were still a couple of hours until dawn, but there was just enough light to make things out. For some reason, the sky seemed brighter than it had in 1955. I learned that it was because of the city lights reflected off the low hanging clouds.

Even with the help of a little pocket flashlight I had with me, it took us a half hour to reach the entrance.

"Look," I said, "We're going to need some transportation. We aren't going to be able to get anywhere if we have to slog around on foot all the time."

"I don't think we've got enough cash to buy a car, not and have any left for other things," Dr. Hollander replied.

"There are more ways than one to get a car," I responded.

"You mean steal one?" The notion seemed to shock her.

"Let's just say, borrow. After all, we aren't planning to keep it."

"Do you have much experience along those lines?"

"A little. I know how it's done. Let's keep walking until we find something."

We walked another fifteen or twenty minutes, leaving the park behind us and entering a more residential neighborhood. I spotted a car, an Oldsmobile. It was a real boat, bigger than a 1955 Cadillac. It was long and low and look like it had seen better days. There was a dent on the fender that had been there long enough for the metal to start rusting. Whoever had been driving it had done a pretty poor job of parking because the front wheel on the passenger side was up on the curb. If I had to take a guess, I would have to say they were drunk, which was all to the good. If the driver was sleeping one off, it might take him a while to notice that the car was missing.

I took a good look around to make sure no one was watching and then went up to the driver's side door and tried the handle. We were in luck, it was unlocked. I opened it and got in after motioning Dr. Hollander to join me. I was wondering if I was going to be able to hot-wire it, but when Dr. Hollander got in, the dome light illuminated a set of keys on the floorboard under my feet. When I tried, one of the keys fit the ignition. I gave it a turn and the engine caught.

Dr. Hollander kept looking around nervously, but no one seemed to have noticed us getting into the car.

"What's the trouble? Why aren't we going?"

"I'm looking for the clutch pedal. There doesn't seem to be one." I hadn't thought about how much cars might have changed in a quarter of a century.

"It's an automatic," Dr. Hollander said. "The shift is the handle in the middle, here. 'D' is for drive, 'R' is reverse, and 'N' is neutral."

"Oh, sure. Makes sense. And the 'P'? What's that stand for?" I didn't think it meant convert the car into a plane, but I couldn't be sure.

"Park," Dr. Hollander replied. I could have sworn there was a smirk in her voice. "Do you want me to drive?"

"No. I can figure it out." I put the lever in drive and we started to move. I gave it a little gas and maneuvered us off the curb. After that, it was easy.

Dr. Hollander played with some controls in the dash and heat started to come out of vents. I hadn't realized how cold I was. We drove around for a while just so I could get the feel of the car.

"What do we do now?"

"I don't know about you, Dr. Hollander, but I could use something to eat. Any chance there might be a diner open at this hour?"

"If we get onto one of the main roads, we should be able to find something. I think if you head that way—"

I followed her directions and soon we turned onto a four-lane road. If the clock on the dash was right it was five-thirty, but there was already a lot more traffic than I was used to. She told me to turn into a parking lot under a big sign that said "Denny's."

Parking something that big isn't as easy as parking the cars I was used to, but I managed. I put the gear shift in park and turned off the engine.

As I got out I told Dr. Hollander, "Lock your door. We wouldn't want someone to steal the car."

She looked at me, and then started laughing. "You're incorrigible Mr. Christian."

"Just practical. I doubt if we could be so lucky twice."

Inside, I asked the hostess if we could have a booth out of the way. She looked the two of us over suspiciously, but motioned us to a booth in the corner and dropped a couple of menus on the table.

Neither one of us said much. I think we were just glad to be out of the dark and the cold. Studying the menu I couldn't believe the prices. Dr. Hollander had said that things would be more expensive due to something called inflation, but I hadn't understood how much. I wondered how long our cash would last.

The waitress came by to take our order. I had ordered eggs and pancakes with sausage links. Dr. Hollander had some kind of omelet.

"So what now?" I asked after the waitress had filled our cups with coffee and left.

"I don't know. You're the detective. I guess we try to find my grandmother before someone kills her." She seemed suddenly unsure of herself.

I thought about it for a minute and then said, "I think the first order of business is to find someplace to hole up. If what you've said is true, we've got a few days until things happen, so we'll need someplace to sleep. We probably should get a change of clothes, too. The way the hostess gave us the fish eye when we came in I suspect that we stick out like a sore thumb."

Dr. Hollander looked up at me. "I think that may be because she thought you were a cop."

"A cop? Why'd she think that?"

"There's something about you, Mr. Christian. Let's just say that plain clothes police officers tend to dress conservatively. For this time, you are about as conservative as it gets."

I admit that I'm no clotheshorse, but I do try to dress respectably. But as looked around at the other diners, I saw what she meant. For one thing, I was the only man in the place wearing a tie. Of course, seeing as it was a diner at six in the morning, that might be understandable.

The waitress brought our food. It was alright, though I've had better. It wasn't really greasy enough for diner food, and it wasn't good enough for classier fare. It didn't matter; I ate it up like I hadn't eaten for days. I noticed that Dr. Hollander seemed to have a pretty good appetite, too.

After we had finished, we lingered over a second cup of coffee. When we had finished that, I paid the bill and left a tip for the waitress that would have bought the whole breakfast in 1955. I guess that was progress.

It was still early, too early to do much of anything, so we drove around some more. I know that Dr. Hollander had said that the future wasn't that much different, but I guess I had expected something more than what I was seeing. I'm not sure what. Maybe people flying around with jetpacks or rocket ships headed to the moon, or something. Instead what the future of 1979 held was pretty much more of the same. The cars were lower and wider and there seemed to be a lot more of them, but they were still cars, four wheels, doors on the sides. They didn't fly or hover or park themselves. The people were pretty much the same, too, except the men seemed to have longer hair and the women shorter skirts. There seemed to be more Negros and Orientals mixing in, too. Other than that, though, the city didn't seem much different than it had in 1955.

While we were driving around, I spotted a car parked in an out of the way location that looked like it hadn't moved in awhile. I stopped, and using my pocketknife as a screwdriver I did a quick switch of plates. I figured that with different plates the car we were driving would be less likely to be spotted as stolen. As for the other one, if it hadn't moved for some time, the owner probably wouldn't realize that the plates were different.

Around nine, Dr. Hollander said, "Turn in here." Here proved to be a Goodwill store.

"I should be able to pick up some different clothes here," she said when I had parked. "I'll need some money."

I handed her a couple of hundred. "You want me to come in with you?"

"No. Why don't you wait in the car? The two of us might look suspicious."

I could see what meant. We didn't exactly look like a likely couple, and the last thing we needed was to attract attention. I was happy that she was starting to think about the practical aspects of what we were trying to do. So I stayed in the car while Dr. Hollander went shopping.

A half hour passed. Then some more. I was starting to wonder if she had run out on me, though the thought didn't make any sense, considering. Finally, she emerged from the store carrying a couple of big shopping bags. She'd gotten herself a coat, too, which she was wearing. She had also picked up a somewhat battered suitcase.

"Get what we needed?" I said as she got into the car.

"Mostly. We need to make one more stop. There's a place down the street that should do."

The place down the street was a K-Mart which seemed to be some sort of standalone department store surrounded by a big parking lot. This time she didn't object to my accompanying her inside. The purpose of this stop turned out to be to pick up toothbrushes and other toiletries. I hadn't given it much thought, but if we were going to hang around 1979 for a few days we would need them. We also picked up some underwear and socks.

It was time to find a place to stay. I headed away from the center of town on the theory that hotels would be cheaper there. Sometime between 1955 and 1979 they'd built a ring road around the city. We found a motel along it that had a sign advertising rooms for $29.95 a night. It didn't look that old, but it was already run down. Not the best sort of place, but the kind of place where they wouldn't ask too many questions.

When I went inside the desk clerk asked for my name and to see some sort of ID. That was a problem, because all I had was a twenty-five year old driver's license and my P.I. ticket. I told him I'd left my driver's license in the car, and that I wanted the room for at least three nights and that I'd pay cash up front. That seemed to satisfy him, though he spent time examining the C-note that I used to pay the bill. On a whim, I signed the register as Mr. and Mrs. John Overholt. The clerk handed over the key and gave me directions to the room which was at the end of the building. We drove down to the end of the room and then I helped Dr. Hollander carry her purchases into the room.

Motel rooms haven't changed much in twenty-five years. I guess you can't improve on perfection. This one had a bed, a dresser, and a cheap table with a couple of shaky chairs. Surprisingly, it came with a television set. Maybe there had been some progress in a quarter century.

Dr. Hollander dumped the contents of the shopping bags on the bed. She'd gotten a skirt, a blouse, and a sweater for herself and a pair of blue jeans and a turtleneck sweater for me. She'd gotten me a navy pea coat and a pair of worn but serviceable gloves as well. I think I'm a little too old for blue jeans, but from what I had seen so far everyone seemed to wear them in 1979.

"So what's next?" she asked after flopping down on the bed.

"Look, we're both beat. You look like you haven't slept in a couple of days. The best thing we could do is to get some sleep. You can take the bed; I'll manage in the chair."

"You needn't. There's plenty of room on the bed." The way she said it, I knew it wasn't an invitation; not that I'd been looking for one.

She stretched out on the bed, turning on her side so she faced away from the center. I took off my jacket and draped it over the back of a chair and slipped my shoes off. She was already sleeping when I joined her. It didn't take me long to drop off, either.

As I woke, I became aware of the warm body next to me. Sometime while we had been sleeping, she had rolled over to her other side so that she was facing me. For the first time since I'd met her the expression on her face was relaxed. It wasn't a bad looking face, either.

A glance at my watch told me that I'd slept for six hours. I wasn't exactly fresh, but at least I was functional. I got up off the bed, trying not to disturb Dr. Hollander. It occurred to me that maybe it was time to stop thinking of her in those terms. I moved over to the chair, and looked out the window into the parking lot. It was getting dark. We'd been in the future for nearly a whole day and all we'd managed was to steal a car and buy some second hand clothing.

What were we going to do anyway? I knew that it was time to come up with a real plan. The first thing to do was find the other Helen Hollander, the grandmother of the woman sleeping on the bed. I was still having trouble thinking in those terms, but I guessed I'd have to get over that. So how were we going to find her?

I turned to the detective's best friend, the phone book. The room had a phone on the nightstand, and in the drawer underneath, I found a directory. It was a year out of date, but I hoped that wouldn't matter. It didn't. A quick look through the

"H's" and I turned up a H. Hollander living at 1233 W. Layton St. Layton Street was down by the campus, which made sense if she was going to the university. There was the only one Hollander listed. If it wasn't a listing for Henry or Harry Hollander, and if she hadn't moved in the last year, our first problem was solved. For a second I considered giving the number a call to see if it was really her, but thought better of it. What would I say? "Hi, I'm a detective from the past here with the granddaughter that you haven't had yet and we're here to save you from the people we don't know who are going to kill you." It didn't seem like that would get us anywhere.

Helen must have heard me moving around, because she woke up and looked over at me.

"I think I found your grandmother. Feel like taking a little trip?"

"Give me a few minutes to freshen up."

"Take your time. We've still got a few days." I didn't add the "until your grandmother is killed." That was implied.

She went into the bathroom. I heard the sound of running water. When she came out, she looked less tired. She'd combed her hair and changed into the skirt and sweater. She looked like she fit in.

I took the hint and changed into the clothes she had bought at the Goodwill. She had a good eye for sizes because they fit pretty well except for the jeans which I found a bit tight. Maybe she liked them that way. When I came out of the bathroom she already had her coat on.

"Where are we going?"

"We're going to do a little reconnoitering. I found an address for an H. Hollander in the phone book. I thought we'd drive by and see what we can see,"

I strapped my shoulder holster on over the sweater I had put on, and then put the pea coat on over it. It looked pretty good when I checked it out in the gritty mirror above the dresser. As long as I kept the bulky coat on it would be hard to tell that I was packing.

Closer in to the campus, the city had changed less than on the outskirts. I knew where Layton was, but they'd made some of the streets one way which caused some difficulties, but finally I got on the right section and drove past 1233. It proved to be a four story apartment building of red brick. It didn't look like anything fancy, but it seemed respectable.

I glanced over at Helen and saw a flash of something in her eyes.

"Recognize it?"

"Yeah. I'm pretty sure. When I was eleven my mom and I lived here in town with my grandmother. I remember walking down this street with my grandmother and her pointing out that building. She told me that she had lived there while she was working on her doctorate."

"You didn't mention this before," I commented.

"I was eleven at the time. I didn't remember any of that until we drove by."

"Fair enough," I replied. "Well, at least we know where she lives. That's something."

"So what do we do now?"

"Now we get something to eat."

We had dinner at a burger joint. It was all bright lights and Formica and tables that were bolted to the floor. They didn't serve alcohol, so I ordered a milk shake along with a burger and French fries. Helen had hers with a Coke. It came to nearly ten bucks for a meal that would have cost less than a buck in 1955. At this rate, the money we had wasn't going to last much longer than the two days we had until the murder we were hoping to prevent.

"I don't suppose you happen to have a picture of your grandmother on you?" I said as I slurped the milkshake through a straw.

"No, but you don't really need one."

"How's that?"

"Because she looks just like me. I've seen photos of her at this age and the resemblance is remarkable. My mother was always remarking on it."

"Well, that should make surveillance easy," I remarked. "You said you lived with her for awhile?"

"Yes. When I was eleven. My mother managed an appointment to the university as a visiting professor. She thought it would be a good chance for me to get to know my grandmother. My grandmother owned a big house just off campus, so there was plenty of room for the three of us. It was the best year of my life, the three of us living in that house. We'd go to concerts and plays and lectures together. It was a pretty heady experience for an eleven year old kid. Three smart, strong-minded women all living together. Real woman power stuff."

"Your grandmother was a professor, too, wasn't she?" I asked. I was trying to get her to open up about her grandmother.

"By that time she was an emeritus appointment, but she still taught a couple of classes for upper classmen. And she was still involved in a lot of political and international organizations."

"Sounds like she must have been really something." Looking at the way Helen's face lit up when she talked about her grandmother made me thing that maybe she really was worth saving.

"She was. You'd know what I'm talking about if only you had had a chance to meet her."

"Maybe I will," I said.

That seemed to bring Helen back to the reality of what we were trying to do.

After dinner we drove back to the motel. Neither one of us was in a talkative mood. Besides, both of us were still suffering from a lack of sleep. I stretched out on the bed, and within minutes I was sound asleep.

I woke to sunlight streaming in through the thin curtains on the window of the motel room. Dr. Hollander was sitting up in bed next to me looking at me. There was a curious expression on her face as if she was studying me. Whatever she saw seemed to amuse her.

"Like what you see?" I asked to distract her.

"Not bad," she replied. "You do seem to have a certain rugged charm."

"I'm glad you approve."

"I'm not sure I'd go that far." She turned serious and asked, "What's the plan?"

"I thought I'd go stakeout your grandmother's apartment building. According to what you've said, whatever is going to happen will happen tomorrow. I'd like to scope out the lay of the land, first. See what her routine is like. If I'm lucky, maybe I'll be able to spot whoever is going to kill her."

"You say 'I'm going.' What about me?"

"You're going to stay here and lay low."

"But I want to be doing something. She's my grandmother, remember?"

"I'm aware of that, Dr. Hollander. The problem is—just how much experience have you had tailing someone? Or maintaining surveillance while not attracting attention?"

She hesitated a moment before answering, "None. But—"

"Look, we don't want to attract attention to ourselves if we don't have to. We certainly don't want to spook your grandmother into doing something that gets her killed. And we don't want to interrupt the time stream unnecessarily, do we? That's what you've been telling me. The fact is that I've been trained to do this sort of thing and I've got a dozen years experience. You don't."

She looked like she wanted to give me an argument, but she knew that what I had just said was right.

"OK. I get the message. I'll stay here like a good little girl."

"Good. I understand you want to be doing something, but we have to be practical. The last thing we want to happen is for these assassins to spot us. There's a good chance that if they are planning a hit for tomorrow, that they've already watching her. If they get a sense that there are other players in the game it might make things complicated. Or it might make them take their shot early, and that's the last thing we want."

"Alright. I get it."

"I don't suppose you have any idea what your grandmother's schedule will be like?"

"Not really. My grandmother was never what you'd call a morning person, so she probably won't be going to campus until later unless she's got an early class, which isn't likely for a grad student. It's more likely that she'll head to her office or the library around mid-morning. But I'm going more on my own experiences at university than real knowledge. It's always possible that she might be working from her apartment today, but from what I remember of her she'd want to get out and see people."

"Fair enough. It's seven-thirty now. I'd better get a move on to be in place when she leaves her apartment."

After stopping for coffee, I drove down to the campus. There wasn't any on street parking near Dr. Hollander's apartment, but there was a parking lot down about a block from which I could keep the front door under observation. The sign on the lot said "Permit Parking Only," but the way I saw it, getting a ticket wasn't one of my major worries at the moment. There were plenty of empty spaces so I parked the Oldsmobile in one facing the apartment building.

I must have sat there for a couple of hours. Plenty of people passed by on the sidewalk, but no one seemed to notice that I was sitting there. The coffee ran out about nine. I was beginning to think I was wasting my time, but then I spotted her coming out of the building.

Dr. Hollander had been right. She and her grandmother looked a lot alike. They could have easily been sisters, even twins. Her grandmother's hair was longer and a lighter color as if she spent more time out in the sun, but the facial structure and build were nearly identical. It occurred to me that this Helen Hollander, the grandmother, was a few years younger than the one back in the motel. I wondered if I'd ever get used to this time travel business.

I was realizing how much styles had changed since 1955, too. She was dressed in tight blue jeans and a loose, bulky sweater and was wearing boots that came up almost to her knees. It didn't match my notion of what a coed wore, but I thought I could get used to it.

There was no way that I would be able to follow her in the car, so I waited until she had gone by and was a half-block down the street, and then got out of the car. I made sure that she hadn't noticed me. Crossing over to the other side of the street I started after her, matching her pace. At that hour the street wasn't crowded, but there were enough pedestrians that it was easy enough to blend in. I was glad that I was wearing the pea coat and jeans that Dr. Hollander had bought. They made me look like just another student. I would have stuck out like a sore thumb in a suit and tie.

It was a pleasant enough day for the first of November, brisk, but sunny. Most of the leaves had fallen from the trees, but there were still piles of them on the ground where they hadn't been raked up yet, and the air had that crisp smell you only get in a northern autumn. I could almost have enjoyed myself if the fate of time wasn't weighing me down.

As we got onto the campus proper, there were more people around. It took more concentration to keep my eye on Helen Hollander, but it was easier for me to blend in. All I had to do was go with the flow. No one seemed to give me more than a glance before moving on.

I followed her into a building on campus. Inside, I had to be more careful not to attract attention, but I'd had long practice at acting like I belonged. I saw her enter one of the classrooms. There were a number of other people inside, so I figured it must be a class. I kept on walking by and left the building by an exit on the other end.

It looked like Helen Hollander was going to be tied up in a class. I was calling her Helen, now, to keep her straight in my mind from Dr. Hollander. The class would probably last at least an hour, so I had some time on my hands. I decided to put it to good use.

On the way to campus I had noted a book store. It seemed like a good place to pick up some camouflage. The one thing that

I had noticed was that almost everyone had been carrying a book or books of some kind. If I was going to impersonate a student I thought I probably should have one, too. I retraced my steps to the store and went in to browse. I had at least an hour to do my shopping. In the stationary section I selected a spiral notebook and a pen. I was headed to the checkout when I passed a counter with used textbooks. I had time to kill, so I poked around the pile until I found one that caught my eye. It was a history of the Cold War. The price was $1.99. I paid for it, the notebook, and the pen and then headed back to the classroom building.

I figured I still had some time before the class was over. Using a convenient planter as a bench I opened the book and pretended to read. As far as any of the passers-by could tell, I was just another student marking time between classes.

It must have been over an hour that I waited around. I actually started to read the book in front of me. I was beginning to wonder if I had missed her, or if she had used another door to leave the building when she finally came out.

I waited until she was a few hundred feet down the hill and then I picked up my stuff and started walking after her. It was getting toward noon, and there were a lot more people moving around. Fortunately, Helen was easy enough to spot. I followed her down the hill and into the Student Union, a big, rambling building along the lake.

Inside, I lost sight of her for a moment. I walked back and forth along the corridor a couple of times and then spotted her at a table in the main hall. This was a large open room filled with tables and chairs. The place was packed with people having lunch, studying, playing cards, or just talking. I found a vacant seat where I could keep an eye on Helen, and spread out my notebook and reading material.

Other than the coffee I'd bought that morning, I hadn't had anything to eat. When I was convinced that Helen wasn't going to move for awhile, I left my camouflage and went and got a sandwich and beer to go with it. My stuff was still there when I got back. To keep my cover, I opened the book and started jotting things down in the notebook. Just another student doing his homework.

A couple of women joined Helen at her table. They looked to be about the same age, but weren't as good looking. It was funny, but I'd never particularly thought about Dr. Hollander's looks with anything other than professional detachment, but I had noticed her grandmother's.

Time passed. I had filled a couple of pages in the notebook. I was actually finding the book interesting. I'd lived through the start of the cold war, actually been a part of it, first at Los Alamos, and then later when I had been stationed in Germany, but it was interesting to see how it had turned out. I wondered if the fact of my reading the book was going to alter history when I went back to 1955.

Along about one, an older man, by which I mean around forty, stopped by the table with Helen and her girlfriends. From the fact that he was wearing a corduroy blazer with leather patches on the elbows, I took him to be a professor of some sort. He chatted amiably with the women, but when he had left, I couldn't miss the snickering on their part. I decided the professor was just another middle aged bachelor with an unrealistic idea of his sex appeal.

The two women got up shortly after that and left. Helen stayed around for a few minutes and then got up as well. I noted that she made a point of cleaning up after herself and dropping the remains of her lunch in a trash bin. I got up, following her example.

After leaving the Union, she made for the library which was just across the street. I followed her inside. She stopped and had a long discussion with someone at the resource desk. I found an empty table where I could keep an eye on her and continued my reading on the Cold War.

After awhile the materials Helen had requested were brought to the desk. She took them and moved to one of the study carrels along the rim of the room. As I could see her from where I sat, I didn't bother to move.

We spent a pleasant two hours in the library reading room. I'd made my way up to the Hungarian uprising. I'm not sure what Helen had been working on, but she seemed satisfied with herself when she returned the materials she had gotten to the desk. It was just before four.

It quickly became clear that she was done for the day on campus and was heading back to her apartment. I was debating whether it was worth following her when I spotted them.

They were easy enough to see if you were looking. There were two of them, dressed in overcoats and matching homburg hats. Even the professor in the Union had chosen more casual attire. They walked differently than the pedestrians around them, too, stepping with almost military precision.

They must have been waiting outside the library, because they had already picked up Helen when I came out the door. They followed her, unhurried, but matching her pace. They could have been two colleagues walking along, except they weren't talking to each other the way that people do when they walk side by side. I dropped back a little so I wouldn't attract their attention.

It was just possible that they weren't following Helen, that it was just a coincidence, but I didn't really believe that. When they turned at the same corner as she did, I was sure. The question was, what were they up to? Was this just preliminary surveillance, or had Dr. Hollander gotten the date wrong, and Helen was about to be killed.

I couldn't take that chance. From the morning, I knew the route that she was taking back to her apartment. I cut over a street and hurried ahead, so that I get between them and Helen without being obvious about it. I was still carrying the books I'd picked up, so with any luck, the two following Helen might mistake me for just another grad student.

When I had gotten ahead of them I caught up to Helen and said calmly, "Helen. It's important that you do what I ask."

She turned to me with a worried look. "Who are you?"

"My name is Christian. I'm a detective. There are two men following you. I have reason to believe they want to harm you."

She started to turn to look back.

"Don't look back just yet. When we get to the corner, I want you to stop and turn towards me as if we were old friends talking. When we stop you can look behind you. You will see two men in overcoats and matching hats."

"This is ridiculous," she protested.

"I wish it were, but I'm serious. Just do as I ask."

We stopped at the corner. Helen did as I had requested. The two men were about a block away. Our stopping had caught them by surprise and they hesitated for a moment, uncertain of what to do. Finally, they crossed over to the other side of the street where they stood, trying to look like they weren't watching us.

"OK, Mr. Christian, or whatever your name is. I see the two men. Frankly, they look like policemen to me."

"Trust me, they aren't. Or at least not the kind of policeman you have in mind."

"You're scaring me, Mr. Christian."

"That's good. Now maybe you'll do as I ask."

"OK. What do we do now."

"I'm going to escort you to your apartment. Once inside, I think you'll be safe for the moment."

"That's not particularly reassuring."

"It's the best I can promise, Miss Hollander. Now let's start walking again."

We continued on towards her apartment. I looked back and noticed that the pair following us had split up. That wasn't good. It probably meant that one of them was trying to get ahead of us so he could cut us off. I unbuttoned the pea coat so that I could get at my pistol.

"Is that a gun?" she asked. Oddly, she didn't seem particularly frightened.

"Yes."

We were about a block from Helen's apartment when the other man appeared in front of us. I noticed that his overcoat had been unbuttoned. I was debating which of the two I should go after first, when I spotted a bus coming down the street.

There was a bus stop right by the apartment building. I was hoping it would stop.

"Listen. When the bus stops, I want you to hurry into your apartment building. I hoping the bus will give us cover."

"And you?"

"I'll do what I have to."

The bus pulled up and three people got off, a man and two women.

"Go," I said.

Whatever the two had planned, the bus had interrupted it. Suddenly there were too many witnesses. The one behind turned around while the other crossed over to the other side of the street and walked away in the opposite direction.

When I turned to look for Helen, she was using her key to open the front door of the building. I followed her inside. She looked at me, not sure of what to do.

"Let's go to your apartment. We can talk there."

We took the stairs rather than the elevator. Her apartment was on the third floor on the corner. She used her key to unlock the apartment door, and when I showed no signs of disappearing, she opened it and let me in.

Once inside, she turned to me and asked, "Alright, who the fuck are you?"

I was shocked by her use of profanity. "I told you, Miss Hollander. My name is Christian, Harry Christian, and I'm a private detective."

"Listen Mr. Hari Krishna—"

"That's Harry Christian, not Krishna," I corrected.

"What kind of name is Harry Christian?"

"It's the name my mother gave me."

She looked at me in disbelief. "You haven't got a clue what I'm talking about, do you?"

"About what?"

"Hari Krishna."

"I don't know any Krishnas."

"Forget it, Harry Christian. You said you were a private eye. Prove it."

I decided I had nothing to lose. I brought out my wallet and pulled out my P.I. license and showed it to her. For good measure I showed her my driver's license as well.

She looked at them in that overly careful way people do when they aren't sure what they're looking at.

"What's your game, Mr. Christian? This license is dated 1955. And your driver's license expires in 1958. Is this some kind of a joke?"

"It's not a joke, Miss Hollander. Look at the pictures."

The pictures on the licenses weren't great, but they undoubtedly bore my likeness.

"OK, I'll admit there's a resemblance, but according to these you're fifty seven years old. You don't look it."

"I'll take that as a compliment," I said with a grin.

"Are you sure these aren't your father's?" she asked. "Or did you send away for them with a cereal box top when you were a kid?" She was getting closer to the truth than I liked.

"No, that's me."

"Fine. Don't tell me. But what is this all about? And who were those two men in the funny hats?"

"I have reason to believe that those two men are planning to kill you, Miss Hollander. I was sent to stop them."

"By whom?"

"I'm afraid I'm not at liberty to divulge that information, Miss Hollander."

"You know, if I didn't know better, I'd suspect you of working for the government, Mr. Christian," she remarked suspiciously. "Only they would have given you better credentials."

"I used to, Miss Hollander. Work for the government, that is."

"But I suppose I can't ask you about that, either."

"I'm really not supposed to talk about it," I replied with a shrug.

She stared at me in exasperation. "You know I'm almost starting to believe you. No one would make up a crazy story like this. Alright, answer me this. Why do those two men want to kill me?"

"I think because they are afraid of you."

"Afraid of me?"

"Of what you will become."

"What I will become? What's that supposed to mean?"

"I really can't explain, and if I did, you probably wouldn't believe me, anyway."

"OK. That's enough of this mysterious stuff. I think it's time that you leave, Mr. Harry Christian."

"I'd rather not. I think it would be best if I stayed."

"What's that supposed to mean?"

"Those two men are still out there somewhere. I didn't scare them off. They're just waiting until there are fewer witnesses around. I'm not sure what would have happened if the bus hadn't come by when it did."

"You're just trying to scare me."

I moved over to the front window and looked out, keeping to the shadows so that I'd be harder to spot. The two men in the homburgs were standing on the sidewalk across the street holding a conclave.

"You think so? Take a look across the street. Just don't get too close to the window." I wasn't really afraid that Helen would be shot, but I didn't know if the two NBT men knew which apartment she was in.

Helen looked out the window. She didn't actually blanch, but I could see that her confidence was shaken.

"OK. For the sake of argument, let's say I accept your conspiracy theory. What are we supposed to do now? Can't you call for backup or something? Isn't that what you're supposed to do in circumstance like this?"

"I'm afraid I don't have much in the way of backup, Miss Hollander."

"That's just great. I'm in danger and all I get is some sort of junior G-man without backup."

"Sorry about that," I replied with a shrug. "Though speaking of backup, there is a call I should make. Would it be alright if I used your phone?"

"You don't have one in your shoe?" Helen asked sarcastically.

I assumed it was some sort of joke, but I didn't get the reference.

When she saw I didn't get it she said, "Sure, go ahead. Call Control or whoever it is."

I went to the phone and dialed the motel and asked for the room. I was put through and a moment later Dr. Hollander was on the line:

"Mr. Christian, I was getting worried. Where are you?"

"I'm with your grandmother. Don't worry, she's alright, but there are a couple of men I think are from the NBT standing around outside on the street. I think it would be better for the moment if I stayed here. I'm not sure when I'll be back tonight, so don't wait up."

"You're sure about the NBT agents?" Dr. Hollander asked.

"No, but if they aren't from the NBT then we've got more than one set of players in this game."

"Do you want me to come there? I can get a taxi or something."

"No. I think your presence would just confuse things. I'm having a hard enough time answering your grandmother's questions as it is."

"If you're sure—"

"I'm sure, doctor. Look, I've got to go, but if you need to get in touch with me you can call," I read her the number from the phone.

"OK. I've got it."

"Good. Be careful if you go out."

"I will."

"Good-bye." I hung up.

"What's with this 'grandmother' business?" Helen asked. Some of her feistiness had returned. "Is that some sort of code name for me?"

"Something like that," I replied evasively.

"You could have chosen something more flattering."

"Sorry, I didn't pick it."

I went back over to the window and looked out. The two men in hats were still across the street, but I could tell they were getting nervous about being conspicuous.

"I take it the NBT are the bad guys?" Helen asked.

"Yeah."

"What's NBT stand for? Is it Russian or something?"

I didn't see any point in lying about it. "It's the National Bureau of Time."

Helen looked puzzled. "Bureau of Time? That makes them sound like clock makers."

"It's a cover name. Like the Manhattan Project."

"You know, Mr. Christian, even when you explain things you don't tell me much. So who are they really?"

"That's a long story, Miss Hollander, and one I can't really get into."

"Of course," Helen said in exasperation. After a moment she added, "You know we can't go around calling each other Miss Hollander and Mr. Christian. For one thing, every time I say Mr. Christian I feel like I'm in Mutiny on the Bounty. Why don't we keep it simple and just use Helen and Harry?"

"I'd like that, Helen," I answered.

While we had talked, I'd kept an eye out the window. The men in the homburgs seemed to have decided they couldn't hang around any longer and were walking away in the direction of the campus.

"They're leaving now."

"Does that mean this business is over?" Helen asked.

"No. It just means that you're safe for the moment."

"So you're still going to hang around?"

"I think I'd better. At least until tomorrow."

"What happens then?"

"If I can keep you alive through tomorrow, I think it's over. At least that's what I hope."

"That sounds reassuring, Harry. What's so special about tomorrow?"

I didn't see any reason to sugar coat it. "That's when you're supposed to be killed."

"By those two agents from the NBT?"

"That's the information that I have."

"But why? Why tomorrow? Why me? What's so special about me? I'm only a grad student. And in philosophy at that. It's not like I'm studying nuclear physics or something like that. What is this NBT that it's agents can go around killing innocent people? And why haven't I ever heard of them before?"

"Those are all good question, Helen. Unfortunately, I don't have answers for most of them. About the only way I can explain it is that the NBT is trying to make history come out the way they want it to and they see you as a potential threat to that plan."

"Me? I don't believe it. It doesn't make sense, Harry."

"A week ago, I'd probably have said the same thing." I didn't see any point in mentioning that the week had happened in 1955.

She was standing there with her hands on her hips like she wanted to say something more, but just couldn't think of what. I had to say that she was taking the whole business better than most people would. Dr. Hollander had been right when she had said her grandmother was a special sort of person.

Suddenly she changed the subject. "Are you hungry?"

"Yeah. A little. All I've had to eat today was a sandwich in the Student Union."

"You were following me? All day?"

"Yeah. From the time you left your apartment."

"OK. I'm telling myself that I'm not going to get upset at that. I guess you were just trying to protect me. That is what you were doing, wasn't it?"

"That's why I'm here."

"Anyway, getting back to food, I don't have much in the apartment. I'm really not much of a cook, either. There's a little Italian place just a few blocks from here. It's mostly just pasta, but it's good and cheap. We could go there. Unless you think it's too dangerous."

"I don't know," I said. "It would probably be better if we stayed here."

"Is it really that bad, Harry," Helen protested. "I'm starting to feel like I'm trapped. I don't want to live that way. The restaurant is only a few blocks. There'd be other people around. It will only be for an hour or so, anyway."

I couldn't resist her pleading. I could see her point, too. An hour earlier and she hadn't been aware of this business. Reluctantly I agreed. "I guess it would be OK. I'll just keep a lookout for anyone wearing a homburg hat."

"I do believe you just made a joke, Harry. Or is that something they taught you in spy school?"

"I never went to spy school, Helen. The one I went to was for anti-spies."

"Another joke!"

"I'm full of them," I replied. Actually, I've never been much of a comedian.

"Do you want to go now?"

I checked my watch. It was half past six.

"Why not? It's probably better to go while our friends in the hats are disorganized."

"Alright. One thing, though. You might want to do something about your gun. Unless you plan on keeping your coat on."

"Good point."

I slipped off the pea coat and got rid of the shoulder holster. The pistol I dropped in one of the coat's pockets for want of someplace better to stash it.

We walked the few blocks to the restaurant. It was in a building that looked like it had once been a corner storefront. Lace curtains had been placed in the big plate glass windows in the front and a gay sign that proclaimed "Maria's" had been stuck up over the front door.

Inside, we were greeted by a woman maybe a year or two older than Helen. She was plump, had long dark hair and a smile on her face that made you think you were family. She grabbed a couple of menus near the door and escorted us to a table at the rear. I pulled out a chair for Helen, mostly so I could sit in one where I could keep an eye on the front door. I hung my coat over the back of my chair so that I could reach the pistol in the pocket if I needed to.

The interior was about what you would expect from an Italian restaurant. There were maybe a dozen tables with red and white checked tablecloths, half of which were occupied. On the center of each table was a straw wrapped Chianti bottle with a candle stuck in it. The walls were hung with old black and white photos of stiff looking couples and staged group portraits.

I took a look at the menu. It didn't hold many surprises, heavy on pasta with red sauce. I don't know that much about Italian food other than spaghetti.

"What's good?" I asked.

"Just about everything," Helen replied. "It's all made from scratch."

When the plump woman with the smile came to take our order I played it safe and had the spaghetti and meatballs. Helen ordered pasta puttanesca.

"After the day I've had I could use some wine. What about you, Harry?"

The last thing I wanted was to get drunk and let my guard down, but I thought Helen deserved some.

"Sure. Why not? Seeing as I'm more of a beer and whiskey man, you choose."

Helen chose a bottle of Montepulciano. It was eighteen bucks which in 1955 would have been a lot, but probably was on the cheap side in 1979.

The dinners came with soup or salad. Considering the weather, we both chose the soup, a minestrone.

The waitress returned a few minutes later with a couple of glasses and the bottle of wine. From the way she opened it, I could tell that she'd done it a few times before. She poured a little in Helen's glass. Helen picked the glass up, swirled it a few times and nodded to waitress who just smiled and poured some of the wine into each of our glasses. I was feeling a little out of my element. I don't usually swirl my rye.

The soup came right after that along with a basket of bread. Helen was right, the soup was great. The bread wasn't bad, either.

"So, Harry, how'd you become a private eye, anyhow?" Helen asked.

I debated what to tell her, but I decided to tell the truth, at least sort of.

"Mostly by accident. It looked like I was going to be drafted, so I enlisted. After basic they asked if I wanted to be in the MPs, that's Military Police. I agreed because it sounded safer than the infantry. After training I got sent to a unit guarding some secret installation in the desert. I must have been good at my job, because after awhile I made sergeant and got involved in doing background checks and that kind of thing rather than manning the front gate."

All that was true, except that the war had been with Germany and Japan rather than the Vietnamese and the secret installation was the Manhattan Project, and what I had been doing was making sure none of the A-bomb secrets got leaked to the Krauts--or the Soviets.

"After the war I signed up for another hitch and ended up in Germany doing counterintelligence."

Mostly my job had been tracking down ex-Nazis, but towards the end we had been more concerned about the GDR and Soviet agents than Germans.

"So that's what you meant by anti-spy." Helen commented.

"Yeah," I replied sheepishly. At least she had been listening, which is more than a lot of women do.

"That still doesn't explain how you became a private eye, though."

"That's simple. When my hitch was up, I didn't reenlist. I figured I had done my bit and I was tired of having to report to someone. Back stateside, with my record and experience, I didn't have any problems getting a P.I. license, so I went into business for myself. I won't say I'm getting rich at it, but I'm doing alright, I guess. At least I'm my own boss."

I was saved from having to talk more about myself by the arrival of the entrees. After that, we both did more eating than talking. For a woman of her build, Helen had a good appetite. I was doing my share of eating, as well. The sauce on the spaghetti was spicy rather than sweet, and the meatballs were good, too. When I asked, Helen explained that they were a mixture of veal and pork. For a woman that claimed she didn't do much cooking Helen seemed to know a lot about food.

There was still nearly half a bottle of wine left when the waitress came to clear the plates. I had had a glass and Helen had had two, which seemed to me to be about the right ratio. From what I could tell, she was one of those women who could hold her liquor. The restaurant was starting to empty out, so there didn't seem to be any rush for us to leave and it seemed a waste to leave wine in the bottle, especially at eighteen bucks. I filled up both of our glasses.

"I think it's my turn to ask the questions, Helen. What's a nice girl like you doing studying philosophy? It seems kind of— esoteric."

She started to bristle, and then saw that my query was serious.

"After all the things that have happened in the world this century, it seems to me that someone needs to ask the big questions. Things like what is the difference between right and wrong? And, how do we ensure that our institutions act in an ethical manner? No one seems to pay attention to issues like that anymore. Philosophy is about more than does a tree in the forest make noise when it falls if no one is around to hear it."

I could hear the passion in her voice as she spoke. I was beginning to understand why Dr. Hollander thought her grandmother was a special person. And why she was worth saving.

We finished off the bottle talking, that is Helen doing the talking and me doing the listening. I sipped at my wine and poured most of the bottle into her glass. By that time I was getting a little nervous about staying out so late. The restaurant had emptied out. I'd already paid the bill and left a nice tip for the plump woman with the smile, and I was thinking it was time to leave when I spotted them.

They had ditched the homburgs, but I was sure it was them, the two men who had been following Helen. They were standing out front of the restaurant, with the street light silhouetting them against the white of the lace curtains in the front window. One of them looked in over the top of the curtain as if checking the place out for witnesses.

I reached into the pocket of my coat and wrapped my hand around the butt of the pistol. Interrupting what Helen was saying, I said, "When I give the word, I want you to get flat on the floor."\

"What is it, Harry?"

"The two men that are after you are out front. I think they are about to come inside. I'm going stop them if I have to."

Helen read enough in my tone not to raise an objection.

The front door opened, the little bell above it tinkling. One of the men stepped through. There was a pistol in his hand, raised the way a pro would carry it. His partner was right behind.

"Now!" I cried. I stood up, my own gun rising as I moved to the side. The chair that I had been in clattered to the floor as it overturned. The lead assassin was moving his eyes from where Helen had been sitting to where I was moving. I fired. Two shots in quick succession. A bullet went by me, shattering the glass covering one of the photos on the wall.

I must have hit him, but I wasn't sure where. He wasn't dead, but I had stopped him, blocking the second man from coming in. The two of us stood there a moment, pistols pointed at each other, then his gun began to waver. I could see blood starting to drip on the floor. He was looking at me, wondering if I was going to finish him off. Slowly he backed out the door. I let him go. I had enough to explain as it was without having a dead body on my hands.

"Helen, are you OK?"

She had hidden herself under the table that had been next to us.

"I'm fine. At least I think so. Can I stand up?"

I couldn't see anyone through the lace curtains in the front window. "I think so."

I went to the front door, looked out, and then stepped out onto the sidewalk. There was no one visible in either direction, though I could see a trail of dark spots leading away to the right. I went back inside, tucking my pistol in the back of my waistband.

Helen was talking to the plump woman who wasn't smiling anymore.

"What happened?"

"I think it must have been a robbery. There were two of them. They burst in with guns. They must have been surprised when they found there were still customers and one of them took a couple of wild shots. I think they panicked and ran then. I guess that was lucky for us."

"But you chased after them," the waitress said suspiciously.

"I thought they might have had a car waiting outside. I wanted to see if I could get their license plate. I guess I wasn't thinking."

"I should call the police."

"Yes, you should," I agreed. "But could you wait until we're gone? We'd rather not get involved if possible."

"Shouldn't you wait?" she said hesitantly.

"Then we'd be witnesses," I tried to explain. "They might come after my friend here."

"I don't know—"

"It will be alright," Helen broke in. "Neither of us really saw anything. It all happened too fast."

The plump woman seemed to put more stock in what Helen said than me. A hint of the smile came back to her. "If you think it will be OK."

"I'm sure it will be," Helen reassured her.

"OK. But I think you should leave now."

"That's probably best," I said trying to sound like I was as shaken as she was. It wasn't that hard. "Maybe we could use the back door in case they're still waiting out front?"

The plump woman looked nervously through the front window.

"Yes. OK."

I grabbed the pea coat, keeping my back away from her to keep my pistol hidden as I put it on. I took Helen by the arm and we stepped through the door at the back of the restaurant into the kitchen.

The back door let out into an alley. I heard the door being locked behind us. It was dark in the alley, but by walking in the middle, we avoided running into anything. I led us to the opposite end of the block and then over a street as we headed back to Helen's apartment.

"I guess I won't be going back there any time soon, which is too bad because the food is good," Helen remarked. There was more excitement than hysteria in her voice.

I kept glancing over my shoulder as we walked, but if the pair was hiding in the shadows, they chose not to make a move on us. We got safely back to the apartment, and with the door locked behind us, I felt I could finally breathe easier.

"Could I use your phone again?" I asked after I had gone around and drawn the drapes on all of the windows. "I need to get in touch with my contact."

Helen just nodded. Now that we were safe for the moment some of the elation had gone out of her as the realization of what had just happened sank in. I dialed the motel. Dr. Hollander must have been waiting by the phone because she answered almost immediately.

"Where are you? I've been worried sick." It struck me how much her voice sounded like Helen's.

"Something came up. There were a couple of men bothering your grandmother. I'm afraid I had to take action."

"Take action? What does that mean?"

"Shots were fired. Your grandmother and I are both alright, but I think it might be better if I spent the night."

"Who fired shots?"

"Two men. They surprised us in a restaurant. I assume they were from the NBT. They didn't stick around."

"But you're alright? Both of you?"

"Yeah. Look, are you going to be OK by yourself?"

"I'll manage. Mostly, I've just been bored. Now I'm a little frightened."

"Don't worry. You should be safe. I don't think they have any idea where you are or even that you are here at all. I'll call you in the morning."

I hung up.

"I still wish you had picked a better code name for me," Helen said.

"It wasn't my choice."

Helen looked at me quizzically for a moment. I couldn't blame her. She found herself in the middle of something she didn't understand and which I couldn't explain to her.

"I know you let me drink most of the wine tonight, but I could really use a drink. Do you want one?"

I knew that I shouldn't, but the truth is that my nerves were on edge. Maybe a shot of something would quiet them down.

"OK.

Helen disappeared into the apartment's little galley kitchen. When she came out she was holding a bottle and a couple of glasses.

"I'm afraid this is all I've got," she said, holding up a bottle of Old Overholt rye with about three inches of liquor left in it. "I normally don't drink whiskey, but a friend left it here after a party."

"Rye will do fine," I assured her. It occurred to me that I might be witnessing the inspiration behind the hero of the books Helen hadn't had a chance to write yet, and that John Overholt wasn't just an alias I'd adopted for the motel registry. It gave me an odd feeling.

She must not have noticed, for she said, "I don't have any soda, but I've got some ice."

"Ice would be fine."

Helen went back into the kitchen with the glasses and I could hear the sound of ice cubes rattling into the glasses. She returned in a moment. The glasses were full. It looked like she had split what was left in the bottle of rye between them. She handed me one of the tumblers and toasted, "Cheers."

I took a sip, and let the whiskey do its work. After that, I shed the pea coat, and put my shoulder holster on again. I wanted my pistol where it would be handy. After I had gotten the rig on again, I took a peak out the front window. The street below was empty. I pulled over a chair so I could sit and still keep a lookout.

"Does this kind of thing happen to you often?" Helen asked. She sounded more curious than afraid.

"Not very," I replied. "I try to avoid shootouts if I can. Mostly I succeed."

"And if you don't?"

"Well, then I shoot back."

"You really do sound like a government agent, Harry," she laughed. It was a good laugh, not a hysterical one. I took a good look at her standing there in her tight jeans and baggy sweater. A man could do a lot worse, I thought. It was odd that despite the fact they looked almost identical, I'd never thought of Dr. Hollander in the same why. It made me wonder why.

"Did you mean what you said on the phone, about spending the night?"

"I really think it would be best. But I'll go if you want me to. I've got a car down the street where I can keep an eye on the place."

"No. You can stay. In fact, I was hoping you would. I'm not sure I'd be able to sleep otherwise."

"Don't worry, I can sleep out here." I had trouble reading her expression. I got the feeling that she was thinking two steps ahead of me and trying to decide which way to go next. "I want you to know, Helen, that you're not a prisoner. I'm just trying to keep you safe through tomorrow."

"What happens then? After tomorrow, I mean."

"I'm not sure, but I'm hoping it means you'll have a long and prosperous life."

"I thought I was the student of philosophy, Harry."

I didn't say anything, just looked out the window.

"Look, there really is some reading that I should do, if that's alright."

"No, go ahead. Pretend I'm not even here. I'll just keep looking out the window."

She picked up a thick book. It looked like it must weigh five pounds. She dug a pair of glasses out of her purse and curled up on the couch with the book. I hadn't known that she wore glasses. I'd say they made her look smarter, but that hadn't really been a problem before she put them on.

I kept watch at the window, but every once in awhile I'd look over to where she was sitting. Whatever she was reading she had immersed herself in it. I wasn't sure she even knew I was there anymore. I turned my attention back outside.

After you've been on enough stakeouts, you learn the trick of focusing your attention so you don't get distracted by stray thoughts. You learn how not to get bored, either. The next thing I knew, Helen was standing up and stretching. The clock on the wall said it was eleven-thirty.

"I've got to get some sleep, Harry. Considering everything, I'd rather not sleep alone." It was more of a statement than an invitation, but I got the hint. She went into the bedrooms leaving the door open.

The street outside the window was empty. The last bus had gone by fifteen minutes earlier. Part of me said that I should keep looking out the window. Part of me said I needed to get some sleep. And part of me—

The first bus of the morning woke me up when it stopped on the street outside. A clock on the nightstand said that it was six-thirty. Helen was lying on her side, her back pressing up against me. My hand was draped loosely over the curve of her hip. She looked as innocent and composed as a baby.

We'd had one brief but intense bout of lovemaking, then she had rolled over and promptly gone to sleep. I must have dozed off a few minutes later. I was tempted to wake her, but decided not to. If things worked out, by this evening I'd be back in 1955, Dr. Hollander would be in 2042, and Helen would still be in 1979. And if things didn't work out? Well, then, nothing would really matter.

She must have sensed that I was awake because she said dreamily, "What time is it?"

"It's six-thirty-five."

"I'm still alive?"

"Yup. And less than eighteen hours to go." As soon as I had said it, I regretted it, but I couldn't take it back.

"Do you really think that?"

"As far as I know. We should just lay low here in your apartment all day and come midnight I'll be out of your hair forever."

"I can't do that, Harry," she said, suddenly serious.

"Do what?"

"Just stay home all day. I've got a meeting with my thesis advisor and you don't skip meetings with Professor Adams. Not if you want to get on with your career."

"Is your career more important than your life?" I asked.

"Yes." She sounded like she meant it. I believed her. She was already up and out of bed before I could counter her.

She went into the bathroom, shutting the door behind her. It hadn't quite been a slam, but the intention was clear. I was to stay out. Out of the bathroom, and maybe out of her life.

I lay there in bed listening to the water run in the shower thinking about what I should do. I could stop her from going out, but that would probably require holding her at gun point. That might work, but it might not. It probably wouldn't, from what I'd seen of Helen. She wasn't the kind of woman to be deterred by some two bit shamus. My best bet would be to get her cooperation and then shadow her throughout the day.

When Helen came out of the bathroom, she was dressed in jeans and a T-shirt. It didn't look like she had anything on underneath. I was beginning to think 1979 might have some good points after all. Still, she wore a look of defiance as if she was ready to toss me out on my ear if I tried to keep her from her appointment with this Prof. Adams.

"Mind if I use your shower?" I asked, trying to exude boyish charm.

"Help yourself." Then she softened a bit. "Will you be staying for breakfast? I think I've got some eggs."

"Eggs would be nice." I pulled on my trousers and headed to the bathroom.

I came out to the smells of cooking. There must have been some bacon in the icebox as well as eggs. There was the scent of coffee, too.

Two places had been set at the table. From the pile of books that had been moved from one of the chairs to the floor I deduced that Helen was in the habit of eating alone. One of the plates held two fried eggs and two strips of bacon, the other one of each. I wondered if that was because she was watching her weight, or because that was what had been in the icebox.

She set a couple of steaming coffee mugs down. There wasn't any cream or sugar on the table. I liked my coffee black. It appeared that Helen did as well.

Neither one of us said much during breakfast, but when I had finished and was staring at what coffee remained in my mug I asked, "What time is this meeting that you've got to go to?"

"It's at two."

"Anything else today that you can't afford to miss?"

"No. Just the session with Prof. Adams."

"OK. How about this? You spend the morning here in the apartment. I tag along to this meeting as your shadow, and when it's over, we come straight back here. After today, I'll be out of your hair. Forever."

"How considerate of you," Helen said sarcastically.

"Look. I'm trying to save your life."

I must have raised my voice, because she looked at me with a startled expression as if everything was just beginning to sink in.

"What do you mean by 'after today?' You've said that a few times. That whatever you are expecting will happen today, and that if I can just get through today it will all be over."

"The information that I have is that the attempt on your life will be made sometime this afternoon. If it fails, there won't be a second try."

Actually, I wasn't at all sure about that. What I did know from what Dr. Hollander had said, was that if Helen wasn't killed that afternoon, then history would have been changed, and the dark world she had visited on her return wouldn't exist. Presumably history would be back to something resembling the one that Dr. Hollander had come from originally, though we couldn't be sure about that. The important thing is that it would be a history where Helen was still alive. For the moment that would have to be good enough.

"But how do you know that? You make this attempt on my life sound like a certainty. It's almost like you think it's preordained. Or like you can see into the future."

Actually, it was more like seeing back into the past from the future, but I couldn't tell Helen that.

"I'm afraid that I'm not at liberty to divulge my sources."

"Geez, Harry, you really do sound like a junior G-man," Helen said in exasperation. "Why are you doing this anyway? What's it to you? Why does it matter?"

"I'm doing this because it's what I was hired to do. Also, I like you. I'd hate to see you dead before your time."

Helen shuddered. "Thanks, I guess. Death, my death, seems so real to you."

"I know this whole business is confusing to you. What I can tell you is that there is someone to whom your survival really means a lot."

"But you can't tell me who or why."

"No. I can't."

For a moment it looked as if she was going to argue some more, then she gave up. "Harry Christian, you are the most frustrating man I've ever met."

After that I helped her clear the table. She said that she had work to do before her meeting. I looked out the front window, but all I could see were a couple of student types that looked like they were waiting for the bus. I watched for awhile to make sure and then called Dr. Hollander.

"Is everything alright?" she asked when she answered the phone.

"It's fine. You're grandmother is fine. Nothing happened last night." I wasn't about to tell the doctor that I'd gone to bed with her grandmother. Besides being awkward, it just didn't seem right.

"What about—?"

"I'm going to be with your grandmother everywhere she goes today. I know what the NBT men look like. I'll keep her safe or die trying."

"What about me?"

"Just stay tight. There's nothing you can do here. Trust me."

"I'm doing just that, Mr. Christian."

"I know. Look, I'll be back after midnight, and then we can both go home."

"I hope so."

I said good-bye and hung up the phone. Helen must have been listening.

"Did you mean that, Harry? About you would die trying?"

"Yes."

"I really think you would. You know they don't make men like you anymore, Harry. You're like something out of an old black and white movie. Like Humphrey Bogart or something."

"I always thought I was better looking than Bogart," I quipped.

"Well, maybe. A little." She went back to her reading.

Nothing much happened after that until we left for the appointment with Prof. Adams. I prowled around the apartment restlessly taking a peek out the window every few minutes until Helen told me to stop it so she could get some work done. After that I cleaned my gun as best I could, and replaced the cartridge I had expended in the restaurant. I had the seven in the automatic, and a couple more tucked into my shoulder holster, and that was it. Not enough for an extended firefight.

We left the apartment a little after one. I was carrying my camouflage of text and notebook, trying to look like just another bored grad student. We got to the building with the professor's office without incident.

"How long is this going to take?" I asked as we entered the building.

"Hard to say. It depends on how much Adams feels like hearing his voice, today. But the sessions usually last about an hour."

"OK. I'll find someplace to wait where I won't attract attention."

I walked her up the two flights of stairs to the floor where Adams had his office and then watched as she knocked and went in. There was a window with a ledge at the end of the hallway. I perched myself on the ledge and pretended to read the book I'd brought. A couple of passersby looked incuriously at me as I sat there, but no one seemed to think it out of the ordinary.

An hour went by, then a few minutes more before Helen emerged from the meeting. From the smug look on her face I took it that it had gone well. She almost didn't notice when I came up besides her on the way down the stairs. It was three-fifteen.

I motioned Helen to pause as we reached the entrance to the building. I stepped outside and took a quick look around, but I didn't see any signs of the men in the homburgs. I indicated to Helen that she could come out and join me.

We followed essentially the same path we'd taken the day before except this time we were walking side by side.

It occurred to me that maybe I was playing things all wrong. That maybe if we would do something different the whole business could be avoided. That maybe if we went to a bar and had a couple of drinks and waited until six to walk back to Helen's apartment, or if we took a taxi or the bus, or just did anything different nothing would happen. But, somehow that didn't seem right. It was as if, if we didn't have the confrontation with the two NBT assassins nothing would be resolved and Helen's life would still be under threat.

As we walked along, I had this feeling we were being followed. I'd look around, but I wouldn't be able to spot anyone, but then a few steps on the feeling would be back. I started to wonder if there were more players in the game than the two men in the homburgs.

When it happened, it happened in almost the exact same way as the encounter the day before. They waited until we were on a residential street with no one in sight except Helen and me. One approached from the rear while the other popped out in front of us. The two of them were about a block apart with us in the middle. The difference this time was that both of them had pistols in their hands.

I reached into the pea coat and pulled out my own automatic. They were still too far away for a sure shot and I didn't want to waste bullets. I looked around for cover, but there wasn't much. No parking was allowed on our side of the street, and the houses were built close to the sidewalk with no lawns to speak of.

The NBT men seemed to know that they had us trapped. Slowly, they moved towards each other closing in on us. I could see the smiles on their faces, just as I could see the fear in Helen's eyes.

"If I give the word or shooting starts I want you to run as fast as you can. Run anywhere and don't look back."

"What about you, Harry?"

"Don't worry about me, Helen, just run."

The men in the Homburgs were about thirty feet away from us. They started to raise their weapons, but just at that moment a car chose to come down the street. Hastily, they lowered their pistols so they couldn't be seen. I took the chance.

"Run."

I didn't wait until the car had gone by. I raised my automatic and fired two shots at the one ahead of us. One of them must have hit him because the body spun and slumped to the ground. I heard the report of another shot behind me. I turned, expecting as I did so to feel a slug tear into me. It didn't. The other man was down as well, but I'd never had a chance to fire at him.

Then a figure stepped out from one of the driveways between houses. He was holding the pistol that had got the second NBT man. I recognized the face. It was Howard Winslow.

I turned to see what had happened to Helen. She was standing frozen up against the wall of a house, but as far as I could see, she was alright. I turned back to look at Winslow, but he had vanished. I thought of trying to follow him, but didn't bother. He'd probably saved my life; and Helen's.

It was then that I realized the bodies of the two assassins had vanished as well. It occurred to me that their TSCs must have had some sort of failsafe so that if the user died, the body would return to the future.

Helen looked at me, her eyes wide. "The body. I was looking at it and it just disappeared. What's going on, Harry? And who was that other man?"

"We can talk later. Right now we've got to get out of here before the police show up."

I grabbed Helen's hand and started to run. I didn't want to hang around and answer questions. Helen hesitated for a moment, and then was running besides me.

We didn't say anything more until we were safely behind the locked door of Helen's apartment.

"Who the hell are you, Harry Christian?" she asked angry and frightened at the same time. "And what happened to the bodies?"

"I don't know what happened to the bodies. I'm as surprised at that as you are. All I know is that they probably went back to where they came from."

"And where is that?" Helen demanded angrily.

"I can't tell you, Helen. And even if I could, you wouldn't believe me."

"Try me, Harry Christian. After what I've seen, I'm ready to believe a lot."

It occurred to me that she deserved some kind of answer, even if it wasn't the complete truth.

"I think they were from the future."

"The future?"

"Yeah. We think that they are part of some sort of time police trying to manipulate history."

"That sounds more like science fiction than reality."

"I know. But how else can you explain the way the bodies vanished? They didn't explode or vaporize or something like that. They just disappeared."

"And you? Are you from the future, too, Harry?"

"No, I'm not," I answered truthfully.

"Then what are you?"

I thought about telling her the truth, but I didn't. Instead, I made something up so implausible she might actually believe it. "Let's just say that I work for a secret government agency that is trying to stop people from the future from messing with time. That's more than I should tell you, but I think you deserve at least that much."

"How do I know you aren't lying to me?"

"You don't, Helen. You've no reason to believe a word I've said. Except for the fact that you're alive right now."

"Yeah, there is that," Helen said shaking her head. "That's how you knew, isn't it? That I was going to be killed this afternoon. You knew that, didn't you?"

"Yes. Or at least I knew that an attempt would be made."

"But how? You said you weren't from the future."

"No, I'm not from the future, Helen. But we have our ways."

"Which you can't disclose."

"No. I really can't. For your sake, Helen. All I can tell you is that in one future you died today, but that future has been averted."

"So what happens to me now, Harry?"

"I don't know, Helen. I really am not sure. But I hope you have a long and productive life."

"You said that before, Harry. That's not really very reassuring."

"No, I guess not."

"So what happens to you now."

"Well, like they say in the westerns, my job is done, ma'am. It's time for me to mosey on."

"I'm never going to see you again after today, am I, Harry Christian?" she asked. She sounded like she regretted the fact.

"No. I don't think that's very likely."

"That's too bad."

"I know."

She grabbed me then and kissed me, long and slow, which made me realize how much I wanted to stick around even though I knew I couldn't.

At that point, the threat from the NBT was probably over. Helen didn't need me as a bodyguard. I could have gone at any time, but I didn't.

We ordered out for a pizza. You can do that in 1979. Helen had a bottle of red wine stashed in her kitchen. It wasn't Italian, but that didn't matter to us. We ate pizza and drank wine by candlelight. Helen talked philosophy, I talked about being a P.I., both of us trying to forget that it would all end at midnight like Cinderella except their wouldn't be a happy ending, at least one that involved the both of us.

I suppose we could have made love one last time, but somehow we never got around to it. At midnight, I put on my pea coat and left. We kissed one last time at the door and then it was over.

The Oldsmobile was still in the parking lot where I'd left it. It hadn't been towed away, but a couple of parking tickets had been stuck underneath the windshield wiper. I got in and drove off. On the way past Helen's building I noticed that the lights in her apartment had been turned off.

Dr. Hollander was waiting for me at the motel. I could only guess how hard it had been for her sitting in that small room not knowing what was happening. I didn't wait for her to ask.

"You don't have to worry. Helen is safe. I left her less than half an hour ago."

"Helen?"

"Your grandmother. After spending a couple of days as her shadow, we got to be on a first name basis." I didn't think I wanted to go into any detail.

"And the NBT agents?"

"As far as I can tell, they're both dead. Their bodies didn't stick around for me to check." I gave the doctor a short version of the encounter.

"Interesting. About the bodies, I mean. Their TSCs are obviously more complicated than mine. Some sort of failsafe to prevent evidence from being left behind."

"Yeah. I figured it was something like that."

"But you shot both of them? You're sure that one didn't get away."

"No. I'm sure. Except I didn't shoot them both. They had me in a pickle, one on either side. I shot one, somebody else shot the second one. I think it was Howard Winslow."

"Howard? He was there?"

"I think so. I got a good enough look at him to be pretty sure."

"What was he doing there?"

"Beats me. He didn't stick around afterwards. He just vanished. Either he ran off or he used his time dingus to vanish like the bodies."

"But my grandmother wasn't hurt?"

"No. I walked her home and stayed with her until midnight. I don't know what's going to happen to her after this. All I know is that she didn't die on November 2, 1979."

"Yes, you're right, Mr. Christian. You can't know how grateful I am for what you've done."

"Forget about it. You were right about your grandmother. She's a wonderful woman who didn't deserve to die. I'm glad I was able to prevent that from happening."

Dr. Hollander looked at as if trying to read what was in my mind. I had a feeling she knew there were things I wasn't telling her. It was odd, her face was so much like Helen's, but the person behind it was so different. Not better or worse, just different.

"Look, doc. If it's all the same to you, I think I've had enough of 1979 for the moment. I'd just as soon wait until I'm fifty-seven to make my next visit. Besides, it's probably only a matter of time before the police track down the Olds outside. I'd rather not have to try to find answers to some embarrassing questions."

"You're right, Mr. Christian. We've done what we came to do. It's time to go back."

I changed back into my suit. I have to admit I had been getting used to walking around without having to wear a tie. When I came out of the bathroom, Helen had the time dingus in her hand.

We embraced and she pressed the button.

We were back in my office. It was still dark outside. From the fact that the bottle of rye was still sitting on the desk where we'd left it, it was still the same night. I looked at the wall clock. It was half an hour after we'd left.

"There's still some rye left in the bottle, doc. Feel like a drink."

"Yes, Mr. Christian. I think I'd like that."

I poured a couple ounces into each of the glasses and then handed Dr. Hollander hers.

"To time."

An odd expression crossed her face, then she smiled and clinked her glass against mine.

"To time."

"So, what's next, Dr. Hollander?"

"It's time for me to return to 2042. I don't belong in this time any more than you did in 1979."

"Do you think it will be different this time? I mean from the last time you went back?"

"I'm sure it will be different, Mr. Christian. I just can't be sure in what way. Between what Dr. Winslow and myself have done, I'm afraid nothing will be quite as it was." There was a note of regret in her voice.

"Don't forget about me, Dr. Hollander. I guess I've got to assume some share of the blame if things have changed."

"I won't forget you, Mr. Christian, but I don't think you can be blamed for what you did. The responsibility lies solely with Howard and me."

There was a moment of awkward silence.

"I'd better get going before I disrupt things more than I have."

"I suppose so. There's no time like the present."

She smiled at that. When she smiled I thought she looked even more like her grandmother.

"I can't thank you enough for what you've done, Mr. Christian."

I held out my hand to her. She took it, but instead of shaking it she pulled me close and kissed my cheek.

Then she was gone.

INTERLUDE
TWO

(2042)

Again, this is the story as it was related to me by Dr. Hollander.

Helen hadn't made the mistake of arriving in the NBT compound outside of Boulder the second time she returned to 2042. She wanted a chance to get the lay of the land before revealing herself to anyone connected with time travel. With this in mind, she had set the TSC coordinates to a place that she hoped would be safe, the backyard of her grandmother's house.

The house had been purchased by her grandmother with the money she had made from the first John Overholt movie. For Helen it had always been a sanctuary from the world, a place of magic and wonder. While she had been growing up, her visits had been frequent, including an entire year when her mother had taken a position as a visiting scholar. When her grandmother had become ill the last few years of her life, her mother had given up her academic post and moved in to take care of her. Her mother had never left, and when her grandmother had died a few years earlier, the house had become hers.

It was eight in the evening when she popped into existence. The house was just as it should be, though the yard looked more overgrown than she remembered. One of the reasons she had picked it as the point of her arrival was that the backyard was surrounded by trees and shrubs that provided a screen against prying eyes. She thought that the plantings needed some attention, but that might just be her imagination. The truth was that her mother was now in her early sixties and in the last few years Helen had been so caught up with the time-travel project that her visits had been few and short.

For a moment after she had arrived, Helen thought about going in through the back door, but she decided against it. Her entering that way might give her mother a shock, assuming that she was actually in residence. Helen realized that she had no way of being sure of that. She had assumed that when her grandmother's murder had been prevented, the time stream would resume its original course, but she knew she couldn't be certain of that.

She went around to the front of the house. There were lights on inside, so someone was home. Climbing the front stoop, she pushed the doorbell next to the heavy oak door. The house had been built in the Tudor Revival style in the late 1920's just before the crash, which for Helen, had always been part of its charm. It wasn't like the houses that other people lived in, but more like something foreign that had been translated to the Midwest.

She could hear footsteps inside and a moment later the porch light came on, and Helen saw a face peering out of the small window set high in the door. The door opened a crack and a thin voice asked, "Yes? Can I help you?"

"I wonder if I could come inside a moment to talk to you," Helen replied.

The door opened wider, and Helen found herself facing a thin woman in her early sixties. It was her mother, but more frail and careworn than she should be. The woman glanced nervously past Helen and then took a shocked look at her face.

"Who are you?" she asked hesitantly. Helen realized that her mother didn't recognize her, at least not as herself.

"I'm not sure you remember me, but I'm a distant relative," Helen extemporized.

"I can see that," her mother said. "You look just like my mother did when she was your age. You'll have to forgive me. For a moment I thought I was seeing a ghost."

"I'm sorry I startled you. Perhaps I should have called first, but—"

"I understand, my dear," her mother said, though Helen wasn't quite sure what it was she understood. "You'd better come in. The curfew, you know."

Helen was beginning to realize that the 2042 she had returned to was not the one she had hoped for.

Once she had come in, her mother locked the door and turned out the porch light.

"I'm forgetting my manners, dear. I'm Harriette Hollander. You can just call me Harry. All my friends do."

"I'm Helen Hollander," Helen said introducing herself.

"How odd. That was my mother's name, too. I had no idea that it was a common family name, though I had always intended to name my daughter Helen if I had ever had one."

"So you don't have any children?" Helen asked perhaps more sharply than she had intended.

"No, I guess I just never met Mr. Right. Not like my mother, your namesake. Please come in and have a seat. You look like you're tired."

"I've had a long trip," Helen replied, trying not to think of just how long it had really been.

Harriette ushered her into a comfortable looking living room and motioned her into a chair in front of the fireplace.

"I've been travelling. I just arrived in town."

"You must be hungry, then. Would you like me to fix you something to eat?"

"I wouldn't want to put you to any trouble," Helen replied though she was famished.

"Oh, it's no bother, dear. Frankly, I'm glad of the company. I've been so lonely since my mother died. And, after all, you are family, aren't you?" It wasn't clear from the tone of the last question in what sense it was meant.

When Harriette got up and went into the kitchen, Helen took the opportunity to examine the room. The house was much as she remembered, though some of the furnishings were different, more fussy and a bit more worn. The thing that struck her most was that there were fewer books in evidence. Both her grandmother and mother had been avid readers on a wide variety of subjects and the bookcases had always been overflowing with volumes.

Despite the similarity in appearance, Helen was realizing that Harriette was not her mother. For one thing, her mother had never been particularly domestic. She had loved to entertain, but there had always been something slapdash about the affairs which had been part of their charm.

This revelation was reinforced when Harriette returned carrying a tray with sandwiches and a teapot. Helen's mother had never made tea preferring, coffee or better yet wine or a cocktail.

The sandwiches were simple affairs of ham and Swiss cheese with a light touch of mustard, but Helen found she had devoured three of them and was on her second cup of tea before she paused. Neither one of them had spoken while Helen was eating, all the while Harriette sipping her tea quietly while she watched her guest.

"Thank you so much for the sandwiches," Helen said. "I hadn't realized how hungry I really was."

"I'm glad you enjoyed it, Helen. You certainly were famished. Now that that's over with, why don't you tell me who you really are?"

Harriette suddenly sounded much more like Helen's mother, more direct, more intelligent.

"I don't quite know what you mean," Helen responded.

"Oh, I'm pretty sure you do, Helen, or whatever your name is. I'm quite familiar with my family's genealogy and I'm certain there aren't any long lost members, and certainly none close enough to bear such a striking resemblance to my mother."

"I assure you—"

"Oh, don't worry, dear. I won't turn you over to the authorities. Not if you tell me a convincing story."

Helen looked at her hostess, reappraising the woman who looked so much like her mother. Just how much could she trust her? She was certainly a much stronger character than she let on. Helen decided that she had nothing to lose by telling the truth.

"Very well, though I doubt if you will believe me."

"I'll try to keep an open mind," Harriette replied, not quite sarcastically.

"I'm the daughter that you never had."

Harriette paused for a moment, suddenly less certain of herself.

"I'm afraid that you will have to explain yourself, my dear. I never had any children."

"Not in this world," Helen said.

For some reason this statement didn't seem to surprise Harriette.

"I take it from that, that you are not of this world."

"No, though perhaps not in the sense you mean."

"I may have phrased that badly. From the way you demolished those sandwiches you are clearly flesh and blood. What exactly did you mean?"

"I am a time traveler."

Harriette raised an eyebrow. "From the future or the past?"

"From the present, just not the one in which we are sitting in right now."

"Could you clarify that?"

"I left 2042 on a mission into the past, 1955 to be precise. When I returned to 2042 after failing my mission I found that things had—changed. The organization that I had worked for had been replaced with another, shall we say, less scientific one. I was held prisoner there until I managed to escape."

"And you came here looking for my help?"

"No, at least not directly."

"Go on," Harriette said calmly. "I must say I find this all very interesting."

"When I returned to 2042, I had discovered that my grandmother, your mother, had been killed in 1979. I suspected that she had been assassinated by my captors to prevent me from being born. When I escaped, I escaped back into the past, where I enlisted the help of a—friend, to prevent my grandmother's murder."

"I take it by my existence that you succeeded?" Harriette commented.

"Yes. I—we—succeeded. My grandmother survived the attempt. I thought that with her alive, the time stream would return to its original path. It's clear, though, that it didn't."

"I presume if it had, I would have a daughter?"

"Yes. Me."

"How interesting," Harriette responded, clearly pondering the implications of what her guest had just said.

"And so you came looking for me." It was a statement, not a question.

"I didn't know who else to turn to. I don't belong in the past, but I don't seem to have a place here in my own time, either. If I turn myself into the authorities, I will probably be imprisoned again."

"Oh, I'm quite certain of that. They have a real penchant for locking people up," Harriette said disdainfully.

"I want to thank you for your hospitality, Harriette, but I probably should be going. I wouldn't want to put you at risk—"

"Nonsense, Helen. After all, if what you say is true, you are my daughter."

Helen looked at the woman who wasn't her mother but was so much like her. She was beginning to think that the domestic middle-aged persona was just a pose.

"I must say," Helen said, "You don't seem surprised by all this."

Harriette looked up, the calm eyes suddenly cold and clear. "No. It explains a lot. I assume that this organization that you escaped from and which tried to assassinate your grandmother, my mother, also has the ability to travel through time?"

"Yes. Why do you ask?" It was Helen's turn to be puzzled.

"There are several reasons. One is, that from time to time, I have been asked by the government to write documents describing in detail the clothing, customs, slang and so on, of various time periods in the last hundred and fifty years or so. You know that was my field of study before the universities were curtailed. Or do you?"

"That was my mother's academic background," Helen responded.

"So I'm that much like her, at least. Anyway, as I said, I've been asked to write these reports on several occasions. I say asked, but I really didn't have much choice in the matter. No one does when it comes to the government. In any case, it paid well and gave the government a reason to leave me alone, for which I was grateful. I always wondered what they were up to. The only reason that I could see for them wanting such information was to enable someone to fit in, go under cover as it were, in those time periods. Of course, the fact that they actually can go back in time explains everything. The checks, by the way, originated from something calling itself the National Bureau of Time. I thought they were using the term in reference to history, but clearly there is a deeper meaning."

Helen thought that the way Harriette was taking the notion of time travel was so like her mother who had always been so rational about everything.

"You said there were several reasons you believe my story. What are the others?"

"The other is much less concrete, I'm afraid. It's just that I keep having these feelings that things have—well-changed. I have these memories, echoes of memories really, of people that don't exist or events that never happened. Is that possible?"

"I have reason to believe that the National Bureau of Time, the NBT, is going back and altering the past to create the present that they want."

"They can do that? I mean change the past."

"Unfortunately, yes. I think that is why they wanted to kill my grandmother. For some reason, they see me as a threat. They wanted to insure that I was never born."

"But they succeeded, didn't they. At least in this version of the present," Harriette commented. "I'm curious, my dear, as to what makes you so dangerous that they would want to wipe out several generations?"

"I don't know. I never trained as a secret agent or anything like that. I was just a member of the team of scientists working on time travel. I'm a mathematician by training. A specialist in knot theory."

"A mathematician? Really? Given your grandmother's and my background I would have thought something more in the humanities," Harriette said with almost motherly interest.

"I guess I have a rebellious nature."

Harriette smiled. "You do take after your grandmother, my dear."

"I like to think so," Helen said. "And my mother."

"Perhaps," Harriette said with a smile. "I'm curious about something, Helen. You said that when you went back to 1979 to prevent your grandmother's death that you took someone with you, someone from the past. Who was he? I assume it was a he."

"Yes. He was a private detective. I had met him on my initial foray into the past. He was the only person that I knew that I thought I could count on, and that knew about time travel."

"I see. What was his name?"

"It was kind of an odd one. His name was Harry Christian."

"And when was this? That you saved my mother? What was the date?" Harriette was insistent.

"Why it was November 2nd, 1979. Why are you so curious?"

"What did your mother tell you about her father?"

"She never spoke much about him. I don't think she knew anything. My grandmother was always evasive about the subject. I gathered that it was some sort of one night stand kind of thing."

"Some sort, yes," Harriette said. "She never said anything to me about him, either. I always wondered what he was like, what kind of man he was. When I was young I imagined him as some sort of dashing spy or agent who had been on some secret mission when they met. Sort of like John Overholt. Your grandmother did write those books in your past, didn't she?"

"Yes. I read them all when I was young."

"So did I. When I was young I pretended that he was my father and that my mother couldn't talk about him for risk of breaking his cover. I wonder—"

"I'm not sure I follow you," Helen said.

"Oh, Helen," Harriette said exasperatedly. "When is my birthday?"

"July 26th."

"And what year was I born?"

"1980. Why is that important?"

"You're the mathematician. Figure it out."

It took a moment for what her mother was getting at to sink in.

"You don't mean—"

"That's exactly what I do mean, my dear. Your grandmother, my mother, is saved by a mysterious stranger and nine months later I was born. It doesn't take a genius, or a mathematician, to jump to the logical conclusion."

"That Harry Christian is my grandfather?"

"Yes. It certainly fits. And it explains my middle name, too. I've often wondered why an atheist would name her only daughter something as unfashionable as Harriette Christianne. Now I know."

"But how—" Helen exclaimed.

"The usual way, I suspect. The two of them were alone together, weren't they?"

"Yes, Harry spent the night at her apartment to protect her."

"And you weren't there?"

"No, I was in a motel at the edge of town."

"It's just as well, dear. I don't think you would have wanted to be there when your mother was conceived, would you?"

"He never said anything—"

"Did he have a chance?"

"No, not really," Helen admitted.

"Tell me, Helen, what kind of man was this Harry Christian? I never had a chance to meet my father. You, evidently, have."

"He was your typical hard-boiled private detective, I guess. Tough, brave, competent."

"Sounds a lot like John Overholt, to me. There must have been more to him, though, to have appealed to your grandmother, or to have gone off through time with you to save the life of a woman he didn't know."

"Yes. I guess he is kind of special at that. It's strange to think that he must be dead now for thirty or forty years," Helen said wistfully.

Harriette looked at the daughter she had never had, trying to judge her.

"You didn't ever—"

"What are you asking?" Helen responded.

"I guess what I'm asking is if you ever slept with your grandfather?"

"No," Helen said. "Our relationship was always strictly professional."

"I'm glad, though, under the circumstances I could understand it."

"I never even thought about it," Helen replied, though of course she had.

Harriette seemed to realize that she had broached a sensitive subject.

"I didn't realize that it was so late, Helen. It's way past my bed time, and from the looks of it, yours as well."

"I'd better be going then," Helen said.

"Nonsense. I've got a guest room upstairs that you're welcome to use. Besides, it's way after curfew and if you were spotted, they'd be sure to arrest you. And neither one of us would want that to happen."

Helen realized how tired she was. After all, she hadn't slept since 1979.

"I'd be grateful, Harriette, but I don't want to put you to any trouble or put you at risk."

"It's no trouble at all, and at my age a little risk is good for you. Besides, you're almost like my own daughter."

Helen helped her take the tea things into the kitchen, and then Harriette showed her to the guest room upstairs. It was the same bedroom that she had always used when she had been a child.

Except this was a room that had never belonged to an adolescent girl. It was furnished in the fussy but sterile way that guest rooms that are never used are furnished. Helen didn't care. She was exhausted, both physically and emotionally. After a brief visit to the bathroom across the hall, she undressed and went to bed.

Helen woke to the smell of coffee and bacon. The clock on the nightstand read 9:30. She had slept nearly ten hours straight. It had been the first really good sleep she had had since before her first trip to 1955. Cradled by the familiar surroundings she felt rested and safe. Except, she knew, she wasn't.

From downstairs came a call, "Helen, your breakfast is almost ready."

She dressed hurriedly, glad that her short hair didn't need much attention.

Harriette was waiting for her in the kitchen as were plates with eggs and bacon on the small table in the breakfast nook along with glasses of orange juice and a pot of coffee.

"I don't normally have much in the way of breakfast," Harriette apologized, "but I thought as long as I had a guest—"

"It looks wonderful, Harriette. Thank you."

The breakfast nook, a small extension off of the kitchen, looked out over the backyard. It was late July and the morning sun played on the flowers and shrubs of the garden. Having breakfast there had always been one of Helen's favorite things when she had been staying with her grandmother.

Breakfast was quiet, the click of fork on plate undisturbed by conversation. Helen sensed that Harriette had something to say, but was waiting until they were finished.

Finally Helen sat sipping the last of her coffee, the sun pouring in through the window casting shadows across the table. Part of her wished the moment could go on forever, but she knew it couldn't. She didn't belong here.

"I want to thank you so much, Harriette. I really needed this."

"It was my pleasure. I've been happy to have you. I don't have much company these days. It almost makes me wish that I had had a daughter. At least if she would have turned out like you."

"If you don't mind my asking, why didn't you?"

"You know, I'm not sure," Harriette answered thoughtfully. "I certainly had opportunities when I was younger. But somehow I never felt—I guess settled is the best way to phrase it—I never felt settled enough to want to settle down. I don't know if it was because of the way your grandmother lived or—Are my mother and your grandmother the same person or are they different? I'm afraid that I don't understand this time travel business very well."

"I'm not sure that I do, either. Not really. I think the answer is that up to some point they are, but something happened that caused things to diverge from what I remember."

"Like meeting Harry Christian?"

"No, I think it must have been after that. It's hard to tell now with the NBT and Howard Winslow running amok in the time stream."

"Howard Winslow?" Harriette said with surprise.

"Yes. Do you know him?"

"I don't really know him, but I've met him several times. I get the impression that he's someone high up in the government, but exactly what his position is seems to be something of a secret."

"I'm not sure we're talking about the same person. The Howard Winslow I know was a scientist on the time travel project, really the man behind it. But now he is in the same position I'm in. He's become detached from the time stream. He was the reason that I went back in time in the first place. He wanted to change history. I was supposed to stop him, but I didn't. I think that was when things started to go wrong."

"That doesn't sound like my Howard Winslow. He's more of a politician than a scientist, and a rather nasty one at that," Harriette said bluntly.

"I think that by what he did in 1955 in saving his grandfather's life, Howard changed his own past so much that the Howard Winslow of the present is no longer the same person," Helen explained. "There are now two Howard Winslows, the one that's here and the other one who is someplace or somewhere else. But they are not really the same person."

"It's all very confusing, isn't it?" Harriette commented, sounding for the moment like the middle-aged housewife she pretended to be.

"You said that you prepared reports for the NBT," Helen said to change the subject. "Just what was in those reports?"

"They were more articles than reports," Harriette replied. "As I said, I covered current fashions, cultural references, slang. All the sorts of things about everyday life that you don't really find in normal history books. Things like what words you can and cannot say in polite conversation, what foods to order, what movies you should have seen. There was nothing about specific people," Harriette said somewhat defensively. "As I said last night, I think it was information to help people blend in. I didn't realize it at the time, but that's the only thing that they would have been useful for."

"Do you remember what time periods they were for?"

"Of course, dear. I'm not senile. There was 1979, of course, and 1955. Let's see, 1941 or was it 42, oh and 1925. Is that important?"

"I'm not sure. 1955 and 1979 are key dates, at least for me. I don't know about the others."

"I didn't think I was doing anything wrong at the time. It seemed so harmless. And it paid well, I have to say, and money was hard to come by after the government downsized so many of the universities."

"They closed the universities?" Helen asked.

"Oh, not completely. They left the practical things like the sciences and engineering alone, but things like history and literature classes were eliminated. They said that history had already happened, so there was nothing new to study and that literature only encouraged decadent thinking. That's why I was surprised when they asked me for those articles. It seemed so frivolous at the time. I had no idea that they were trying to alter history. Of course, dictators have always tried to do that, but previously they could only change what was in books, not what really happened."

"Don't blame yourself. You couldn't have known what they wanted them for," Helen said.

"Thank you dear. Coming from you that makes me feel a little better about it," Harriette said. Then a strange smile came to her face. "Of course, even not knowing, I committed my own little acts of sabotage."

"Sabotage?" Helen asked.

"Yes. I'm afraid I added little extra details. Things that weren't true but which they wouldn't be able to check easily.

Like the fact that in 1979 men all wore Homburg hats. I suppose that any agents they sent back to then felt foolish at first."

"I'm sure they did," Helen agreed.

"Have you thought about what you're going to do?" Harriette said after a pause.

"Not really. I was hoping that things would be different, that I would belong again—"

"But you don't, do you. I would love to have you stay, Helen, but I'm afraid that just isn't possible. The police are bound to discover you sooner or later. The first time they asked to see your identity card—well, you don't have one, do you? A card or an identity. They'd put you in prison—or worse."

"I know. And I wouldn't want to jeopardize you."

"Don't worry about me, dear," Harriette said. "Could you go back to 1955? With this Harry Christian?"

"You mean my grandfather?"

"Well, yes, I guess I do. It would be easier for you to blend in back then. They were less fussy about papers and such."

"But I don't really belong there, either."

Harriette paused for a moment. "You know in all the time travel stories they make it sound so romantic, to go back in time and see ancient Rome or sail on the Titanic or whatever. It's a lot more complicated than that, isn't it?"

"Yes. I'm afraid it is," Helen agreed with regret.

"Don't worry, my dear. We'll think of something," Harriette said reaching across the table. Then something seemed to strike her. "There's something that might help you decide. I'll just be a moment."

Harriette disappeared into the living room. Helen could hear the sounds of her rummaging through drawers. After a moment she returned holding a large envelope.

"I'd almost forgotten about this," Harriette said. "It came several weeks ago. It was addressed to Dr. Helen Hollander. I didn't want to open it. I thought that it was for your grandmother, but now I wonder if it really was meant for you."

"But how could anyone know that I would be here? I don't even really exist!"

"I don't know, my dear. But there is one sure way to find out." She handed the envelope to Helen.

The envelope was addressed to "Dr. Helen Hollander" with the street number of her grandmother's house. There was an embossed return address that looked like it was probably for a firm of lawyers. Taking her butter-knife, she slit the envelope open. Inside was a single sheet of paper and a smaller envelope. Unfolding the sheet of paper she read:

Dr. Helen Hollander:

Enclosed you will find an envelope that was entrusted to our firm in 1925 for delivery on this date to this address. I know that this must seem an unusual arrangement but those were our instructions. I have no idea of the contents as per instructions the letter has remained unopened in the firm's safe since it was received. Of course, I was not with the firm at that time, but I believe that it was my great-grandfather that accepted the letter in 1925 from a gentleman by the name of Howard Winslow. While our firm can take no responsibilities for the contents of the letter, I hope that it will prove of some use or benefit to you.

Sincerely yours,
Frederick Hoyt
Partner Hoyt, Jackson, & Schmidt

Helen fingered the enclosed envelope. It certainly looked as if it could have lain in a safe for over a hundred years. The only writing on the outside was her name written in faded ink. She stuck the knife under the flap and slit it open, the ancient paper parting easily. She read:

August 21, 1925
Dear Helen:

I have no idea whether this will ever reach you, but I am desperate enough to pin my hopes on what is for all intents and purposes a note in a bottle tossed on the sea of time. I'm stuck here in 1925. Something has gone wrong with my TSC, and given the primitive state of electronics in this era I have no hope of repairing it. If you eventually read this, I beg of you to come and rescue me from this god-forsaken time period.

I know that you may not feel you owe me anything. Indeed, you may feel the complete opposite. I want you to know that I had nothing to do with the attempt on your grandmother's life. That was the idea of my alter-ego. When I became aware of the mission to kill her, I traveled to 1979 to prevent its success. You can ask that detective, Christian, about that if he hasn't already told you about it. If it wasn't for me, he and your grandmother might both have died in 1979.

I have come to the realization that time travel is inherently dangerous, not to the time traveler, but to the fabric of time. If you have returned to 2042 and are reading this, then you are aware of what I mean. You must trust me that that was never my intent. My only motive in travelling back to 1955 was to prevent the death of my own grandfather. As your own foray to 1979 was occasioned by a similar motivation, you should understand. Unfortunately, I didn't realize that my actions would have such profound consequences, consequences that I now deeply regret.

That is why I am pleading with you to come to my aid. Perhaps the two of us working together will be able to devise some way to repair the situation and restore the time stream to what it should be. I can only hope that you will listen to my plea with a sympathetic ear.

If you do decide to rescue me, I can be found at 1537 Erie St. on August 23. I realize that this request, given its nature, is somewhat ironical, but please hurry.

Yours sincerely,
Howard Winslow

Helen read the letter over twice, then handed it over to the woman who was not her mother. Harriette read it slowly, then gave the letter and envelope careful study.

"This isn't a joke, is it?" Harriette asked.

"No, I don't think it is," Helen replied. "It seems all too like Howard."

"The paper and ink seem appropriate to the period. I've studied enough documents and letters from the 20's to know that."

"Oh, I've no doubt that it's genuine—"

"You just aren't sure whether he means it, are you?"

"No. It could just be a trick. Or an attempt by Howard to get his hands on my TSC."

"TSC? I take it that's what you use to travel through time?"

"Yes."

"And his is broken?"

"It's plausible. The one he stole was a prototype. It wasn't intended for repeated use."

Harriette handed the letter back to the woman who wasn't her daughter. "I think it would be best if you took this with you when you go. It might be awkward for me if they came looking for it."

"I wouldn't want that," Helen acknowledged. She carefully refolded the letter and returned it to its envelope.

"So what are you going to do?" Harriette asked, sounding for all the world like Helen's mother.

Helen paused for a moment, then drew in a deep breath.

"As you said earlier, I can't stay here. I may as well be in 1925 as any time. Maybe Howard actually does have some notion as to how to fix time. It's worth a shot. I don't see that I have anything better to do."

"No, I don't think you do. I hope you succeed, Helen. I rather like the idea of my having a daughter if she turns out like you. When will you be going?"

"As your father once said to me, 'There's no time like the present.' Of course, I think I will make one stop on the way. In 1955."

Harriette nodded and said, "I think that would be wise, my dear."

Helen went upstairs to retrieve the TSC from her bedroom. When she came down, she embraced Harriette and then pressed the button.

PART FIVE

(1955)

Effie had gone home and I was sitting at my desk reading the paper trying to catch up on the news. The last few days, since Harlan Winslow hadn't been killed in fact, had been pretty much of a whirlwind, and left me out of touch. As I scanned the front page I had the feeling that there was something that I was missing, but I couldn't quite put my finger on what it was.

I looked up from the paper and saw Dr. Hollander standing there. I hadn't heard the office door open, but then the doctor wasn't in the habit of using it. I hadn't really noticed before, but it struck me again how much she looked like her grandmother.

"Geez, doc, couldn't you at least knock. You nearly gave me a heart attack."

"I'm sorry, Mr. Christian, but unfortunately the TSC isn't equipped with that function. Perhaps in the next model—"

"Do you think that's a good idea, doc?"

"What do you mean?"

"There being a next model. It seems to me that that time dingus has caused enough problems as it is."

The comment caused her to pause a moment, as if deep down she agreed with me.

It had been less than twenty-four hours since we'd parted, but there was something about her that was different. She seemed sadder than she had been but oddly more at peace with herself. It made me wonder what had happened in 2042.

"Perhaps you are right, Mr. Christian."

"I take it that things didn't go so well in 2042?"

"Why would you say that?" she asked.

"You're here, aren't you?"

"Yes, I see your point."

"So what happened?"

"Nothing much, really. I had a nice visit with my mother. The only thing is, she never had a daughter. Or any children for that matter."

"That must have been awkward."

"Less than you would think. My mother is a very open minded woman."

"Then you told her about the time travel business?"

"We talked about a lot of things. That was one of them." The way she answered me made me think that there was something she was leaving out. I've questioned a lot of people in my time, enough to know that whatever was on her mind, I'd have to let her tell me in her own time.

"So obviously your grandmother survived long enough to have your mother, but something happened so that you were never born."

"That's about the size of it. I don't know why, exactly, but it seems my mother never met my father, so there is no me."

"And the rest of it? 2042 I mean?"

"It's different," the doctor said with a sigh. "And not for the better. The NBT seems to have become a sort of secret police. If anything, things were worse than the first time I went back to the future. Not only do they get rid of anyone they see as a threat, but they are going back in time to prevent their enemies from ever existing."

"Seems to me that would be kind of dangerous."

"That's an understatement, Mr. Christian," Dr. Hollander said grimly. "You can see why I couldn't stay in 2042. My very presence would have put my mother's life at risk."

"We wouldn't want that," I said which elicited an odd expression on the doctor's face.

"No, we wouldn't." Again, I had the feeling I was missing half of the conversation.

"So you couldn't stay in 2042. Why come back to 1955? I would have thought there would have been better times to retire to."

I had an idea of what this was building up to, and I could see that Dr. Hollander was trying to broach the subject. Finally she just came out and said it.

"I'm afraid I need your help again, Mr. Christian."

"Oh? Why me? I'm no scientist and I'm certainly no historian."

"But you have proven yourself in the past. Or the future. Don't sell yourself short, Mr. Christian. You are both capable and resourceful. More importantly, you are the one person in all of time that I can trust."

"I'm not sure about that, but let's hear your sales pitch. What do you want me to do?"

"I need you to go back to 1925 and help me rescue Howard Winslow."

"Howard Winslow? Let me get this straight. Are we talking about the same Howard Winslow that hired me to prevent his grandfather from getting killed? The guy that you came back to 1955 to stop? Didn't he steal one of the time dinguses? Isn't that what started this whole mess?"

"Yes, that Howard Winslow. I'll also point out that it was Howard Winslow that showed up in 1979 to keep an NBT agent from killing you."

"Point taken. So why does he need rescuing?"

"His TSC had stopped working and he's stranded in 1925."

"And how did you find this out?"

"He wrote me a letter. In 1925. He gave it to a firm of lawyers with instructions to post it in care of my mother in 2042. It was waiting for me when I visited her."

"How could he know that you were going to show up?"

"I don't know, Mr. Christian. Maybe he just assumed that sooner or later I would end up visiting her. Maybe he was just desperate and casting notes in bottles out into the sea. For all I know he might have sent out multiple notes hoping that one of them would reach me. All I know for sure is that a letter was waiting for me at my mother's. She thought it was meant for my grandmother because she didn't know that I even existed."

"OK, that explains the how, but what about the why? How can you be sure this isn't some kind of trap? Maybe Howard Winslow is trying to get his hands on your time dingus. Maybe it's a plot by the NBT to get rid of you."

"I'm pretty sure that the letter was authentic. It was in Howard's handwriting. I know him well enough to know that. And the paper the letter was written on looked like it could be a hundred and twenty years old."

"OK. So the letter came from Winslow in 1925. That still doesn't mean it isn't a trap."

"That's why I need you, Mr. Christian. I need you in case it is a trap."

"I'm glad you have confidence in me, Dr. Hollander. I'm not so sure I do. I messed things up here in 1955 and I had to be bailed out in 1979. Seems to me I'm not really cut out for this time travel business. Besides, is it really such a good idea to rescue Winslow? Maybe things are better off with him stranded in 1925. Have you thought about that?"

Dr. Hollander took a deep breath. "Trust me, Mr. Christian, I have thought about it. Let me ask you this. Is it any safer to leave Howard stranded in 1925? Think about it for a moment. A brilliant scientist with knowledge of a hundred and twenty years of scientific and technological advances and foreknowledge of more than a century of political and social upheaval. Just think of the kind of mischief that might occur, even unintentionally."

"OK. So say we rescue Winslow. What then? Do we bring him to 1955? It seems to me all of your arguments still hold except with thirty years lopped off of them. Or do the two of you go back to 2042? Twice that hasn't worked out so good for you. So when? 1979? 1999? 12,000 B.C.?"

"I get it, Mr. Christian. I don't know. That's why I need to go back to 1925 and talk with Howard. He realizes that his actions in preventing the death of his grandfather have compromised the time stream. He wants to undo that, if possible. He seems to think that if the two of us put our heads together maybe we can fix things. But he can't do anything if he's stranded back in the twenties."

"I don't know, doc. Maybe you're right—"

I was interrupted by Dr. Hollander snatching up the paper that I had set down on the top of my desk. Some headline had attracted her attention. She read for a moment and then flipped the paper back a few pages to where the story continued. Finally, she put it down on the desk turning it so I could read it and pointing at a small article below the fold.

NEW GOVERNMENT DEPARTMENT OPENS

Dr. Harvey Winslow assumed the post of director of the new National Bureau of Time, a federal government department that is to be in charge of perfecting improved methods of measuring time.

When the article continued on page six there was more in the same vein and some background information on the new director.

"What about that?" Dr. Hollander asked accusingly.

"What about it?" I countered.

"Do you remember hearing anything about this National Bureau of Time before? And why do we need a new department to improve methods of measuring time? Don't we already have a National Bureau of Standards and a Naval Observatory? No, this is something different. It's a cover name for time travel research. Just like the Manhattan Project was the cover name for the atomic bomb."

I knew a little about the Manhattan Project. I'd been part of it. I could see what the doctor was saying.

"I bet this bureau didn't even exist for you before you met Howard Winslow for the first time," the doctor exclaimed.

"You mean the past, my past, has been changed?"

"I don't know, Mr. Christian, but I don't remember any NBT in my history books. I don't know whether this had something to do with Howard being stranded in 1925 or not, but something has changed time. That's why we need to go back and rescue him!"

"You'll have to bear with me, doc. I'm still coming to grips with this time travel stuff. How can something not exist in my past and then all of a sudden exist?"

"Have you ever heard of Schroedinger's cat?"

"What's a cat got to do with anything?"

"It's a famous thought experiment in quantum mechanics. There's a cat that's in a box with a poison capsule. If the capsule is broken the cat is dead, if it isn't, the cat is alive. Except in quantum mechanics, you can't know whether the cat is alive or dead until you open the box, so until you open it the cat is both dead and alive."

"That sounds crazy to me, doc."

"That's quantum mechanics. Common sense doesn't apply. But what I'm saying is that until I read that letter from Howard Winslow the NBT was like that cat. It didn't exist and it did exist. When I read it, that froze the past so that the NBT existed starting sometime in 1955. And that's why we have to go back and rescue Howard. If we don't, time is going to keep getting mixed up more and more."

"I still say it sounds crazy, doc, but after what I've been through I'll take your word for it."

"Then you'll help me?"

"Do I have a choice?"

"We all have a choice." The way she said that made me feel again like I was missing half the conversation. I decided to call her on it.

"OK, doc. Since you popped in here again you've had something on your mind that you haven't said. I don't know what it is, but if you want me to go traipsing back to 1925 with you, I think now is the time for you to spit it out."

I may have sounded more angry than I was, but I wanted to get Dr. Hollander's attention. I must have succeeded because she paused as if she was making a big decision.

"You're right, Mr. Christian. There is something on my mind, and you are right that it needs to be out in the open if we're going to work together."

"I'm glad you agree, doctor."

"Why didn't you tell me you slept with my grandmother?"

That wasn't exactly what I had been expecting. My first thought was how did she know? As far as I knew, the doctor hadn't had any contact with Helen. My second thought was why did it seem to matter so much to her? Was it possible that the doc was in love with me and that she was jealous of her own grandmother?

"I didn't tell you because I didn't think it was something you needed to know. We didn't have much time together after the fact, either. How did you find out?"

"Because my mother told me."

"Your mother?" I was confused. "How does she figure into this?"

"My mother's birthday is July 26th. She was born in 1980. As my mother told me, do the math Mr. Christian."

I couldn't figure out why the doc was so angry with me. I couldn't see what she was getting at, either. Then it dawned on me.

"You mean--?"

"Yes. My mother, Harriette Christianne Hollander is your daughter. And I'm your granddaughter."

I hadn't been expecting that. Not in a million years. Or twenty-five. I'd never married, never had a kid that I knew of, and now I had one that was born a quarter century in the future.

"I don't know what to say, Dr. Hollander."

"You don't have to say anything. I'm not blaming you. There was nothing you could do about it. It's just that I never knew my father, and growing up I didn't have a grandfather like other kids. I guess I kind of imagined that he was some mysterious figure like John Overholt. And then to find out—"

"That your grand dad is a two bit private eye from 1955—"

"Don't sell yourself short, Mr. Christian. It's just that it's been a lot for me to deal with on top of everything else that's happened."

"Look, I understand, I think. If I'm going to have a granddaughter, I'm glad she turned out as well as you did."

A strange smile came to her face. "It's funny, that's what Harriette, the woman who wasn't my mother, said. It's kind of romantic in a way. The mysterious stranger coming out of nowhere to save my grandmother's life. It's no wonder she wrote all those John Overholt books, Mr. Christian."

"I'll have to read one some time, to see what she really thought of me. But I guess I'll have to wait twenty-five years for that. And don't you think it's time that you stop calling me Mr. Christian? We are family, after all."

"What should I call you? Grandpa? That doesn't seem right, somehow."

"How about Harry." I didn't add that I was going to keep calling her doc. Somehow, I couldn't see me calling her Helen. Especially now that I knew—.

"Alright—Harry."

"So what's the plan, doc?"

It turns out she hadn't had time to make one. I phoned down to the diner to have some dinner sent up along with a couple of cokes. We were still hashing out the details of what we were going to do when the boy from the diner showed up with the food.

I had ordered the special of the day which turned out to be meat loaf, mashed potatoes and peas. Maybe not the greatest meal, but I figured that we both could do with something substantial. Dr. Hollander seemed to agree as she dug into hers with gusto.

"You know, Harry, I had breakfast only a few hours ago," the doc said as she washed down the last with a swig of coke.

"I guess that's the problem with time travel."

"One of the more minor ones," she responded.

I could see that she still had something on her mind.

"You know, I really don't know very much about you, Harry. It seems that I should, you being my grandfather."

"What do you want to know?"

"Well, how did you end up being a private investigator, for one? It seems like you could have been anything."

"Anything other than a private eye, you mean."

"No, that's not what I meant," she said in embarrassment. "But how did you become a P.I. That is what it's called, isn't it?"

"Sometimes. When people are being polite. Mostly it was by accident."

"What do you mean?"

"I knew I was going to be drafted when the war started, so I enlisted first. They needed M.P.s , that's military police, and someone decided I'd make a good cop. It wasn't bad, really. Safer than the infantry except on a Friday night. Anyway, I got sent to a secret base in New Mexico, a place called Los Alamos, to work security. At first it was just manning the front gate, but then I got detailed into more serious stuff like making sure that the scientists didn't leak word about what they were working on. There were a few spies hanging around, some German, some Russian. I think we caught most of them. Then they let off the bomb and the cat was out of the bag.

"After the war they sent me over to Europe, which was OK except things were pretty much a mess. Mostly I was doing background checks on scientists that wanted to emigrate, making sure that they hadn't been Nazis and that they weren't Soviet agents. It wasn't bad work most of the time. I made sergeant and probably could have gone to O.C.S. if I had wanted to, but after six years I decided that I'd had enough of following orders, so I didn't reup when my enlistment was up. Back in the states, I realized that being an investigator was all that I really knew how to do. With my military background, I didn't have any trouble getting a P.I. license, so I set myself up in business, and here I am. Not much of a story, is it?"

"Oh, I don't know, Harry. It sounds like you were part of making a lot of history."

"Instead of breaking it?"

"Yes," Dr. Hollander said, suddenly serious.

"Look, we've got a lot of things to do tomorrow. We should both get some sleep. Let's go back to my place."

Dr. Hollander gave me a funny look.

"Don't worry. You can have the bed. I'll sleep on the sofa."

"OK, Grandpa."

I didn't get much sleep that night. I had a lot on my mind. I was still getting used to the idea of my having a granddaughter which was especially difficult considering that she was nearly the same age as me. Actually, that wasn't so hard to deal with. Dr. Hollander was the kind of offspring one could be proud of, and from what she had said, her mother hadn't turned out so bad, either. Not that I had had much to do with either of their upbringings. I had to attribute the way they had turned out to Helen, the woman I would love so briefly twenty-five years in the future.

What was really on my mind, though, was our planned excursion to 1925. From what I had seen and what the doctor had told me, intervening in the past never seemed to turn out as intended, even when the motivations were noble. Winslow's persuading me to save his grandfather had set all sorts of unanticipated and undesirable things in motion, and even my saving Helen's life hadn't resulted in what we had tried to achieve. Not that I would have changed that for anything.

But now, we were going back to 1925 to rescue Howard Winslow. Was that really such a good idea? Or would leaving him there result in changes for the worst? Did it really matter? Would going back change things, or would it leave them the same because we had already showed up in 1925 and did whatever it was we did? Somehow, that didn't seem right, but if even Dr. Hollander wasn't sure about these things, I was sure that I didn't know enough about the workings of the time stream to know how things were going to turn out.

I lay there, my mind getting tied up in knots thinking about it until I must have finally dozed off.

I woke to the smell of eggs and bacon. It took me a moment to realize that it was my apartment I was in, and that the person doing the cooking was my granddaughter. My back was stiff from sleeping on the sofa, and when I stood up I could hear my back creak. What did I expect? After all, I was a grandpa.

"You're up," Dr. Hollander said. "I wasn't sure if I should wake you. You seemed to have had a restless night."

"Nothing that a cup of coffee won't fix," I replied.

She set a couple of plates of eggs and bacon on the table and came back with a pot of coffee. It occurred to me that I could get used to having Hollander women fixing me breakfast, though I knew that that was never going to happen.

She waited until I had finished eating before asking, "So what do we do now? You seem to have some ideas as to how to proceed."

I paused for a moment to gather my thoughts, then explained, "We left a lot of things to chance when we went to 1979. Too many things could have gone wrong. We could have been arrested with a stolen car for one thing. I want to be better prepared before we make the next trip."

"What did you have in mind?"

"Well, for one thing I think we should be dressed for the part before we go. We'll fit in from the start and we won't have to waste time trying to get outfitted once we get there. And we won't have to spend money doing it, either. And that's another thing. My money was still good in 1979, but I don't imagine anyone is going to accept 1950's currency in 1925."

"What did you have in mind?"

"Trying to buy the right kind of cash from a coin dealer is out of the question. It would be too expensive, for one thing. But we should be able to pick up some period jewelry for not too much money. Not real expensive stuff. Costume jewelry. Stuff that is out of style now, but which we should be able to pawn in 1925 without anyone asking questions. That should be enough to get us walking around money, at least."

"You seem to have thought this through pretty well," Dr. Hollander said.

"Yeah. I guess I have."

"That's why I wanted your help, Harry."

For a moment when she said my name I thought about how much she sounded like her grandmother. I had to remind myself that she was a different woman. That she was my granddaughter.

To hide my thoughts I said, "I know that we've got plenty of time, but we should get going."

I helped her clean up the breakfast things and then got ready.

As we were leaving the apartment building, we ran into my neighbor, Mrs. McGinty who gave us the fish-eye. I knew that she didn't approve of me and could imagine what she thought about catching me in the hallway with a woman at nine in the morning. I thought about giving her some story about the doc being my cousin from Topeka or something, but decided it wasn't worth it. Nothing I could say was going to change her mind about me.

There was a second hand clothing store a few blocks from my place. Most of the stock was more recent, mostly post war or late thirties, but they did have some older things too. Dr. Hollander had a surprisingly good eye for styles, and what would be appropriate for 1925. It didn't take her long to pick out a suit that fit me. The pants were a little baggy for my taste, but I trusted her judgment. She came up with a shirt and tie, as well.

Finding something for her to wear proved more difficult. Most of what they had was too dressy for day time wear. She spent a lot of time going through what they had on the rack before finally selecting a dress that met her approval. She managed to find shoes and a bag, as well. She even dug up one of those ugly hats they wore back then. The total for the pair of us came to just over sixty bucks. Time travel was proving to be expensive. Between what we were spending here and what we'd gone through in 1979, I wasn't making anything on the case.

As we walked out of the shop I asked, "How'd you learn so much about period styles? That seems odd for a mathematician."

"I picked it up as a kid. My mother always had stacks of books and magazines with photos of clothing and furnishings from throughout the twentieth century. That was her area of expertise, after all. I remember looking at all the pictures and thinking how wonderful it would be to live back when the pictures were taken. Little did I know—"

"Yeah. That you'd actually get the chance. Has it lived up to your expectations?"

She looked at me oddly for a moment before replying. "It's a lot more—complicated—than I imagined as a child."

"You have a talent for understatement, doc."

Our next stop was a pawn shop that specialized in jewelry. At first the owner wasn't particularly helpful, but when he saw that Dr. Hollander knew what she was talking about, he became more cooperative. The two of them spent nearly an hour going over tray after tray of rings and things while I mostly stared at the junk hanging on the walls. When they were done, she had come up with an assortment of broaches, pins and rings that would fit into her purse. It came to a hundred and twenty bucks. It looked like a bunch of out of date stuff to me, but the doctor seemed satisfied with herself. The owner seemed happy, too and said we should come back anytime.

After that, we headed back to my apartment.

When we got there we tried on our purchases. It felt a bit like getting ready for a costume party, not that I'd ever done that much. The suit fit alright, though dealing with the separate shirt collar gave me a bit of a problem. I strapped on my shoulder holster, put on the suit coat and looked at myself in the bedroom mirror. The bulge from the automatic was hardly noticeable. Seeing as our destination was 1925, I figured that most people would try to ignore a man with a heater under his jacket.

My notions of the era were pretty sketchy. I'd hadn't been much more than a toddler in 1925, and most of what I knew I'd picked up from watching old gangster movies. I knew that selling booze was illegal, but that people drank more of it than had before Prohibition went into effect. The impression gained from the movies were that the streets were dominated by speeding cars full of Tommy-gun wielding gangsters but I suspected the reality would be quite a bit different. 1925 was before the Crash and the Depression, so we'd be going to a relatively prosperous time where everybody was trying to make a killing in the stock market.

As I was pondering all this, Dr. Hollander came out of the bathroom where she'd been changing. She looked different, more feminine in sort of an understated way. I had to admit, that she really had a knack for period styles. The dress didn't do her figure justice, it was cheap and plain, the sort of thing that would have been worn by shop girls or secretaries, but she could have stepped out of some old photo. She'd done something with her hair, too, to make it look like one of the 'bobs' that had been popular in the 'twenties. She certainly didn't come off as a 'flapper.' More like someone that worked hard to make ends meet. That was probably just as well. We didn't want to attract attention.

"Well, what do you think?" she asked, after doing a twirl.

"You're asking me? The last time I was in 1925 I was three. But from what I know, I think you'll do fine. What about me?"

She gave me a critical going over. When she stepped in close and adjusted my collar and tie, I could smell the scent of her hair. I had to remind myself again that she was my granddaughter.

"You look very dapper, Mr. Christian. We need to do something about your hair, though."

She went back into the bathroom and came out with my comb. She spent a few minutes fiddling with my hair, slicking it back and trying different parts. Finally she seemed to be satisfied.

I took a gander at myself in the mirror. She certainly knew her stuff. I'd learned a few things about disguises working in intelligence, but nothing like this. Looking in the mirror was like looking at my father.

"You should fit right in, and I can hardly see that pistol you're wearing."

"Speaking of which, do you still have that automatic I gave you?"

"It's in my handbag."

"And the jewelry?"

"It's all in there as well."

"Looks like we're about ready then. When do you want to go."

"You said it yourself, Mr. Christian. There's no time like the present."

"I guess so."

She pulled the hat onto her head, and took one last glance at herself in the mirror. I was standing right behind her. We could have been a couple in an old family portrait.

She pulled out the TSC and made whatever adjustments it was she had to make to land us in 1925 and then she stepped close and put her arms around me.

Then she pushed the button.

PART SIX

(1925)

We'd learned a few things from our excursion to 1979. Instead of landing in the woods, we'd picked as our point of arrival a dead end alley not far from where my office would be located thirty years in the future. By doing so, we didn't have to worry about obtaining transportation. In 1925 there would be fewer automobiles around and even fewer that wouldn't be missed if we stole them. I wasn't convinced that I'd be able to get one of those cantankerous machines started, either.

If the TSC had worked as planned, we'd timed our arrival for nine-thirty in the morning, as well. That way we wouldn't have to stumble around in the dark. We'd also attract less attention walking around than we would in the early hours of the morning.

The alley we had picked had a short, right angle dog-leg that kept us out of view from the street. The alley still existed pretty much unchanged in 1955, and I had done a quick reconnaissance before we'd left to judge its suitability. Luck was with us, there wasn't anyone else in the alley; not that that had been likely, the only thing in the alley were a few trash cans. After we separated we took a moment straighten our clothing and then walked out of the alley onto the street.

We paused a moment to adjust to the bright sunlight after the dimness of the alley. I looked up and down the street, but if anyone noticed a couple emerging from the alley, they didn't give any sign. On the corner there was a drug store with a clock projecting out in front above the sign. It read "9:42", pretty close to when we had planned. I set my wrist watch to match. I hadn't bothered to get a pocket watch. Dr. Hollander had assured me that since the World War wrist watches had become commonplace.

One thing that struck me was that things were dirtier. Maybe it was the fact that most of the heat was supplied by burning coal which left a residue of ash on everything, or maybe it was just that there was less of an effort to clean things up. There was a pile of horse droppings in the road, too. The automobile was less ubiquitous, and only a few were parked along the block.

"What now?" Dr. Hollander asked.

"First we need to get some walking around money. There should be a pawn shop around the corner."

We weren't that far from my office, and I would be walking these streets a lot in thirty years. Though I'd never had to avail myself of its services, I'd passed the shop hundreds of times. One thing I remember were the words "Est. 1912" painted in gold leaf on the shop window.

My memory hadn't been faulty. The pawn shop was right where I remembered it. It didn't look much different except maybe that the ukulele and cameras and other items in the front window would be considered antiques in 1955.

We entered separately. I'd thought it would arouse less suspicion that way. A little bell over the door rang for each of us. A moment later a short man came out of a room in the back. He looked just like you would imagine the owner of a pawn shop would look. I pretended to examine the collection of musical instruments in a cabinet against the side wall while Dr. Hollander approached the counter.

"Good morning, miss. What can I do for you?" The tone was friendly enough, but in the reflection in the glass of the case, I could see the proprietor eyeing the doc up.

"I've got a few pieces of jewelry that I'd—I'd like to sell." I wasn't sure if Dr. Hollander was just acting the part or if she was really as nervous as she sounded.

"Oh?"

"Yes," she said, sounding more determined. She opened her bag and started laying them out on the counter one by one.

The proprietor produced a jeweler's loupe from the pocket of his vest and began the examination of the jewelry.

"Hmm. Some nice pieces, miss. Good workmanship. Not so expensive you understand. No precious stones, and mostly cheaper alloys. But that's what people seem to like these days. There are quite a few pieces here. Nearly a dozen. May I ask how you came by so many and why you want to sell them? You said you wanted to sell and not pawn them, didn't you?"

"Yes. I assure you they aren't stolen. They are all legitimately mine. It's just that I—I need the money."

I could see the wheels going round in the shop keeper's head. Dr. Hollander, even with her twenty-first century accent sounded and acted like an educated woman, but he could sense that something wasn't quite right.

"I'm not sure that I can help you out, miss. A man in my position has to be careful, you understand. Maybe if you could tell me a little more about how you came by this jewelry?"

Dr. Hollander looked around nervously trying to catch my eye to see what she should do. I decided to intervene.

"Look, mister. I don't mean to butt in, but can't you see the lady is embarrassed at being down on her luck. Can you blame her? I ask you, does she look like a thief?"

"And who might you be, sir?"

"Me? My name is Overholt, John Overholt. I just came in because I'm thinking about taking up the fiddle. But I couldn't help overhearing you and the lady—"

"And you don't know this lady?"

"Never saw her before," I lied. Being a detective, I'd learned to lie pretty good over the years, but I had a feeling the old guy wasn't buying it. I couldn't say that I blamed him. It probably did look pretty fishy.

"So it's really none of your business then, is it, Mr. Overholt? But it is mine."

"Maybe not, but I'd like to see the lady get a square deal." I don't know for sure, but I think the pawn broker sensed that I had a gun under my jacket.

"So what would you suggest I do, Mr. Overholt?" he asked nervously.

"Look, you said yourself the stuff isn't real expensive. Not the kind of thing a thief would take if they had the choice. More like gifts, say. Why don't you quote the lady what you think is a fair price. Then she can either take it or leave it."

"There's something in what you say, mister." He took another look at the jewelry, figuring what he could sell each item for. Finally he asked, "You want me to give you a price for everything or do you want to know what each piece is worth?"

"Just one price for everything, please."

"Eighty-four dollars. That's the best I can do. You understand, these pieces don't have much intrinsic worth, not like a diamond ring or something—"

"Eighty-four dollars is fine," Dr. Hollander said. "I'll take it."

"Give me a moment," the proprietor said, as he retreated into the back room. For a minute I wondered if he was going to call the police, but then I heard the sounds of him opening a safe. He reappeared holding a small stack of notes.

He counted out the money, fives and tens along with four silver dollars. Dr. Hollander picked up the bills and stuffed them into her handbag.

"Thank you."

"You're welcome, miss."

Dr. Hollander left the shop. I waited a moment to make it look good.

"You said you were interested in a fiddle, Mr. Overholt?"

"I think maybe I've changed plans. I'm thinking of taking up the tuba, instead. I'll let you know when I've made up my mind."

I gave the old man a wink and walked out.

I caught up with Dr. Hollander down at the corner by the drug store.

"I probably should have gotten more. Maybe if we had only tried to sell one or two pieces at a time—"

"Relax, doc," I said cheerfully. "You did fine. Getting rid of the stuff one piece at a time would have taken us all day. As it is, we've got plenty of walking around money. Remember, this is 1925 and eighty-four bucks will go a long way."

"So what do we do now? Try to find Howard?"

"One thing at a time, doc. This drug store probably has a lunch counter. We should grab something to eat before we look up Winslow."

As I had predicted, the drug store did have a lunch counter. As it was still quite a bit before noon, there were plenty of stools open. We chose two at the end where we'd be out of earshot of the waitress. The selection on the menu posted on the wall behind the counter was limited, but the prices, at least in comparison to those in 1955 were quite reasonable. The daily special was advertised as roast beef with gravy and mashed potatoes which sounded safe if not exciting. We both ordered it when the waitress came around along with a cup of coffee.

While we waited for our lunches, I said to Dr. Hollander, "You know Winslow a lot better than I do. How do you think we should play this?"

The doc thought for a moment before replying. "I think we should take him at his word. At his core, Howard is a rational man. I think he realizes now that disturbing the time stream has unintended consequences. I feel he wants the future to go back to the way it was as much as I do. The very manner in which he contacted me strikes me not so much as an act of desperation, but as part of a well thought out plan."

"Sending a letter to be delivered more than a century later isn't an act of desperation?"

Dr. Hollander smiled. "Not for someone with Howard's understanding of the time stream. It wasn't random act like throwing a bottle with a message in the ocean. He planned for it to be delivered to me. And you have to admit the plan worked. After all, we're here, aren't we?"

"I guess you've got a point there, doc. So you think we should just go to the address Winslow gave you and knock on the door?"

We were interrupted by the waitress dropping two plates of food in front of us. It looked less appetizing than I had hoped; two thin slices of roast beef and a small scoop of mashed potatoes with a lumpy, brown gravy drizzled over both. I took a tentative bite. It didn't taste as bad as it looked. The coffee was black, strong and a bit bitter, but I've had a lot worse.

Dr. Hollander must have been hungrier than me, because she dug right in. As she seemed more interested in eating than responding to my question, I joined her. It was as I was mopping up the last of the gravy with the roll that had come with the meal that she finally gave me an answer.

"I don't see that we have a lot of choice in the matter. It's August 23, the date that Howard said that he'd be expecting me. We don't have much time for any preliminary surveillance. I'm not sure that that would do us much good, in any case. I assume that we're going to make contact with him no matter what, if only to get our hands on the prototype TSC."

"That's alright by me, doc. I just wanted to make sure that that's what you wanted to do."

I picked up the check the waitress had dropped on the counter. The specials had been thirty cents each; the coffee had been a dime a cup. I flipped one of the silver dollars we'd gotten from the pawn shop on top of the bill and stood up.

"Shall we, doc?"

The house numbering and street names hadn't changed much from 1925 to 1955, so we didn't have any trouble finding 1537 Erie. It proved to be a three story apartment building nestled in a block of similar buildings.

The front door opened to a small foyer. The mailboxes for the apartments were stacked on one of the walls. I read through the names posted on the boxes, but none of them read "Winslow."

"What do we do now?" I asked.

"You saw the letter. This is the address he gave. And it is August 23—"

"Could he have gotten the year wrong?"

Dr. Hollander was about to answer when a woman poked her head out of one of the apartment doors.

"Can I help you?" she asked somewhat suspiciously

"I hope so," I said trying to sound harmless and friendly. "We're looking for Howard Winslow. He wrote us this address, but I don't see his name listed on any of the mailboxes."

"That's because he doesn't have an apartment. The owner has been letting him use the cellar for some sort of radio project he's working on. You'll probably find him there now. Just go down to the end of the hall and take the last door on the left. But mind the stairs, they're kind of steep."

I said, "Thanks for your help, ma'am," but by the time I had finished she'd closed the door in our faces.

"Friendly sort," I commented. Dr. Hollander didn't say anything.

We followed the directions. When I opened the last door on the left, there was a steep, narrow staircase lit by a dim electric light bulb with a naked filament suspended from the ceiling by a cord. It cast just enough light to see the treads of the stairs. We descended in single file.

The cellar was what you'd expect in 1925. There was a big coal fired boiler that wasn't operating at present, it being August. There was an assortment of broken furniture, old trunks and other junk, all covered by a layer of coal dust. Other than the light bulb at the foot of the stairs, the only illumination seemed to be coming from the front of the building.

I called out, "Winslow? Are you there?"

At almost the same time, Dr. Hollander said, "Howard, I'm here."

I could hear someone stirring up front. I found my hand reaching for the pistol I wore under my coat.

"I've been expecting you." The voice was the one I remembered as belonging to Howard Winslow. "Come on up front."

We walked towards the light.

Winslow was sitting at a sort of work bench on which sat what looked like the remains of a half dozen radio sets. The only thing he had in his hands was a large soldering iron. I relaxed a little and withdrew my hand from my coat.

"I suppose I could ask you what took you so long, but we all know that the question would be irrelevant." Winslow said that as a joke, but it was the kind of humor I'd heard during the war. He was thinner looking than he had been when he had hired me in 1955 and paler looking, too. He had punctuated the sentence with a cough, which considering the coal dust all around wasn't surprising.

"How long have you been here, Howard?" Dr. Hollander asked.

"You mean in 1925? Six months, nearly seven."

"But how did you get here?"

"You really mean why, don't you?"

"Well, yes, I guess I do," the doc replied awkwardly.

"To make a long story short, after I saved your grandmother I went back to 2042. You obviously did, as well, or you wouldn't be here. I don't know how it was for you, but things hadn't really improved. I had hoped that by preventing your grandmother's death, the time stream would correct itself, but we both know that didn't happen. Knowing that there wasn't a place for me in 2042, I headed back to 1955. That's when it happened. Something in the TSC went blooey. I found myself in February 1925 with no useable money and a dead TSC. I can tell you it gets damn cold in February before global warming."

I didn't understand the last bit, but I got the general idea

"Why didn't you send a message to rescue you earlier?" Dr. Hollander asked.

"The first few months I was just trying to survive. Whatever I earned was just enough to get me enough food to keep me alive and maybe someplace to sleep where I wouldn't freeze. It's only been recently that I have saved up enough money that I could approach a lawyer and have some confidence that a letter might get through."

"But why wait until now?" I interrupted. "Why not have us come rescue you when you first arrived?"

Winslow looked at me and shook his head. "Because I've learned my lesson. I'd already lived through the first half of 1925. If you had come back any earlier to save me, that would have made another change to the time stream. You should realize by now, Mr. Christian, that that's not a good idea. By the way, I apologize for getting you into this business. Helen and I at least had our eyes open when we started, you were just shanghaied."

"Think nothing of it. It's been interesting to say the least." I looked at Dr. Hollander. Winslow looked puzzled for an instant, but then must have realized that there was something unspoken between the doc and me. I'm not sure that he got it right, but that didn't really matter.

"I must say, Mr. Christian, that you've proved yourself more adaptable than most men would have," Winslow commented. The admiration, if that was what it was, was still grudging. He might have had a rough time of things since he'd become stranded in 1925, but he hadn't fully lost his arrogance in the process.

"Yeah, well I guess I've seen a few things in my time that give me a certain perspective." Having witnessed the first A-bomb blast and the ruins of post-war Europe first hand, I'd learned to live with a lot of things, even time travel. "Look, what's the situation here?"

"Perhaps it would be simplest if I recount my adventures since arriving in the 'Roaring Twenties,'" Winslow said.

"Tell it any way you want," I replied curtly. Dr. Hollander looked like she didn't quite approve, of my manner, but then I didn't know Winslow as well as she did.

"As I said earlier, it was February when I was deposited here by the broken TSC. I can only surmise that there had been some sort of overload that had disabled one or more of the circuits on the TSC. As my arrival was unplanned, I was dressed for 1979 and I didn't have any currency on me that would be useable in 1925. It didn't take me long to discover that my twenty-first century skills and knowledge were useless. Being able to program a computer or design advanced electronics isn't of much use in a world where computers haven't been invented and transistors and integrated circuits don't exist. Even my knowledge of physics wasn't relevant. Too much of it depended on principles that haven't been discovered yet. That first month, I managed to survive, barely, by taking a sequence of menial jobs, dish washer, bus boy, whatever.

"I managed to find more or less steady employment in a speakeasy owned by one of the local gangsters; a gentleman who goes by the name of Buster O'Toole, though if he's Irish, I'll eat his hat. As I said, I was employed in cleaning up around the place, moving stock around, that kind of thing, not the criminal end of the business. No one paid much attention to me; I was just another bum down on his luck. I don't know how much you know about this time, but the illicit liquor trade is pretty cut-throat. About the time I started at the speakeasy there was a gang war going on over who would provision the booze in town. A group with backing from Chicago were trying to take over from the local mobsters. Let's just say their methods weren't subtle.

"One night as I was cleaning up and O'Toole was tallying up the receipts three men showed up, armed with a couple of guns apiece. They shot O'Toole's bodyguard and got the drop on him. No one there, including O'Toole, paid attention to me. They certainly weren't expecting someone mopping the floors to be armed. I was still carrying the same pistol I had used to kill the NBT agent in 1979. I knew I couldn't count on the gunmen leaving any witnesses alive, so I pulled out my pistol and shot them."

"Just like that?" I asked.

"Just like that," Winslow replied. "Like I said, they weren't really paying attention to me. O'Toole was grateful, though I think he still had suspicions about me. I'm pretty sure he suspected me of being an undercover Treasury agent or something. Not that a lot of men didn't learn how to use a gun during the war. In any case, I found myself promoted on the spot to be one of O'Toole's crew.

"That beat scrubbing floors, but I had ambitions beyond being a hired gunsel. The life of a gangster isn't nearly as glamorous as it's portrayed in the media, particularly when there's a turf war in progress. I had no great desire to remain in 1925, either. Even you, Mr. Christian, must think of it as somewhat primitive."

"Maybe," I replied noncommittally, "I haven't had a chance to see much of it, though Prohibition is a bit of a downside."

"Oh, it's easy enough to get booze if you know the right people. But to get on with my tale. I wanted to get back to 1955—"

"Why 1955?" I interrupted.

"I would have thought that obvious. 1955 is the fulcrum of this whole business. Specifically the moment when my grandfather wasn't killed. I realize, now, that my interference in that event was a grave mistake, an act of hubris on my part. Our only hope of ever restoring the time stream is to go back to 1955 and undo that moment. Don't you agree, Helen?"

There was a twinge of regret when I heard him use that name, but then I realized he was referring to Dr. Hollander. She looked at him for a moment, as if wondering how far she could trust him. "I'm not as convinced of that as you are Howard, but I don't rule out the possibility."

"Wait, are you both talking about returning to 1955 to make sure that Harlan Winslow dies from a gunshot fired from the alley on Third St.? Wouldn't that be murder?"

Winslow shook his head. "Believe me, Mr. Christian, I regret the necessity of that fact more than you can imagine. We are talking about my own grandfather. But, yes, that is what we are talking about. But can you really call it murder. He was supposed to die. It was the very fact that he didn't that has disturbed the time stream in the first place."

I was having trouble with Winslow discussing the death of his grandfather so dispassionately. Maybe that's because I'm not a scientist, but when I looked over at Dr. Hollander I could see that the notion bothered her, as well.

"Maybe you should get on with your story. We can figure out what our plan is later," I said, trying to avoid an impasse.

"I had improved my prospects, at least temporarily, but, as I said, I wanted to leave 1925 as quickly as possible, and not just to correct the time stream. The current situation here is hardly stable. Sooner or later the Chicago mob is going to take over the town, and when they do, that will be the end of O'Toole. It probably will be the end of all those working for him as well. I'm sure that you are familiar enough with the era to know the sort of things that happened in a gang war?"

"You mean like the St. Valentine's Day massacre?"

"Precisely. I made arrangements to send the letter to Helen's mother in 2042 in hopes that it would reach you, but I couldn't count on that plan succeeding. As a backup plan, I set about trying to repair the TSC. As you can imagine, that has proved difficult. I wasn't even sure exactly what was wrong with the device. I've been forced to improvise even the most basic of test equipment. Buying the necessary parts takes far more money than I was making as one of O'Toole's henchmen. I've managed to convince him to invest in what I've described as an 'improved type of radio set.' O'Toole agreed to loan me some money, I think he was rather flattered by the idea of becoming a legitimate businessman, but I'm afraid that his patience is wearing thin. I suspect that he is hoarding his resources in the eventuality that he has to make a hasty departure. Hence these rather Spartan working conditions. You can see now, why I was so relieved when you arrived to rescue me, Helen. I have to admit, I wasn't expecting Mr. Christian to be accompanying you."

"We couldn't very well leave you here, Howard. Especially when you mentioned your willingness to work together to restore the time stream to its original state. As for Mr. Christian, he's proved himself both adaptable and useful. Besides, he's more intimately tied to this business than you realize."

"Oh?"

"Yes. He happens to be my grandfather."

Winslow looked at me appraisingly. "I see. Obviously in 1979. That was quick work, Mr. Christian. I underestimated you."

There was a moment of embarrassed silence.

"Just so I get this straight, in addition to wanting our help in making sure your grandfather dies in 1955, you've landed us in the middle of a mob war?"

Winslow looked at me oddly, then said, "Yes, I think that sums it up succinctly."

"Just checking. Has either of you eggheads thought about the implications of what will happen if we succeed?"

"I'm not sure I follow you, Mr. Christian. What are you getting at?"

"Okay. Say Harlan Winslow dies on a Friday night on Third St. What happens then? Does time travel not get invented? Do you and the doc not go back to 1955 and try to hire me? Do I not travel through time to 1979? And if I don't, just who is Dr. Hollander's grandfather?"

"I confess that I've been so concerned with getting out of 1925 that I haven't given much thought to the consequences. I've been assuming that in restoring the time stream, things would just work themselves out. Obviously Helen was born because she exists. Perhaps the truth is that she isn't your granddaughter after all. Or maybe it's like Schroedinger's Cat, where she both is and is not your granddaughter."

"There you go with that damn cat, again. That just doesn't make any sense."

"I'm afraid, Harry," Dr. Hollander said, trying to calm me down, "that there is a lot about time travel that doesn't make sense. Not in the conventional meaning of the word. You have to remember that we're new to the workings of time travel and we haven't mastered all the nuances, yet."

I didn't take kindly to being lectured to by my own granddaughter, if she was my granddaughter, that is. "Well, just maybe, before we go off half-cocked and try to keep Harlan Winslow from not getting killed, you should give some thought to those nuances. It seems to me that ignoring nuances, or pretending they don't exist is what has gotten us into this mess."

The two scientists looked at each other in stunned surprise.

After a moment, Winslow said, "You know, Helen, I think our detective friend is right. Maybe we should give some thought as to what will or will not happen when we return to 1955."

"My grandfather can be quite astute at times," Dr. Hollander said quietly. "That's why I asked him to come with me." She turned to me then, "You're quite right, Harry. We do need to discuss the ramifications."

"Good," I commented, feeling smug with myself, though I'm not sure that was warranted.

I won't try to recount the next several hours of conversation. I don't remember much of it, and I understood even less. All I know is that there was a lot of scribbling and waving of hands and occasional raising of voices.

It was hard to tell time in the cellar, but when I looked at my wristwatch I realized that it was after five. I waited until there was a lull in the discussion and then interrupted:

"Look, I don't know about either of you two, but I'm getting hungry. I wouldn't mind a drink, either, as long as it doesn't come out of a bathtub."

The two of them looked at me as if they had forgotten that I was there.

"Harry's right, as usual," Dr. Hollander said. "If there's one thing I've learned flitting through time is that one should eat when the opportunity presents itself. You never know when you'll get the next chance."

Winslow chimed in, "I agree, Helen. There's an Italian restaurant down the street a few blocks, Mr. Christian, that will make dinners to go if you ask. The food isn't half bad if you like tomato sauce. And if you say 'Buster sent me' they'll even add a bottle of whiskey to the order. But make sure it's something that was brought in from Canada. The local stuff is plain awful at its best."

"Sure," I said. "I wasn't adding much to the discussion, anyway. Down the street, you say?"

"Yes. To the left as you go out the front entry," Winslow answered, sounding almost too agreeable.

I made my way out of the cellar. After the stuffy confines of the basement, the fresh air in my lungs felt good. It was a nice August evening, not too hot or humid, just the kind of night for a pleasant stroll.

The restaurant was more like three blocks away rather than two. I didn't need the sign above the door that said "Mama Rosa's" to know it was the place Winslow had meant. When I went in, I saw that there were a handful of customer's sitting at mismatched tables covered with red and white checked tablecloths. From the red liquid in juice glasses on the tables, it didn't look as if anyone was too concerned about Prohibition.

A middle aged man with a white apron and a black moustache came up to me and asked, "You wanna dinner, meester?"

"A friend of mine said that you could make food for me to take home."

"Sure. We can do that. We gotta big pan of lasagna. That okay?"

"Sure. I need enough food for three."

"No problem. It take just a coupla minutes."

"Buster, that's my friend, said that you could also maybe supply me with something a little extra. Something from up north."

"Sure. No problem," the waiter said with a wink. "For a buck extra, I give you a bottle of wine, too. Good stuff. I mak'a it myself."

"That would be swell."

"Sure. Just you wait."

The waiter went back into the kitchen.

While I was waiting, I got to thinking about getting back to 1955. One thing was bothering me. According to the doc, the time dingus had a limited carrying capacity. She'd said that two people were pretty much the limit. If we couldn't get Winslow's TSC working that might be a problem. We could do it in relays, of course, but could the person left behind on the first trip really trust someone to come back for him. It was kind of like the puzzle of trying to get a wolf, a goat, and a cabbage across a river in a boat that would only hold two of them at a time. Leave the wolf alone with the goat and the wolf would eat it. Same with the goat and the cabbage. I couldn't remember the solution. I was still thinking about it when the waiter returned with a big sack that smelled of garlic, tomato, and basil.

"Here you are, meester. Lasagne, some nice bread, a bottle of vino, an' a pint of Canadian hooch. Three dollars for the food, one for the vino, and two for whiskey. Another buck for the plates and forks, but if you bring them back you get that back. Seven bucks total."

I pulled out a sawbuck and handed it over saying, "Keep the change."

"Thanks, meester. You can keepa da plates."

I was still thinking about the boat puzzle while I was walking back towards the apartment building smelling of garlic. I was pretty sure that I could trust Dr. Hollander. I wasn't nearly as sure about Winslow. What I really wasn't sure about was with the two of them together. After all, what if the time dingus stopped working on the trip back to 1955? If Dr. Hollander and Winslow made the first trip, would they risk coming back for me? They might figure that I would have the best chance of surviving in 1925. I was still working on a solution when I stopped before the front steps of the apartment building.

What had caused me to pause was a long, black touring car parked in front of the building. I noted that it had an Illinois license plate. It looked like one of those cars that come careening around a corner in gangster movies with tommy guns blazing from the back seat. I wasn't an expert on twenties car models, but it struck me as too upscale for the neighborhood. It was pointed the wrong way and the engine had been left running. Like someone was planning a quick getaway.

I set the sack with the food down on the steps and reached inside my jacket for the automatic pistol I was carrying. Inside, there was no one in the hallway. Quietly I covered the distance to the rear of the building, listening for anything out of place. That's when I heard the shot coming from behind the cellar door. In the confined space of the hallway it echoed like a cannon. It sounded like it had come from a large caliber pistol, probably a .45.

With the automatic in my right hand, I opened the door with my left. In the dim light at the foot of the stairs I could see a man standing turning his head to look up at me. He was carrying what looked like a Luger. As he swung the pistol up towards me, I fired. Twice.

At least one of the shots must have gone home because the body dropped. I worked my way down the steps trying to see into the depths of the cellar. At the foot of the stairway, I did a quick check of the man I had shot. He was dead. I picked up the Luger from where it had fallen. It hadn't been fired. I stuffed it into the pocket of my jacket, and moved out from under the light.

From the front of the cellar, I could hear the sound of soft sobbing. I thought it was coming from Dr. Hollander. I couldn't tell if she had been hurt or not. I knew there had to be at least one more gangster down there, but I wasn't sure if there were more. The car outside could have held half a dozen.

I started to work my way towards the front of the cellar, moving along the side of the building. The light was still on over Winslow's workspace, but between the junk and the coal furnace, I couldn't get a good look in that direction. I could hear soft footsteps. It sounded like only one man. He was moving slowly down the center of the cellar towards the rear of the building.

I finally got a glance at him around the edge of the furnace. He was a big man, big enough that the Colt automatic in his beefy hand didn't look out of place. He looked like he knew how to use it, too.

If I had been smart, I would have taken a shot then and there. But that wasn't the way I had been trained. I called out, "Drop the gun and raise your hands."

He didn't. Instead, he swung around firing a shot in my direction. It hit the boiler of the furnace, which was probably the only thing in the cellar tough enough to have stopped the slug. I didn't give him a chance to fire again. The first shot didn't stop him, so I fired again. And again. The third one dropped him.

"Doc, are you okay? Are there any more of them?"

"I'm alright," she answered after a moment. Her voice was shaky but not hysterical. "I think there were only the two of them."

I went to check on the big man. He was dead. My last shot must have hit him in the heart.

I went to the front of the cellar. Dr. Hollander was standing over Winslow's body. There wasn't much doubt about it, but I checked anyway. He was dead. At least that resolved our dilemma. We wouldn't have to worry about having to get three people back to 1955.

"He just shot him, Harry. In cold blood. He just came up to us, pulled out that gun and shot. He didn't even say anything. He just shot. I think he was wondering whether to shoot me, too, when you showed up."

"Good think I did, doc. Look, I think we'd better get out of here. If the cops show up we'll have a tough time explaining ourselves. Besides, there's not much we can do for Winslow."

Dr. Hollander looked from me to the body and back. She seemed to pull herself together a bit.

"You're right, Harry. There's nothing we can do."

I looked around at the table Winslow had been using as a workbench. The prototype time dingus was sitting there, it's back cover open.

"There is one thing we can do, doc. I don't think we should leave the other time controller where it can be found. They might not be able to make it work again, but it might give someone ideas."

She looked at the time dingus, then at me. "Yes, you're right, of course."

"Can these things stand heat?"

"Not much, why?"

"The furnace is cold for the summer, but there's a separate boiler for hot water. If I smash the TSC and throw it in the firebox, would that take care of it?"

"Yes. That would do it."

I grabbed Winslow's TSC. I gave it a good whack with a wrench that was lying there. I could hear the glass of the front display crack. I hit it again to make sure. I didn't know a lot about how the thing worked, but I think I did a pretty good job on it. As an afterthought, I picked up a notebook that was lying open on the table as well. I found a rag to protect my hand as I opened the boiler door and tossed the time controller and the notebook inside. For good measure I tossed a hunk of coal in after them.

Returning to Dr. Hollander I said, "Well, that should take care of that."

She was still looking down at Winslow's body. "Maybe not."

I wasn't sure if she was still in shock over his death. "What do you mean?" I asked.

"While you were gone he told me that he'd made a copy of his notebook. He said that he had mailed it to Harlan Winslow's father. I think that notebook is where Harlan must have gotten the idea for what he was working on in 1955."

I think my jaw must have dropped. We'd gone back to 1925 not just to rescue Winslow, but also to remove any knowledge of time travel from the period. Now Winslow was dead and I had had to kill two men, and the notes and plans for a time travel device were still out there waiting for Harlan Winslow to find and implement. We might as well not have come.

"Well, there's not much we can do about it now, doc. The police will be showing up any moment. Let's get out of here."

Dr. Hollander pulled her TSC out of her handbag and set the destination coordinates for my office in 1955. Then she nodded. In the distance we could hear the wail of a police car siren.

I pulled her close to me, not just to make the jump, but to comfort her.

She pressed the button.

INTERLUDE THREE

(1955)

We popped back into my office. There was just one problem. It wasn't my office. Oh, it was the same room, alright, the same dingy paint peeling of the walls, the dame dirty window looking out onto the street below. It was pretty much the same street, too, though at one o'clock in the morning it was kind of hard to tell. But the same diner still occupied the ground level corner across the street at one end of the block and a drug store was at the other end of the block just as it always had.

But it wasn't my office that we'd landed in. For one thing, the furniture was different. Not better or more modern, just different. The desk looked like it was cherry rather than oak and the top was neater than I had left it. I tried the lower right hand drawer where I kept my bottle of whiskey, but the drawer was locked. So were all the other drawers. I never locked my drawers, there's no point. Anyone with a paperclip and a screwdriver can open the typical lock on a desk drawer.

I could sense that Dr. Hollander was also aware that something was wrong. Winslow's death had shaken her up pretty badly. She'd been through a lot and there was a frightened look behind her eyes that hadn't been there the first time she had walked into my office.

"What's wrong?" It wasn't hysteria that was in her voice, but there was fear.

"This isn't my office," I replied trying to keep my own panic in check.

"You mean the TSC took us to the wrong place?" she asked doubtfully. "Or the wrong time?"

"No, I have a feeling that the time dingus is working just fine. This is the room that was my office, and unless whoever occupies it now doesn't keep up their calendar, it's the right date, too." I pointed to the desk calendar aligned neatly above the desk blotter that was turned to the date we had set the TSC for. "It's just that this isn't my office anymore."

"Then whose is it?"

"I haven't got a clue. Let me do a little detecting."

My detecting consisted of picking up one of the business cards that were in a holder next to the desk calendar. It read, "James. H. Pettibone, Accountant." It gave an address and phone number as well. The address was mine, the phone number wasn't. I showed the card to Dr. Hollander who took it and stared at it.

There was a phone directory in the bookshelf that sat underneath the window. When I turned to the listings for accountants in the Yellow Pages, I found Pettibone's name. The phone number in the listing was the same as the one on the card. The directory was for 1954, so Pettibone had been in the office for at least a year.

I was a little afraid to do it, but I thumbed through the directory to the page for private investigators. It was with some relief that I found a listing for The Harry Christian Agency. The phone number was mine, but the address was the Jefferson Building which was two blocks over. At least I appeared to still exist in this time stream, though I wasn't sure what the implication would be of there being two of me. I remembered that the doc had said something about there being a reaction if we got too close together, but she'd said a lot of things about time that I hadn't really understood.

"It's a good thing that we chose to arrive here after midnight. We would have had a hard time explaining ourselves to Mr. Pettibone if we'd zapped in while he was still working."

"How can you joke at a time like this?" Dr. Hollander said. I think the irony of the question was lost on her. "Don't you realize what this means?"

"Calm down, doc. After all we've been through, now is not the time to panic. I realize that something that we did, or Winslow did, back in 1925 has changed things in 1955. Maybe not by much, but enough that this isn't my office anymore. The question is, what are we going to do about it?"

"What do you mean, what are we going to do about it? What can we do about it?"

"I don't know, doc. I'm just a two-bit gumshoe. You're the mathematician. I was kind of hoping you'd have some ideas.

Presumably there's a private investigator by the name of Harry Christian who has an office a couple of blocks from here. It might cramp his style if I were to show up at his office tomorrow morning."

"You can't do that!" Dr, Hollander said. She said it loudly enough that I hoped that the night watchman was on some other floor.

"I know that, doc. That's why I asked you what we were going to do about the situation."

"You're asking me? In case you haven't noticed, I haven't been doing so well so far. Everything I do just seems to make things worse."

I realized that Dr. Hollander had gotten to the point that she was doubting herself. I could understand that. I was on the verge of a case of the heebie-jeebies myself except that I knew that that wouldn't do us any good.

"Maybe that's true, doc. But we've got to do something. We both know we can't just leave things as they are. For one thing, Mr. Pettibone is going to be walking in through that door in a few hours and he's going to have some questions that will be hard for us to answer if we're still here."

Oddly, that statement seemed to cause the doc to sober up.

"You're right, Mr. Christian. We can't stay here. We must do something. I'm just not sure what." For a moment I was afraid that Dr. Hollander was going to give into despair again.

"Well, we've still got a few hours to figure it out."

"Yes, you're right as usual."

That wasn't exactly the response that I'd been expecting, but I could sense that the doc had some kind of idea forming, so I didn't interrupt.

She sat down at the desk and grabbing a blank piece of paper from a neat stack to the left of the desk blotter she started to write away. I couldn't understand any of it. To me it looked like a cross between someone trying to figure out their income taxes and those diagrams football coaches draw up to explain plays. There were lots of circles and arrows and calculations in the margins. The circles had dates in them, dates that I knew like

1925, 1955, 1979, and 2042. The arrows connected the circles in a complex web that I could halfway follow knowing where the doc and I had been. As to the calculations, well, as they say, they were all Greek to me, full of funny letters like the ones I remembered from high school physics class.

Dr. Hollander was at if for over an hour, filling up sheets of paper, shaking her head and crumpling them up before tossing them into the wastebasket and starting over. It occurred to me that Pettibone might wonder what it was all about if he saw them in the morning, so I calmly pulled them out, flattened and folded pages and stuck them in my jacket pocket.

Finally, Dr. Hollander set the pen back in the pen holder, straightened up, and said, "I think I know what we have to do."

"What's that?" I asked, trying to sound encouraging.

"Howard was right. This whole tangle of the time stream started when you prevented Harlan Winslow from being killed. What we have to do is go back and make sure that you don't succeed in that."

"I don't get you, doc."

"It's simple, really. We have to go back to that alley on Third Street that Friday and kill Harlan Winslow."

I could see that Dr. Hollander was deadly serious about what she was proposing.

"Are you serious, doc? There's got to be some other way?"

"I'm afraid not. At least not that I can come up with. I've tried looking at the alternatives, but I'm afraid that that is the key point in time. Correct it and things will go back to being what they were. Leave it and time becomes a tangle with uncontrollable consequences."

"I might be a lot of things, doc, not all of them good, but I'm not a murderer."

"I didn't mean that you'd do the killing, Mr. Christian. That could cause problems. You are already on the scene as it were. I'm the one that will have to fire the fatal shot."

"Have you ever killed a man before, doc?"

"No. But I will. I have to, Mr. Christian. There's no other way. Believe me." I could see that she meant it.

"Okay. But what about the original killer? The one in the alley. What are you going to do about him?"

She just shook her head sadly. "Think about it for a moment, Mr. Christian. Who was the person in the alley? You couldn't find them when you looked after you had saved Harlan Winslow's life. The police never found the shooter, either, in both timestreams, the one where Harlan Winslow dies, and the one where he doesn't. That's because the shooter disappeared. I'm pretty sure that that's because I'm the shooter in the alley. I've been the shooter all along."

"That's crazy, doc."

"Haven't you learned one thing about time travel, Harry. It's all crazy. That's why we've got to stop it."

I was trying to wrap my head around the whole business. It wasn't easy.

"Okay. What's going to happen if you do kill Harlan Winslow? What happens to me? For that matter, what happens to you? If you succeed, how am I going to go to 1979 and become your grandfather?"

"I don't have an answer to that. I wish I did. Maybe things will work out somehow. I don't know. In the world I came from, Harlan Winslow died and I was born. Hopefully, that's the way it will go back to being. Maybe when the time stream gets untangled, you aren't my grandfather. I rather hope that isn't the case, because I was just getting used to the idea, but I don't see how that can possibly be. I just don't know enough. All I know is that we have to go back and try to make things right again."

"Why do I have to go back? Why do I have to be there?"

"Because the ends of all the loose threads have to be present at the moment when Harlan Winslow is killed. If they aren't— well, I don't think things work out the right way."

"But won't there be two of me? This me, and the other me, the one trying to keep Harlan Winslow from being killed?"

"If I've figured things out right, the two of you will merge back into a single individual, one who never travels in time." She paused for a moment. "Of course I could be wrong."

"And you, doc? What happens to you at that moment?"

"I disappear. I will have never existed. Or maybe I will exist but never leave 2042 to travel back in time."

"You're willing to take that chance?"

"I have to take the chance, Harry. No matter what it means for me personally. Too many lives have been changed."

I looked at her illuminated by the light of the desk lamp. She looked so much like her grandmother. The woman that I would never see again, never have seen. And I knew she was right.

"Let's do it."

PART SEVEN

(1955)

Dr. Hollander had set the controls of the TSC so that we appeared at the far end of the alley off of Third Street at six o'clock on the Friday Harlan Winslow had/hadn't been killed. That would give us time to get situated and check things out. I still wasn't completely convinced that Dr. Hollander was going to be the person to fire the shot from the alley, but unless some unknown party was going to show up later, there weren't any other candidates, so I decided that the doc must be right. Maybe that just showed that I was getting used to this business of time loops and knots and whatever. There was something else that was bothering me, but I just couldn't put a finger on it, so for the time being I just let the feeling nag at me.

Standing in the shadows in the alley, it was kind of creepy thinking that an earlier version of me was sitting in his car out on Third Street waiting for something to happen. Especially when that something was us. The whole business was hard to grasp. Subjectively, it had been less than two weeks ago that Howard Winslow had first walked into my office, but in those two weeks I had traveled twenty five years into the future and thirty years into the past, been shot at and shot back several times and had a daughter I'd never have a chance to meet.

Dr. Hollander must have sensed that my mind was wandering, because she asked, "Getting cold feet?"

"It's not that, doc. I'm just trying to understand things. I don't think the human mind is meant to handle the complexities of this time travel stuff."

"You're probably right, Mr. Christian. Just as we can't really visualize more than three spatial dimensions no matter how we try. That's where mathematics comes in."

"I'll take your word for it, doc. Do you know what time it is?"

She looked at the readout on the TSC.

"According to this it's six-fourteen."

I set my watch to match. I'd been doing that a lot lately.

"You're sure that Harlan Winslow will be crossing the mouth of the alley just after seven?"

"I'm sure, doc. I'm checking my watch every five minutes or so while I'm sitting in the car out there on Third Street. Winslow turns out the lights in his workshop just after seven and comes out and starts to walk toward the bus stop at the end of the block. The bus comes by at 7:11. Even after the shooting, I was still able to get him on that bus. It must have been 7:05 or 7:06 when the shot was fired. Just as he gets to the alley, I call out his name. That's what makes him stop so that the shot misses. If that's any help."

"I'll keep that in mind, Mr. Christian."

"What do you think is going to happen, doc?"

"What do you mean?"

"What happens if you don't miss this time?"

"I have to admit that I'm not really sure. I think that time will go back to the way that I remember it happening. At least that's what I'm hoping for."

"That isn't very reassuring, doc."

"I would have thought you'd have realized by now that nothing is really certain, Mr. Christian. But what I think is going to happen—well, imagine a string with a really complex knot in it with multiple loops and crossings. The time stream is the string and those loops and crossings are you and me and Howard going back and forth through time and crossing each other's paths. Now think of the knots as being kind of loose. As you pull on the ends of the strings, the knots tighten up. If you pull hard enough, eventually the knot shrinks to the point that you can't even tell that it's there. It's just an indistinguishable bump in the string. Well, that's what I'm hoping will happen."

"Okay. I get that. But what happens to us?"

"That's harder to say. I think that for you there will be a kind of convergence. At the moment that Harlan Winslow is shot, this you and the you sitting out there in the car will merge back into one person and everything that has happened to you in the last week will shrink like a knot pulled tight."

"Will I remember any of this? Any of what has happened?"

"I don't really know. Probably not. It will be like nothing ever happened."

"I guess I can live with that," I said shaking my head. "You haven't said what you think is going to happen to you, doc."

"That's a bit more problematic. Maybe I'll be back in the 2042 that I knew; the 2042 before I traveled back in time the first time."

"And if not?"

"I may just disappear. Or be left on an orphaned piece of the time unattached to the past or the future. I just don't know."

"And you're okay with that, doc?"

"I don't think I have any choice. I can't leave things as they are."

The brave resolve in her voice made me proud that she was my granddaughter.

"Doc. There's one thing still bothers me. If you manage to fix things, how is it that you even existed to come back in the first place. I mean, if I don't travel forward to 1979 and—you know?"

"Sleep with my grandmother?" Dr. Hollander completed with a hint of an impish smile.

"Yeah. To put it bluntly."

"I don't have an answer for that. Somebody was obviously my grandfather, but I told you, my grandmother never spoke about him, either to me or to my mother. Maybe there was, or there will be, a real John Overholt. If it's any consolation, I was actually getting used to the idea of your being my grandfather."

It was starting to sink in that if we pulled this business off, that for me, none of this would have happened. I wouldn't travel into the future or into the past. More importantly, I would never meet, have met, Helen Hollander, never have spent that one night with her. I think that that was what bothered me the most.

"Something else just occurred to me, doc. Say this works, and things go back to the way they are supposed to be. Does that mean that in the future, in 2042, Howard Winslow is going to steal the prototype TSC and come back to 1955 to hire me to save his grandfather and that we'll just repeat this whole thing over and over again?"

Dr. Hollander looked at me with wide eyes. I don't think the idea had even occurred to her. She paused for a moment deep in thought and then answered, "I haven't got a clue."

She stood there for a moment before continuing, "Maybe there will be some little thing that is different that will cause things to turn out differently, but for all I know, this sequence of events could have already played out repeatedly an infinite number of times. There is no way to tell."

There wasn't much to say after that. Nervously, I looked at my watch. "It's 6:40."

Dr. Hollander straightened her shoulders. She pulled out the .32 revolver that I had given her, and checked it.

"I think it's time for you to go, Mr. Christian. I want to thank you for everything you've done."

"What do you mean?"

"In a few minutes, your earlier self is going to be at the end of this alley. There's a chance that if the two of you get too close to each other that something might happen. We talked about this once. I can't risk that happening. I'm sorry. I could use your moral support, but it's best that you aren't here when I shoot."

"You're sure about that, doc?"

"Yes. Trust me, grandpa."

She reached out, putting her arms around me and kissed me gently on the cheek. It was too dark in the alley to see, but I thought I had felt tears on face as we had touched.

I wasn't in any position to argue. Dr. Hollander had a better idea of how these things worked than I did. We separated and I began walking to the far end of the alley. As I looked back, I could just make out the shadow of the doctor standing there, the revolver held loosely in her hand by her side. She was maybe twenty feet from where Winslow would pass in front of her.

I didn't know where to go, so I just started walking up the street. I got to the corner and turned. Something was still nagging at the back of my mind, but I was in such turmoil that I couldn't figure out what it was.

Without thinking, I found myself at the bus stop that Harlan Winslow would be approaching in a few minutes. In the light of the streetlamp I looked at my watch. It read 6:59.

Looking down the street I could see the car where I was sitting three quarters of a block away. As I watched I saw the light in Winslow's workshop turn off, and a moment later the tall lanky form came out of the building. I heard the sound of a car door quietly opening and a man, me, get out of the car and start walking towards Winslow.

It was at that moment that I realized what had been bothering me. Dr. Hollander had a .32 revolver. The newspaper article she had shown me that first time we met had said that Harlan Winslow had been shot with a 9 mm. parabellum and that an empty cartridge casing had been found at the scene of the crime. The difference in caliber and the fact that a revolver doesn't eject the casing meant that Dr. Hollander wasn't going to be the one to kill Winslow. It would be someone else. Someone with a 9 mm. automatic pistol, one like the Luger that I was carrying in my pocket.

I started running down the street towards Winslow. My other self was catching up with him as they approached the mouth of the alley. I could hear me call out Winslow's name. I saw him turn and look behind himself. He crossed the alley and stepped back. I pulled the Luger out of my pocket and began to raise the weapon pointing it in Winslow's direction. A shot rang out from the alley. Winslow started. I fired.

There was a moment of confusion. For the briefest instant I felt as if I was looking down at the scene, at the two versions of my body, then I found myself standing over Harlan Winslow's body, my .38 automatic in my hand. I could tell that he was dead; the parabellum round had gone through his heart.

I ran into the alley, but no one was there.

Dr. Hollander had been wrong about one thing. I hadn't lost the memories of the last few days traveling through time. They were like the recollection of a dream so vivid that even after waking it seemed real. I hadn't forgotten her. I hadn't forgotten Helen.

I realized that I didn't have much time. The police were going to be showing up in a few minutes and there were still things that I had to do. I rummaged around Winslow's pockets and found his set of keys. Grabbing his briefcase I headed back towards his workshop.

There was one thing that I was certain of, and that was that time travel was too dangerous, too uncertain, to allow it to exist. If Harlan Winslow's work had provided his grandson with the inspiration or knowledge to implement it, then I had to destroy all of his notes and apparatus, and I had to do it now before the police showed up.

At the front door of the building, I fumbled with the keys until I found the right one. In the distance, I could hear the sound of a siren drawing closer.

Fortunately, there was no one inside the building. I went to the room that was Winslow's workshop, unlocked the door and went inside. I found a desk lamp and turned it on, adjusting the shade so that I had enough light to see by but so it wouldn't attract attention from the street.

There was some sort of half assembled apparatus sitting on a bench in the middle of the room. I grabbed a hammer from a tool chest and began to smash the thing. I pounded on it until I was gasping from my exertions. I don't know how much damage I managed to inflict, but it would be hard to put the pieces back together again.

I began to work more methodically. I searched all the drawers for papers, blueprints, anything that might possibly provide a clue as to how to build a time stream controller. I tore them up into fragments and piled them on top of the broken apparatus. The contents of the briefcase joined them. Rummaging around, I found a can of naphtha which I poured over onto the papers making sure that all of them were drenched in it.

Then I used my lighter to set it all on fire.

I got out of there fast, climbing into the car that I had left parked across the street when I had gone to follow Winslow. I was having a hard time keeping my memories straight, those that were real and those that were—

What were they? Had I really traveled in time? Was it just a dream? A hallucination? I wasn't sure anymore. I drove away slowly just as a police cruiser pulled up to the alley and the body lying there.

I drove around for a while trying to get things straight in my mind. It wasn't easy. I'd just seen a man get killed right in front of me. Or had I shot him myself? I wasn't too clear about that. I pulled over to the curb and checked my pistol. The clip was full and it hadn't been fired. But I had the distinct impression that I had raised a pistol, another pistol, a Luger, and pulled the trigger. But if I had fired the shot, where was the gun?

And why had I burnt Harlan Winslow's papers and destroyed his workshop? It had seemed important at the time, to prevent the secret of time travel getting out. But that seemed pretty improbable. There was no such thing as time travel, was there? Then why did I remember 1925 and 1979 as if I had been there, and Dr. Hollander—and Helen?

Driving around wasn't doing me any good. What I really needed was a drink, preferably a stiff one. I saw the neon sign of a cocktail lounge, and found a parking spot just down the block.

The place was dark and nearly empty, but it was still early, not even eight. I ordered a double rye from the bartender. He looked at me oddly, but poured the whiskey. I noticed that the bottle was Old Overholt. Why was that important? I found that my hand was shaking as I brought the glass up for the first sip, but it steadied after I felt the bite of the rye.

As I sat there drinking the whiskey, I tried to sort things out. I had two sets of memories in my head. One set leading up to the shot from the alley, and another set from that moment—and running into the future before looping back—to the moment when I had fired the Luger. Unless I was going crazy, it didn't make sense.

The bartender must have noticed my condition because he asked, "You okay, buddy?"

"Yeah. Sorry, I guess I'm not myself. I just lost a friend."

"Sorry to hear that," he replied perfunctorily.

"Say, you got a phone I can use?"

"There's a pay phone back by the johns." He pointed to the rear of the place with his thumb.

"Thanks."

"You need change?"

I stared at him for a moment, not sure what he meant, then replied, "No, I've got enough."

I found the phone and dialed Howard Winslow's hotel.

"Could I speak to Howard Winslow, please?"

"Who?" The person who answered sounded bored.

"Howard Winslow. I'm not sure what room he's in, but he's a guest there."

There was a pause while the desk clerk looked it up.

"Sorry. There's no Howard Winslow registered. You sure you got the right hotel?"

"Yeah, I'm sure."

"He must have checked out then. I just came on duty, so if he checked out earlier, I wouldn't know."

"Could you check the register?"

"I already did. He's not in it. You sure you got the name right?"

"Yeah."

"I can't help you then. Sorry."

"Thanks." I hung up.

So Winslow had checked out. But I'd known that because I'd called the hotel before, hadn't I? I'd tried to call him to tell him that his cousin was alright. But his cousin wasn't alright. He was lying dead on Third Street. And he wasn't his cousin but his grandfather because Howard Winslow came from the future just like Dr. Hollander. Except according to the desk clerk, he'd never checked into the hotel. Was that because he hadn't stolen the prototype TSC and traveled back to 1955 from 2042? And what the heck was a TSC?

I went back to the bar and ordered another rye. This time I told the bartender to put some ice and a splash of soda in it. This seemed to make him feel better.

So what was I going to do? I could go to the cops, but that might lead to questions to which I didn't have answers. As far as I knew, there wasn't anything tying me to Harlan Winslow. It didn't look like Howard Winslow was going to be around to tell them anything, and there hadn't been any witnesses to the shooting except for me—and Dr. Hollander, but she hadn't stuck around, either had she? But where was she?

A good question. What if it was all true? What if she was a time traveler from the future? What if she really was my granddaughter? What had I done when I'd fired the shot that killed Harlan Winslow? Was she back in 2042 where she had a loving mother and a career? Or, had I exiled her to some unattached fragment of time where she was doomed to repeat the same events over and over again because there weren't any others? I didn't have an answer.

"Ready for another one?" the bartender interrupted.

"No, I'm fine. I think I've had enough for tonight."

I settled up the tab and went home. Alone.

I was in a good mood as I headed to the office the next Monday. The fine spring weather was holding, and I'd managed to put any doubts I had behind me. There had been a report of Harlan Winslow's death in the Sunday paper, but there hadn't been any mention of me. The police didn't have any clues except for a single shell casing from "a Luger or similar type pistol" that had been found in the street. The fire at the dead man's workshop was mentioned, but the authorities weren't sure if the two were connected.

When I asked Effie if there had been any calls, she answered that there hadn't been. No one was waiting in my office, either.

1979

(FOR QUANTUM-MECHANICAL REASONS THIS STORY HAS TWO ENDINGS, BOTH OF WHICH ARE TRUE. IT IS LEFT TO THE READER TO CHOOSE THE ONE THEY PREFER.)

Epilog A (1979)

I was back in 1979, only this time I hadn't used a time dingus to get there, I'd just lived the intervening twenty-five years. Those years had taken their toll, too. I was fifty-seven, balding, maybe a little overweight. I'd been married twice, neither marriage lasting more than a couple of years. I'd given up being a private eye along the way and gone to work as an investigator for an insurance company, mostly arson. The pay wasn't bad, the job came with benefits, and the work was interesting. It meant that I traveled a lot, but only in space.

There are times when I think that the whole time traveling business was just a well remembered dream. But most of the time it feels as if it had been real, and that feeling has continued to haunt me over the years. Not that I have any proof that it had ever happened. There wasn't anything tangible that I could hold in my hand, not even the Luger with which I had killed Harlan Winslow. But I have the memories of Dr. Hollander, Harold Winslow, 1925, and Helen—mostly of Helen.

That's what I was doing there on Halloween 1979. It had been a few years since I'd been back in town. Like I said, I traveled for work, all over the Midwest, and I was based out of Chicago. The job had brought me back, a fire at a cold storage facility that had proved to be a careless accident and not arson. My work was done, I didn't have anything to do, it was a crisp fall afternoon. I couldn't help myself; I had to see if she was real.

So that was how I came to be walking along the street that ran past Helen's apartment building. I'd spotted her coming out of a building on campus, the same building that I remembered from the last time I'd been in 1979. She looked the same as I remembered; tight jeans and baggy sweater, boots and long blonde hair. I followed her at a discrete distance, making sure she didn't spot me. I was a little out of practice, but some things you never forget.

I wasn't my intention to contact her. At least that's what I told myself. I just wanted to make sure that she got home safely. I kept looking around expecting two guys wearing Homburg hats to appear, but they didn't show. If I'd done my work right back in 1955, the NBT would never exist.

Helen had almost made it to her apartment when he showed up. He was a man in blue jeans and a navy pea coat. For a moment I got a chill thinking that I was seeing an echo of myself, but then I got a good look at his face. It wasn't me. He was the right age; early thirties and the same general build as I had had at that age. But he wasn't me.

The two of them seemed to know each other. They stopped to chat on the corner. From their body language it looked as if the encounter was casual and friendly. I had to cross to the other side of the street to avoid being obvious. I don't think either one of them noticed me as I walked past them. I went about a block and then turned to look back just in time to see the two of them entering Helen's apartment building.

I found myself wondering if they'd go out to dinner at the little Italian restaurant and then go back to Helen's apartment for drinks. Would Helen write a series of thrillers based on the man in the pea coat? Would she one day have a granddaughter named after her who became a mathematician?

I realized with some sadness that it was none of my business. I was no longer a part of the story. I walked back to my hotel and had a drink in the bar, rye on the rocks.

Epilog B (1979)

I was back in 1979, only this time I hadn't used a time dingus to get there, I'd just lived the intervening twenty-five years. Those years had taken their toll, too. I was fifty-seven, balding, maybe a little overweight. I'd been married twice, neither marriage lasting more than a couple of years. I'd given up being a private eye along the way and gone to work as an investigator for an insurance company, mostly arson. The pay wasn't bad, the job came with benefits, and the work was interesting. It meant that I traveled a lot, but only in space.

There are times when I think that the whole time traveling business was just a well remembered dream. But most of the time it feels as if it had been real, and that feeling has continued to haunt me over the years. Not that I have any proof that it had ever happened. There wasn't anything tangible that I could hold in my hand, not even the Luger with which I had killed Harlan Winslow. But I had the memories of Dr. Hollander, Harold Winslow, 1925, and Helen—mostly of Helen.

That's what I was doing there on Halloween 1979. It had been a few years since I'd been back in town. Like I said, I traveled for work, all over the Midwest, and I was based out of Chicago. The job had brought me back, a fire at a cold storage facility that had proved to be a careless accident and not arson. My work was done, I didn't have anything to do, it was a crisp fall afternoon. I couldn't help myself, I had to see if she was real.

So that was how I came to be walking along the street that ran past Helen's apartment building. I'd spotted her coming out of a building on campus, the same building that I remembered from the last time I'd been in 1979. She looked the same as I remembered; tight jeans and baggy sweater, boots and long blonde hair. I followed her at a discrete distance, making sure she didn't spot me. I was a little out of practice, but some things you never forget.

I hadn't been my intention to contact her, but I found myself quickening my steps trying to catch up to her.

"Excuse me, but are you Helen Hollander?"

She turned to look at me. She was a little uncertain at being accosted, but she faced me with the same inner confidence that I remembered.

"You don't know me, but I'm a friend of someone in your family. When they heard I was going to be in town, they suggested I look you up. I found myself with some time on my hands, so here I am."

Even as I said it, I knew that it sounded pretty lame. It was the sort of line that a con-man or sociopath would use.

"I'm afraid that I don't know you, Mr.— "

"Harry, Harry Christian," I replied.

She laughed. It wasn't quite the reaction I had suspected. It wasn't a mean spirited laugh, though. It was just that my name had struck her as funny. I guess I should have expected that.

"That's not your real name, is it?"

"I'm afraid so."

"What kind of name is Harry Christian."

"It's the name my mother gave me."

She looked at me in disbelief. "You haven't got a clue what I'm talking about, do you?"

"About what?"

"Hari Krishna."

"I don't know any Krishnas."

"OK. Prove it. Prove that you're Harry Christian."

I reached into my jacket and pulled out one of my business cards. She took it, examining it with interest.

"This says you're an insurance investigator. Is that like a private eye?"

"Something like that, only I work for an insurance company."

"That sounds interesting." She sounded dubious but curious.

"It can be. Sometimes. Sometimes it just means finding out that there was bad wiring or someone forgot to put the cap on a can of paint thinner."

"And you really know one of my relatives?"

"Several of them. Quite well, as a matter of fact. You could say I'm almost an uncle."

"How is it that I've never heard of you? I think I'd remember the name."

"It's been awhile. I travel a lot for business."

"Oh. Well it's been nice meeting you, Harry Christian, but I'm afraid I've got to get going. I've got an important meeting with my advisor tomorrow that I have to prepare for."

"Of course. I understand. It was nice meeting you, too."

I was about to walk away, but then I said, "Look, it's obvious that you don't me from Adam, but I assure you that I'm mostly harmless. I haven't been back in town for a long time and I really don't know anyone. If I remember right, there's a little Italian restaurant a few blocks from here. I'd like to buy you dinner. I promise I'll get you home in plenty of time for you to prepare for your meeting tomorrow with Prof. Adams."

"How did you know my meeting is with Adams?" she asked suspiciously.

"I am a detective, after all," I responded.

"Just who are you, Harry Christian?"

"Would you believe me if I said I was a time traveler?"

For a moment I thought she was going to storm off, but then she started to laugh.

"You're incredible, Harry. Or is that incorrigible."

"Take your pick. But have dinner with me. Please."

"Alright. But only if you promise to explain yourself."

"It's a deal."

We dropped off her things at her apartment. It was just as I remembered, a mixture of neatness and messiness with books piled everywhere. From there we walked to Maria's. She had the pasta puttanesca; I had spaghetti and meatballs, for old time's sake. I let her order a bottle of Montepulciano. We both had the minestrone.

We talked all through dinner, Helen telling me about her studies and me recounting some of my more interesting cases. I never did have to explain my remark about being a time traveler, which is just as well. It was nearly eight when we finished the last of the wine.

"It's been great, Harry. I've really enjoyed myself, but I have to get home and study."

"I understand. At least let me walk you home. It's more or less on the way back to my hotel, anyway."

"If you insist."

Our exit was much quieter than the last time. I paid the check, grabbing the receipt for my expense report. Then I walked her back to her apartment. There was an awkward moment when I was unsure whether we'd just shake hands or she'd give me an "avuncular" peck on the cheek. Instead she said:

"Would you like to come up to the apartment for a drink, Harry? I'm afraid that all I have is a bottle of Old Overholt that someone left."

"I'd love to."

Author's Afterword

A Detective out of Time is not the book that I set out intending to write. As originally envisioned, it was to be a romp through time with the title character assuming the role of hard-boiled detective in different eras. Somewhere along the way, probably while I was writing Part Two, the story got hijacked by the characters and transformed into something much darker and more serious.

This isn't that unusual an occurrence for me. Some of my best writing has been when the story and the characters take on a life of their own. I often find that characters which I have created as minor figures designed to play a particular role in a plot, acquire a back story, personalities, and motivations far beyond my original intentions. That is part of the fun of writing. In *A Detective out of Time* it is the three generations of Hollander women that came to dominate the story, changing it from a thriller to a novel focused on questions of loss, responsibility and sacrifice.

I won't make the claim that there is any new or original contribution as far as time travel goes in *A Detective out of Time*. The subject of time travel paradoxes has been examined in a serious, and less than serious, manner at least since the 1930's by any number of well known authors. Both the consequences of time looping and the so called "butterfly effect" have both been addressed numerous times. What I have done, I think, is to explore the human side of this subject, not just in the reactions of Harry Christian, but also the effect the problems of time travel have on Dr. Hollander.

I believe I once read a comment by Dashiell Hammett to the effect that if he knew how a story would turn out, there would be no point in writing it. I couldn't agree more, and that certainly was the case with *A Detective out of Time*. The novel is nothing like that which I sat down to write. I may yet get around to writing that story. I even have a tentative title selected, *A*

Detective in Time, but for the time being, this is the story I am left with. I hope you enjoyed it.

   Greg Fowlkes

Special Preview!

A Fictional Detective Trifecta

~ Novellas Featuring
the Fictional Detective ~

Now available from The Fictional Press
www.TheFictionalPress.com

A Fictional Detective Trifecta: The Fictional Detective Speaks with the Dead

My name is Frank Slade. I'm a private detective. At least I think I am. Oh, I'm sure I'm a private dick, but some things about my last case have caused me to question my reality. I'm a man without a past. Before a few months ago there's nothing to prove I ever existed, no paper trail, no public record. My own memories from that time are all kind of vague and hazy. And generic, like they were details created by someone making them up. Like maybe someone named Ezekial O. Handler, the mystery writer that got bumped off not too long ago by his publisher. Oh, there are a few people who claim to have known me, like Flannigan, a police detective, but when I checked into it, his past is no more substantial than my own. Handler wrote me a letter in which he claimed he was responsible, that he had created me to avenge his death by means of some spell he had gotten out of an old book, just like he had created Flannigan, Armand the ex-jockey who operates a newsstand downstairs, a female impersonator named Josephine LaTouche, and Janet Nielsen, my fiancée and Handler's old girl friend. It was a pretty wild claim, even if it did seem to fit the evidence. But Handler had proved to have a good idea of the events that followed his death. If I were a thinking man, it might have bothered me, wondering whether I was real or not, but I'm just a simple private gumshoe and the whole thing is just too existential to worry about.

The current reality is that I'm a private detective with an office in a low rent building in a not particularly nice part of town. The office is what you'd expect would come out of the imagination of a mystery writer known more for his lurid titles than his high literary style. Of course, it's also just the sort of office a not terribly successful P.I. might rent. There's the frosted glass in the door with my name in peeling black paint, the second hand furniture, the bottle of bourbon stashed in the desk drawer.

It's the kind of office that you've seen at the start of a dozen mystery movies and read about in more pulp thrillers than you can count. I won't describe it in detail, you can visualize it perfectly without really trying.

Like I said, I'm a private dick, though my fiancée is trying to get me to quit. It's too dangerous she says, and after Handler left her the rights to his last book, the one published after he was killed, it's not like we're going to need the money. She says I should try my hand at writing, detective fiction stuff, says I'd be a natural at it, and wit the Handler connection I'd have no problem finding a publisher. What the heck. I might as well give it a try, so here goes. This is an account of my most recent case as it actually happened. It might even be real.

I was sitting in my office going through my files. This was a couple of weeks after I'd solved the Handler murder. That case had left me with a lot of unanswered questions about the nature of reality and I'd gone into a kind of funk that ended up in a week-long drunk. After I'd sobered up I came to the conclusion that no matter what the truth was, there was nothing I could do about it and I might as well just get on with life. After all, it wasn't shaping up as such a bad life. Janet and I were talking about getting married. Janet is the kind of dame men dream about; tall, good looking with curves in all the right places. She was smart and had money, too. We'd be fixed for life with what Handler had left her in his will.

I was thinking about getting out of the business, and was trying to tie up loose ends. I wasn't really looking for any new cases, but I was still listed in the phone book and business directory and it still said "Private Detective" under my name on the frosted glass in the office door. I wasn't completely surprised then, when there came a tentative knock on that door. It was a woman's knock, quick, light, not so much demanding attention as imploring for it.

I stood up, stashed the bottle of bourbon and the glass in the bottom drawer and went to open the door. The last time I had done that, the woman had been Janet, a leggy blonde with looks straight out of a fashion magazine. My visitor was nothing like that.

She was a big woman, not fat, but ample, probably in her mid fifties. She was dressed expensively in a dress and coat that actually fit her and made her seem thinner than she really was. Her hair had been styled recently in one of those cuts that women who can afford it wear. She reminded me as much as anything of the heavy set broad who always played the older rich dame in the Marx brothers movies. You know the one I mean, the one who never seemed to get the jokes.

"Mr. Slade?" she asked tentatively.

"That's me. What can I do for you?"

"I believe you are a—a private detective?"

"That's what it says on the door, though I'm thinking of getting out of the racket."

"Oh—I'm sorry. I thought—" I could see she had trouble on her mind. I never could turn down a dame in trouble, even an older one.

"Please, come in. The least I can do is hear your story. After all, you came all this way down here to talk to me."

"That's very kind, Mr. Slade." She entered the office and took the chair facing the desk. Despite her size she moved with a certain kind of grace. I shut the office door and sat in my desk chair.

When I was seated she said, "I don't quite know where to start."

"Why don't we start with the simple things. Like your name."

"Yes. Of course. I'm Geraldine DuVille. My husband was Herbert DuVille. He ran a trucking business, Tri-State Transportation Services, until he died recently."

"My condolences, Mrs. DuVille. Just what did you want to consult with me about?"

"Well, it's like this, Mr. Slade. Some time before his death, my husband took on some partners. He needed some capital to expand the business."

"How was the business doing, if you don't mind my asking?"

"Quite well, I think. I never bothered too much about the business. I left that to Herbert. But we had always lived quite comfortably. Herbert was a good provider." I could hear the love in her voice. "I'm not sure why Herbert felt the need to expand, but he seemed to think it was important."

"And these partners he brought on? Were they on the up and up?"

"They seemed to be at first. They were just going to invest some money and leave the running of the business to my husband. But after awhile they wanted to become more involved. He never said anything about it, but I could tell that Herbert wasn't altogether happy with the situation."

"Any particulars?"

"As I said, Mr. Slade, I never involved myself with the business. And then Herbert died, and that changed everything."

"Just how did he die?"

"An accident, or so I thought—"

"But something has caused you to change your mind?"

"I'm getting to that. The arrangement as I understand it was that my husband retained fifty-one percent of the company while Mr. McClure and Mr. Trentino split the remainder of the shares between them. However, there appears to have been an unfortunate clause placed in the contract by which they invested. In the event of the death of any of the partners, their share of the company would be split between the surviving partners. The result was that when my husband died his share of the company went to Mr. McClure and Mr. Trentino, and I was left with nothing."

"Your husband didn't leave anything to you?"

"Oh, no, Mr. Slade. I don't want you to think that. He left me the house, of course and some investments. There was also a large insurance policy that he had taken out shortly after we were married. I don't want you to think that he left me a pauper. I may not be able to live quite as well as before, but I shall get by. But it's the thought of the company that Herbert worked so hard to build just going to those— others that bothers me."

"You've talked to a lawyer about this, haven't you?"

"Yes. He said that it was an unusual agreement, but it seemed perfectly legal. He didn't hold out much hope for litigation, I'm afraid."

"I'm sorry about your troubles, Mrs. DuVille, but I'm not quite sure what it is you want me to do?"

"What I want you to do, Mr. Slade is come to a séance."

"A séance?" I said with surprise. It was about the last thing I had expected.

"Yes, a séance, Mr. Slade. I know that this may sound to you like a strange request, but I have been in touch with my husband, and he wishes to speak with you personally. There is something that he wants to tell you."

"You've talked to your husband? At a séance?"

"Yes."

"And he asked for me?" I couldn't keep the skepticism out of my voice.

"Yes. He was quite particular about that point. At the last session he asked for you. That's why I came down here, Mr. Slade. I assure you that I don't normally employ private detectives."

"I didn't think you did, Mrs. DuVille. I admit that I have very little experience with these kind of things, but isn't this an awfully specific request for someone who is dead to communicate."

"I assure you, Mr. Slade, that this séance was not a silly parlor game like those Ouija boards. The Professor is a very serious person."

"The professor?"

"Yes, the medium. Professor Longwell. He's quite well known, Mr. Slade."

"I'm sure he is." Probably by half the bunko squads in the state, I thought to myself.

"I detect a note of doubt, Mr. Slade, but I am willing to pay you for your time, whatever your standard rate is. Please, won't you come? I'm a desperate woman." She seemed on the point of tears.

"It's a hundred dollars a day. Plus expenses."

"What's a hundred dollars?"

"That's my standard fee, Mrs. DuVille. When is this séance?"

"Tonight, if you can make it. I'm sure I can arrange it with the Professor. He's been so helpful."

"I'm sure he has. As it is, I am available tonight. What time?"

"Would nine o'clock be possible?"

"That shouldn't be a problem." Janet was going to fix me dinner, but we'd be done in plenty of time.

"Fine. Here's the address," she handed me a card with her name and address.

"Tonight, then. And don't worry, you can pay me after the séance."

"Thank you, Mr. Slade. I'll be waiting for you."

She rose and I escorted her to the door.

After she left, I thought about the deal. Was she just some poor widow being preyed upon by a charlatan? Or was there more to this séance business? I didn't really believe in ghosts. On the other hand, I didn't not believe in them either. I'd seen enough strange things lately to keep an open mind. Of anyone in the world, I was the last to question the reality of such things. Or the reality of anything, for that matter.

I remembered reading about Herbert DuVille's death in the papers, but couldn't recall any of the details. It hadn't made much of a splash, just a few column inches in the financial section. The death had been ruled an accident. A jewelry heist the next day that had left two dead had pretty much seized my attention along with that of just about everyone else in town.

I decided to give my favorite flat-foot a call. He worked the homicide squad, and if there was anything about DuVille's death that hadn't made the papers, he'd be the one to know.

The phone rang three or four times before a voice announced, "Homicide, Lt. Flannigan." He didn't sound happy. Like he wasn't getting enough sleep.

"It's Frank. Got a minute?"

"Oh, sure, Frank. I've got plenty of time for cheap private dicks. After all, that's what we're here for, isn't it?"

"I can sense that you're busy, so I'll make it quick. What do you know about Herbert DuVille's death?"

"DuVille? It was ruled an accident. Some boxes fell on him at his warehouse or something like that. Why the interest?"

"His widow was just in my office. Apparently her husband has something he wants to tell me."

"Her husband, huh? Wait a minute. Is this some kind of gag, Slade? Her husband's dead."

"It's no gag, Flannigan. Or if it is, it's on me. She wants me to attend a séance. She claims her husband is going to communicate with me from beyond."

"Beyond what?"

"You got me."

"You're not taking this seriously, are you Frank?"

"I don't know. Like I said, his widow was in my office wanting to hire me. She seemed kind of upset. The way I figure, it's probably some huckster trying to take advantage of a poor widow that just happens to have some money. I thought I'd go to this séance and maybe find the hidden wires or whatever."

Flannigan said, "I thought you were thinking about getting out of the P.I. business, Frank."

"Yeah, I am. Janet doesn't like the idea of me putting myself in danger. But how much risk can there be at a séance?"

"I don't know, Frank. Some of these older dames can get some crazy ideas."

"I think I can protect myself. By the way, you wouldn't know anything about a Professor Longwell, would you?"

"Who's that?"

"He's the guy that's holding the séance. The medium."

"Not my line, Frank, but I can ask the guys in Bunko if they've ever heard of him."

"That would be swell, Flannigan. I'll be at Janet's until about 8:30."

"A hot dame like that, and you want to run around messing with ghosts. If you ask me, you're the crazy one, Frank."

"I get that a lot. Let me know if you find out anything. I'll let you get back to your corpses, Flannigan."

I found myself talking to a dead phone. Flannigan had cause for being short of patience. He had been putting in long hours working the jewelry heist murders. A salesclerk and the store's owner had been found dead. Over a million in prime ice was missing, too, without much in the way of clues.

I looked at the clock on the wall. It was getting late, and Janet was expecting me for dinner. I didn't want to disappoint her.

A Fictional Detective Trifecta is available now from The Fictional Press. Find it on TheFictionalPress.com, or buy it on Amazon.com!

BOOKS BY GREG FOWLKES

From the Wizard at Law Series:
The Laws of Magic
Trial by Magic

From the Murder on Mars Series:
Blood Red Sands of Mars
A Death at Station Alpha
A Corpse in Hut Town
Murder at the Mars Club
Blackmail Under a Dark Star

From the Fictional Detective Series:
The Fictional Detective
A Fictional Detective Trifecta

Star City Stories: Space Opera Noir Featuring Frank Sladek

The Uncorrupted Corpse

Tequila Visions

Cargo From Paradise

Ice Viking

From the Wizard at Law Series by Greg Fowlkes

The Laws of Magic

Egil Njalsson was an aspiring lawyer. A lawyer with a difference. Not only had he passed the bar, but he had an undergraduate degree from the most prestigious school of magic in the country, the California Institute of Thaumaturgy. Needless to say his caseload and clients tended to the unusual. Like witches; or vampires. And the opposition, well they were likely to be demons. But Egil Njalsson had sworn an oath to uphold the law of the land, and... *The Laws of Magic*!

Trial By Magic

Egil Njalsson is just another practicing attorney. Except, that is, for the occasional unusual client. Such as the ghost who retained his services using e-mail. Or the wolf who has been cursed by an Indian shaman to turn into a human during the full moon. Or the Leprechaun who is facing the loss of his saloon. Even when the clients are human, they have unusual problems like the Creole chef accused of making a rival a zombie or the scientist accused of transmuting a man into a statue of silicon. Yet somehow, Egil manages to resolve all his client's problems whether legal or magical. Of course it helps that he is a wizard as well as a lawyer.

Trial by Magic includes five new tales from the same world as *The Laws of Magic*.

FROM THE MURDER ON MARS SERIES BY GREG FOWLKES

BLOOD REDS SANDS OF MARS

On Mars the wind was rising. The grains of sand could be heard abrading the thin aluminum skin that was the only protection against the outside. On the far side of Olympus Mons a prospector lies dead in the sand. Inspector Erik McKernan, head of the handful of men that make up the small Martian police force must find the killer while threading the maze of corporate and international politics that govern the planet, and he must do it while trying to survive . . .*The Blood Red Sands of Mars!*

A DEATH AT STATION ALPHA

Station Alpha, a remote Martian research facility isolated by a planet wide dust storm. When one of the scientists is found murdered, it falls to Inspector McKernan to determine which of the remaining twelve people at the station wielded the fatal weapon. But, as the crime was committed in a locked laboratory with no possible access and all the suspects would seem to have unbreakable alibis, it will take all his skills as a detective to solve the puzzle of *A Death at Station Alpha*. Thirty years in the making, the long awaited sequel to *The Blood Red Sands of Mars*.

A Corpse in Hut Town

Hut Town is the remnants of the original Martian settlement; a collection of inflatable buildings abandoned by the Trust Authority and the mining corporations and now occupied by those catering to the baser needs of miners and construction workers in for a spree. But when a corpse is found in one of the service tunnels, Chief Inspector McKernan is called in.

He has plenty of questions. Who's body is it? How did they die? How did they get to Mars in the first place, and why weren't they missed? And the most important one on the Inspector's mind— are there any more bodies down there?

Murder at the Mars Club

The Mars Club was the sanctuary of the rich and powerful on Mars, so when one of the members is found dead, Chief Inspector is called in to solve the case as discretely as possible. Will the solution of the case prove to be the one man he'd least like to implicate?

FROM THE FICTIONAL DETECTIVE SERIES BY GREG FOWLKES

THE FICTIONAL DETECTIVE

Mystery writer Ezekial O. Handler has been killed in a suspicious car crash. Private detective Frank Slade has been hired by Handler's beautiful girlfriend to investigate. Handler, seemingly with a premonition of his death, has left a trail of clues. Can Slade discover the murderer, or will he instead uncover a secret that will shake his existence to the core?

A FICTIONAL DETECTIVE TRIFECTA

The Fictional Detective has gotten out of the Private Investigator game. Instead, he's trying to write hard-boiled masterpieces such as *Death Buys a Condo*. But despite the fact that the door of his office now says WRITER, some of his clients haven't gotten the word. And a strange lot of clients they are. A man that only contacts him during séances because, well, he's dead; a female impersonator who has inherited a house that's just a little too haunted for the market, and a small time gambler who's trying to end an affair with Lady Luck.

Three All New Novellas featuring the Fictional Detective!

The Fictional Press
www.TheFictionalPress.com

The Fictional Press is a small, independent press specializing in the publication of fictional works by emerging authors. If you are interested in bringing your fictional works to life in print as well as electronically, contact us! We can help!

Find out more at www.thefictionalpress.com.